LYING FOR KEEPS

OFF-LIMITS LOVERS
Book Three

LORE TOWNSEND

LN
P

Lying for Keeps
Paperback Edition

Love N. Books Press
An Imprint of Wolfpack Publishing
1707 E. Diana Street
Tampa, FL 33610

www.lovenbookspress.com

Edited by My Brother's Editor

Lying for Keeps was originally published as Savage Lover in 2024 by Lore Townsend

Paperback ISBN 979-8-89567-635-6
Ebook ISBN 979-8-89567-634-9
LCCN

OFF-LIMITS LOVERS
Book Three

LORE TOWNSEND

LNP

Lying for Keeps
Paperback Edition

Love N. Books Press
An Imprint of Wolfpack Publishing
1707 E. Diana Street
Tampa, FL 33610

www.lovenbookspress.com

Edited by My Brother's Editor

Lying for Keeps was originally published as Savage Lover in 2024 by Lore Townsend

Paperback ISBN 979-8-89567-635-6
Ebook ISBN 979-8-89567-634-9
LCCN

For anyone who's ever seen what they wanted and gone after it, consequences be damned…

Before We Begin...

This love story leans a bit to the dark side, incorporating bedroom games that would potentially be very dangerous for the participants. It's all in good fun (oh, how fun it is...), and I know you're going to love it.

That being said, while I've done my best to include safety and consent wherever necessary, this is a work of fiction and should not be taken as a guide or manual for the BDSM lifestyle. The characters in this story get up to hijinks that may not be safe or recommended to try between your own sheets or in your own backyard without preparation and conversations about safety, if at all. (Seriously, stay indoors during major storms please.)

As well, while BDSM is referenced in the book, the characters do not belong to the lifestyle or participate in activities that reflect the values and reality of true BDSM dynamics. These are fictional characters living their fictional lives in messy ways.

Potential content warnings:

- **Primal chase scenes**
- **CNC that is explicitly consented to ahead of time but not in the moment.**

This book is a wild ride. If you need someone who understands to talk to along the way, you can find us in Lore Townsend's Romance Club on Facebook. I'm in the group often and will be happy to answer questions and chat about books or expand upon content warnings if needed.

Lore

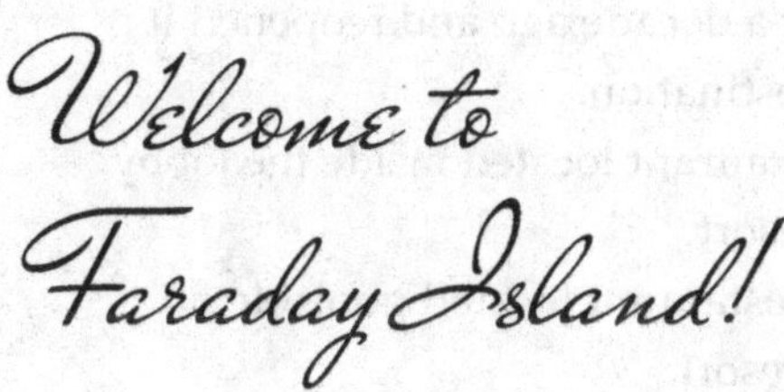

If this is your first time checking into The White Sands Resort, you're in for a wild ride. Ben and Victoria's love story is not to be missed. Please be sure to read the author's note with content warnings before diving in! Here's a series cheat sheet, just for fun.

The owners of The White Sands Resort:

- **Dominic:** The chef
- **Sam:** The general manager
- **Ben:** The lawyer
- **Avery:** The wild card

- **Reina:** Dominic's fiancée. You can read their love story in *Off the Menu*.
- **Franzeska:** Avery's girlfriend. You can read their love story in *Shameless*.

Places you'll go:

- **Faraday Island:** a fictional tropical island with the climate and geographic features of a small island off the coast of Belize (where I was when I started writing this series)

- **Saubry Village:** The town on Faraday Island.
- **Merit Island:** The small island next to Faraday where the guys own a house.
- **The White Sands Resort:** The four guys purchased the abandoned resort over a decade ago and reopened it as a high-end beach destination.
- **Raft:** The high-end restaurant located inside the lobby of The White Sands Resort.
- **Reef:** The casual fare restaurant located poolside on the lower level of the resort.

Lying for Keeps

Rule #1

YOU COULD FUCK HIS DAD

VICTORIA

"Holy shit, girl. You are not going to believe this."

Sally holds up her phone, where she's got the Instagram app open. It's Ainsley's profile, of course, and he's posted a photo of himself at a beach resort with a woman.

A beach resort that's definitely not on Faraday Island.

And a woman who sure the fuck isn't me.

Guess that explains why he didn't show up last night.

Biting my lip, I try to keep my emotions from showing.

"What a fucking dick," she mutters to her phone screen, shaking her head and sinking deeper into the tropical print cushions on her rattan-framed chair.

I snort trying to take a drink of my mojito and kick my bare feet up onto the low, wooden table between our chairs in the shady beach bar, watching my silver-painted toenails glitter in the light from the coconut lamp hanging overhead. "Couldn't have said it better myself."

"What are you going to do?" Sally loves gossip, and this shit is gold.

"What can I do?" I shrug as my insides slowly turn to stone.

It wasn't that I expected Ainsley, the rich, young trust funder, to be my forever. I just expected a little…I don't know. Respect?

I should have known better.

No, damn it. I did know better. The guy didn't take the time to remember anything about me. He barely remembered my name.

And not my last name.

After two months of…hanging out.

"I could never figure out why you chose that fuckboy anyway. I mean, you could seriously have any guy on this island," Sally says, not looking up from her phone.

I would generally try to dissuade people from stereotyping someone like that, but it's hard to argue with her right now.

Two months of practically living together, spending every night together, and the man wouldn't even consider calling me anything other than a friend.

"I'm just not looking for a relationship right now…"

The words threaten to burn a hole through the lining of my skull as they play over and over in my head.

I will not cry.

Will. Not. Cry.

"It's a really low blow." Her tone is sympathetic. Probably more than I deserve.

"I knew better," I finally manage.

"You keep saying that, but I'm not sure it's entirely true. I mean, you two were hanging out for a while. I don't think it's unreasonable for you to have thought that maybe it would turn into something." Good ol' Sally, always on my side.

"Maybe it wouldn't have been unreasonable for someone else, but this is me we're talking about. This is how it always goes with guys. Either I like them, and they're unavailable, or they like me, and I'm not interested."

"And your solution is to just keep hanging around the

unavailable ones for a while, hoping they become available?" She sounds less sympathetic now.

I shake my head and sigh. "I know it's stupid. I sometimes think they just need time. Like, I'm going to prove myself worthy of girlfriend status or something." I wave off her eye roll. "I know it's pathetic, and I'm stupid, and I fell for another one. You can save me the lecture. The punishment is built in."

"I get hanging out with someone who isn't ready to commit thinking maybe it will turn into something. I mean, if we didn't do that, I'm not sure any of us would be in relationships. It's not like guys are posting 'message me if you're ready for marriage and kids because I sure am' in their dating profiles. They have an internal security system, and it goes haywire when a new girl hangs around for more than one night. That's all normal. What's not normal is the way you just take it."

"As if I have a choice."

"Of course you have a choice. If you're going to play the game, you gotta be as much of a player as those assholes." She takes a long pull on her straw and starts to grin, playing absent-mindedly with the bright pink paper umbrella. "You know what I think you should do?"

I roll my eyes, knowing full well that whatever idea she's come up with is not something I'm going to do.

"Find someone else to fuck and post a pic of the two of you on your Instagram," she says far more matter of fact than the statement deserves.

I can't help but smile. It's such a Sally thing to say. I have no doubt that's exactly what she would do. "It hardly seems like he's stalking my Instagram feed right now."

She shrugs. "You never know. I mean, pics don't just appear on the app automatically. He took the time to upload it, even typed out a caption." She scrolls down and grimaces. "Ick. You should not read that."

I grab for her phone, but she pulls it away.

"No, seriously, Vic."

I flop back into the big, comfy chair and lay my head back, closing my eyes.

It's fine. I'll be fine.

It's just…why does this kind of thing keep happening?

I know that on some level Sally's right. All the girls I know go through this kind of thing with guys. But it seems like they always end up finding someone who thinks they're worth taking themselves off the market for. Me…not so much.

"You could fuck his dad."

I don't even bother to lift my head or open my eyes. "Great advice. Thanks, Sal."

"No, seriously. He's sitting right over there looking hot as hell."

My head snaps up, and I follow her gaze over to the bar where, indeed, Ben Adams, one of the resort's owners and a super-rich lawyer from the States, is sitting alone in a dark suit.

"Who wears a suit to a beach bar in the tropics?" Sally muses, reading my mind. "You should go take it off him."

I laugh at her brazenness. "I'm not fucking anyone's dad."

It's not that I'm holding out hope that Ainsley will come back to Faraday and explain that this whole thing was just some giant misunderstanding, but…I mean, he could.

Right?

"Well, you gotta do something. You aren't doing yourself any favors letting guys walk all over you like this."

"So, I go fuck his dad, and then all the future guys will take one look at me and think *'don't mess with that one, she's a dad fucker.'*"

Sally cracks up. "Dad fucker!"

I sigh. "I'm so glad my heartbreak keeps you amused."

"Don't start with that shit, girl. As soon as you call this heartbreak, you've given the bastard far too much power over you."

I bite my lip and consider. She's right, of course. I'm in no way brokenhearted over the loss of my most recent non-relationship.

It's just…

I pound the rest of my cocktail.

"You know what I'm going to do?" I ask.

Sally sits up excitedly, feeling the new energy that's coming off me.

"I'm going to go tell his dad what a douchebag his son is."

"Oh, yeah, girl. That's a perfect plan."

The fact that she agrees so readily gives me a moment of pause. She isn't exactly the person I take life advice from. But in the end, I shake it off.

Sally's excitement is palpable as I stand and smooth my short black dress down over my thighs.

"Wish me luck."

"You don't need luck. You're a fucking knockout."

I toss her a grateful smile and turn to make my way over to the bar.

The man in question is sitting alone with two empty seats on either side of him at the otherwise full bar. Like he's someone to be feared.

He's certainly a formidable presence. Even with his back to me, I can feel the power radiating from him. It could be the obvious strength hiding underneath those expensive-looking clothes, but I think it's more than that. He's broody, as if shadows emanate from him in all directions.

I slide onto the tall, wooden chair directly to his left and lean on the bar, head tilted in his direction. "Hey."

His head turns to me, eyes meeting mine directly.

I'm struck dumb by the intensity in those dark brown eyes, momentarily unable to breathe.

I watch, breath held, as his eyes drift down my body to where my elbows rest on the bar, and then briefly toward my legs and then back up to my lips. His expression is not what I'm used to seeing on the faces of men checking me out. If anything, I'd say the guy looks sad.

His eyes touch on mine briefly once more before he turns his full attention back to his drink. "Hey."

The exchange is so unexpected that it takes me a second to process. My whole reason for coming over here vanishes as I sit beside this man who is definitely dealing with something heavier than whatever silly shit I've got going on.

"Are you okay?" I fully planned to start reading him the riot act about his playboy son, but now, I just can't.

His face turns toward me again just enough for me to see one corner of his mouth tick up. I catch his eye for a split second.

"Yeah. I'm just having a hard week."

"Do you want to talk about it?"

He inhales deeply and lets it out before turning his head back to me. "You want to hear about my problems?"

I shrug.

I mean, the honest answer is no, I want to tell him about my problems, but the guy just looks so forlorn…and so fucking hot.

Like, so hot.

I can see from my vantage point that his cream dress shirt is unbuttoned enough to show off a patch of dark hair gracing his skin. His face is every bit the dashing hero I grew up fantasizing about, even more so than Ainsley. As a matter of fact, this guy looks like what you would get if you fed a picture of Ainsley into an AI generator and requested it turn him into a Mafia boss/underwear model. Dark hair, dark eyes, and five o'clock shadow I have a feeling isn't usual.

Shit, if this is what Ainsley is going to look like in twenty years, maybe I should reconsider giving up on him over one stupid pic.

"It doesn't look like you have anyone else to talk to."

That earns me another sad smile. The man glances to his right and then back at me. "I suppose that's true enough."

"So, come on. What does the king of the island have on his mind that's so bad it's causing him to drink away his sorrows in a bar alone?"

His eyebrows lift at my insinuation that I know exactly who he is. "King of the island, huh?" His tone lightens as I apparently amuse him. I suppose it's a step in the right direction.

"Don't change the subject."

His smile widens, and I can't help but return it.

"Can I buy you a drink?" he asks, glancing down at my empty hands where they rest on the bar.

I should say no, but obviously, I don't. "Sure."

"What's your poison?"

"The bartender knows." I don't know this sassy, confident woman I've apparently turned into, but I like her.

Seems Ben likes her, too.

He holds my gaze with a look so long and deep I nearly melt before he turns to signal the bartender to bring me another with just a few gestures of his hand.

My drink arrives, and I fall on it like a life raft.

Play it cool, girl.

But why? This isn't a date or even a guy I want to impress.

I try to shut my mind up with a graceful chug of the strong, tart cocktail. I have no idea what's going on, but I'm here for it.

"Now, are you going to tell me what's gotten that pretty face so long?" I ask.

Seriously, who am I right now?

I get a real smile out of Ben now, big and glorious. It lights up his face, transforming him from broodingly hot to storybook prince handsome. I almost have to look away.

"That's better," I coo.

Who knew I could coo?

He shakes his head, looking back down at the glass in his hands.

I wait patiently.

"Sometimes, life just doesn't go the way you expect. And there's nothing you can do but accept it."

Cryptic and not offering any real information, but I nod anyway. "I know how that is."

His face turns back to me, the expression sly, amused even. "Oh, do you? What would a young woman like you know about life not turning out as planned? You've hardly even begun."

It's my turn to shrug. I may be young, but I have a fair idea about how hard life is. The last thing I'm going to do right now is start on my own sob story, though.

"You'd be surprised," I say anyway, just to stay in character.

"Well, I suppose that could be true." His eyes flick to mine and then down at my cleavage where they rest for a full beat. I try to hold still under his gaze, and it takes my full concentration. "It wouldn't be the first surprise I've gotten tonight."

His eyes raise to meet mine and his look officially has a name. It's desire.

This guy wants me.

Ainsley's dad thinks I'm picking him up at the bar.

Shit.

"Pretty girl like you got a name?"

"Victoria."

"Victoria. Victory. Name fit for a queen."

What the actual fuck.

He's flirting with me.

"I'd ask for yours, but we both know that's not necessary."

He nods his head, accepting my statement as truth.

"So, Victoria, what brings you to The White Sands tonight?"

I take a long breath and let it out as quietly as I can. This is the part where I tell him the truth.

Right?

"Getting a drink with a friend."

His eyebrows tick up just a hint. "And what brings you to the island?"

He's fishing here, and I have a feeling I know what he wants to know. I take another sip of my drink, the strong liquor flaring into courage as it burns through my body. "Same as most people, I suppose. The sun, the sand, the ocean. And the fitness studio."

That earns me a smile, and I relax just a bit. Telling the truth feels steadying, even if it's not enough truth for him to actually know anything.

"Fitness junkie, huh?"

I shrug. "You're clearly no stranger to the gym."

He looks at me sidelong then, a shadow passing over his features that I can't read. "You could say that."

I have no idea where to take this. I'm too far gone to just come out and tell him the truth about why I came over here, and I'm still not sure if I have the gumption, or even the true desire, to keep taking this interaction in the direction it seems to be heading.

I mean, if this was any other guy on the planet, I'd be all for it. Who wouldn't? Hot, older guy, clearly safe and trustworthy, since he owns the damn resort. He would be the perfect escape for the evening.

The thought of being alone with him in some fancy rich-person bedroom and getting to slip off my dress and blow his mind with my hot-as-fuck-Pilates-instructor body has me shifting a bit in my seat.

I mean, it wouldn't even have to be a revenge thing. I'm certainly not the kind of person to snap a pic of myself in bed with someone's hot dad and post it on the internet. What if I just pretended this guy was someone else?

I glance down at his left hand where it cradles his drink, trying to detect even a hint of a tan line on that ring finger. I can't remember if Ains ever mentioned his mother, and nothing would throw cold water on this faster than learning this guy is married.

Maybe I can sneak to the restroom and Google him just to be sure.

Ben follows my gaze and rubs his thumb thoughtfully across the base of the finger, the way you would spin a ring if it was there.

My breath catches as I wait for him to confirm my suspicion and release me from the act of complete madness I'm considering.

Instead, when he meets my eye, he gives the smallest little shake of his head. It's not a lot, but it's enough. Not married. I believe him. I mean, he has to know he can't lie about that kind of thing. Or anything, really. Between the nosy staff and the internet, I bet I could find out just about anything I want to know.

He's silent for a long moment, still watching his thumb graze over his ring finger.

There's something to the movement, and the look he's giving it, that hints at a deeper meaning, and I can't help but be curious.

He must be divorced. Maybe recently divorced and still sad about it.

Well, even better.

A sexy night with a hot stranger is just what he needs to start getting over her. I'd be doing him a favor. A public service of sorts.

When he looks up again and meets my eye, I no longer see sadness or even hesitation. The desire is back.

Well, that makes two of us, buddy.

"I'm not sure what the next step is here," he says finally, head cocked to the side so he can look at me.

"The next step is that you take me home with you."

His eyes hit the ceiling for a moment as he tips his head back and sighs. "Well, I can't do that. But I can probably get a room here at the resort for us to spend some time in."

"Okay."

Oh my god. I am freaking out right now.

"Do you work here?"

It takes me a second to process his question with my brain currently on overload.

"What? Oh, no. I don't work here."

"Say the words—I am not a White Sands Resort employee."

"I am not a White Sands Resort employee."

He considers my face for a long moment. "Would you say that under oath?"

"If you advised me to, I would."

He shakes his head. "Fuck," he mutters, so low I barely catch the word.

I am going out of my mind with excitement and nerves. All I can do is watch and wait for him to decide.

"I'm going to go to the front desk. If you're here when I get back..." he trails off, seeming unsure of what to say.

"I'll be here," I tell him. Sure. Confident.

For a second, I think he's going to change his mind, but he just shakes his head and walks out of the bar.

The second he disappears through the doorway, Sally runs to my side.

"What the fuck?" she hisses excitedly, grabbing both of my hands in hers.

"I don't know! I mean, I guess I kinda picked him up. He's going to get us a room. How did this happen? What the fuck?"

Sally squeezes her eyes closed and squeals silently in glee. "Girl, just go with it. That is like the most eligible bachelor on the island. Hell, in the world! Just go up to his room and do whatever he tells you to do."

"Will you Google him really quick and make sure he's divorced?"

Sally's face breaks into a grin. "I don't need to Google him. I know, and it's even better. He's widowed."

I grimace. "How is that better?"

She rolls her eyes. "No other woman drama. Besides, it was ages ago."

"Should I tell him about Ainsley?"

Sally looks like I just slapped her across the face. "What the fuck is wrong with you? No, you don't tell him about Ainsley. Screw Ainsley. He's a spoiled little boy. You are about to bed yourself a real man." She closes her eyes and proactively vibrates with excitement for me. "You've got this, Vic."

But do I?

It's too late for any more pep talk. Sally spots him coming back into the bar over my shoulder and quickly walks away.

Ben returns to his seat, watching her go. "Friend of yours?"

I nod.

"What does she think of all this?"

"She thinks I should go up to your room and do whatever you tell me to do."

I surprised him with that, and I relish the brief, unguarded look my statement puts on his face. It's quickly replaced with his all-business, stern face. "And what do you think?" he muses.

"Wouldn't you like to know."

He nods, holding my gaze tightly with his own piercing stare. "Yeah, I sure would."

I shrug and say nothing.

After a full beat, where I've all but convinced myself that he's going to bail, Ben reaches into his jacket pocket and pulls out a red keycard. He sets it on the bar between us.

"This is the key to the penthouse suite upstairs. If you hit R in the elevator, it will take you there."

We both look at it, and when I finally glance up, I find him staring at me once more.

"I'm not going to go up with you. That would be…too much. You can head up when you're ready, and I'll meet you there."

"And if you don't show up?"

A little smile flashes across his chiseled features. "If I don't show up, you can enjoy the best room in the resort all to yourself. Order room service, swim in the rooftop pool."

"Okay."

He sets his fingers back on the keycard where it rests on the dark bar, tapping them three times. I watch, mesmerized.

"Okay," he says finally.

I swallow hard as he rises from his seat and stands beside me. The touch I've been waiting for finally comes—one hand lightly resting on the bare skin of my shoulder. I look up into his eyes as his warm skin burns into mine.

And then he's gone.

Rule #2

BE CAREFUL WHAT YOU WISH FOR

VICTORIA

I make my way up to the penthouse after another short freak-out with Sally. She makes sure my phone is charged, assures me that the resort staff works twenty-four hours a day, and reminds me she's just a phone call away if I need help.

It's not that I'm scared of the guy. Not exactly. It's just hard not to feel like I'm a walking lie, going up to the man's room with an invisible load of baggage that he for sure, one thousand percent would want to know about if given the option.

Baggage that would change his mind about our little rendezvous.

"All the more reason to keep your mouth shut," Sally told me before disappearing into the night a little while earlier.

I suppose she's right, although if my goal for talking to Ben was to tell him off for raising such a douchebag son, then what is my sleeping with him going to accomplish? It's not like I'm going to tell Ainsley about it to make him jealous, am I?

I shake the thought off quickly. I'm really not like that.

So why the fuck am I here?

I rise from the white chaise lounge where I collapsed after entering the penthouse to do my brooding. I should just go.

I should definitely go. The fog of insanity that apparently overtook me at the bar has lifted, and I can see this decision for the terrible one that it is.

I head for the front door.

"Going somewhere?"

I spin to find Ben standing across the room, making a drink at the low, wood sideboard next to a set of open patio doors.

"Oh…yeah."

He lifts his eyebrows and holds out a glass. I can see now that he was making a drink for me. It looks an awful lot like the mojito I was drinking downstairs.

Don't go over there and take it, Victoria. You're leaving.

But what could one drink hurt?

I walk over and take the glass from him, not meeting his eyes. My purse dangles from my shoulder.

"Did you think I wasn't coming?"

I shake my head, still avoiding his eyes. It's not hard. There's plenty to look at in the incredible room now that I take a moment to look at something other than my own terrible life choices. The view. The pool. The freaking bed. It's breathtaking.

"You thought I was coming and decided to leave before that happened."

The confident woman from the bar seems to have abandoned me. I shrug.

"You've changed your mind." The statement from Ben is so final, so resigned, I can't help but look up to see the expression that goes with it. He looks calm enough. His sad eyes from earlier are still gone, thank God. He just looks…pensive.

Why that is so hot, I can't even begin to process, but it is.

He's looking at me like I'm an expensive piece of art. Something he plans to admire. Enjoy. Not like a man who's going to try to talk me into sleeping with him with vague insinuations about a future relationship.

My purse slips from my shoulder to my hand. "I was just... This is kind of a lot for me."

He cocks his head to the side. "First time?"

My eyes go a bit wide, and he smiles. "First time getting taken up to a hotel room after flirting in a resort bar?" he clarifies.

I nod.

"Well, if you choose to stay, it would be my honor to show you the ropes."

Well, shit.

Just his words send desire coursing through my body. What this man is offering, promising, I want it so bad. When was the last time I was really and truly taken care of by a man? Um, never. And here is this one, easily the most handsome man on the planet, offering me a night of...whatever he wants.

Hell, I bet he won't even make me choose what we do.

It's that thought that sends me over the edge. "Okay."

"Okay you'll stay?"

"Maybe just for one drink?" My voice comes out soft and unsure. I have got to find the confidence I had earlier if I'm going to make it through tonight.

Ben glances down at the glass in my hand, and I follow his gaze.

Empty.

How the hell did that happen?

When I look up, he's watching me again. "Why don't you come over here?"

Oh fuck. Oh fuck, oh fuck, oh fuck.

I walk over and set my glass down on the bar. I set my purse down next to it.

And then, like I'm on death row, I walk slowly until I'm inches from the man. I can feel the heat of him, even in this tropical weather. He's a dark sun—pulling me in.

He doesn't touch me at first, simply walks all the way around my body. I follow him with my eyes as long as I can and then spin my head to watch him come around the other side. He looks me up and down, an expression of pure desire written across his handsome features.

"Perfection."

I say nothing.

"You know, when I asked if it was your first time leaving the bar with someone, I should have told you that it may as well be mine."

My eyes lift to his at this unexpected statement. He offers another of those small, tight-lipped smiles.

"I don't make a habit of picking up young women in bars."

"I'm not that young."

"You are plenty young."

"Do you want to see my ID?" I feel a bit of my fire coming back as I grow more comfortable with his proximity. With our very private situation.

The smile grows just a bit as he shakes his head. "No. The fact that you were drinking in one of my bars is proof enough for me."

His words bring back the memory of my first time at one of The White Sand's bars. I had to run home to get my driver's license after being denied entry without it, something that had never happened to me outside of the US. This man and his rules must have been the reason for that.

I wonder what other rules he has.

Probably has one about sleeping with his son's exes.

I shake off that thought and look up to find Ben watching me curiously.

"What?" I ask.

"Just curious."

"About me?"

"Yes."

"What do you want to know?"

"What changed your mind?"

"About waiting here for you? Or about staying just now?"

"Staying."

I bite my lip as I consider what to say. There are so many ways I could play this night, so many ways this could go.

But there's only one way I want.

"I thought you might…tell me what to do."

"And that's what you want?"

I nod, unable to make myself speak.

He considers me, taking a step back and folding his arms. "Men your age don't tell you what to do enough?"

"Never."

He raises his eyebrows.

"They can never make decisions about anything. I feel like their mother."

That earns me a soft laugh, and I look up into his eyes once more.

They're on fire.

"Letting go of control can be a dangerous game, Victoria."

"You seem pretty trustworthy."

Another breathy laugh, and Ben shakes his head. "I guess that much is true. But I don't like the idea of you picking up guys in bars and then going up to hotel rooms with them so they can order you around."

Just the hint of displeasure from him about my behavior—the concern he feels about my safety—is enough to make the decision for me. As if it hadn't already been made.

"I told you it was my first time."

"And your last?"

I lock eyes with him once more. "We'll see."

He holds my gaze for a long moment, and I can see the warring factions in his mind.

After what feels like forever, he blinks. "Get on your knees."

I obey, using my hands to help myself down in my short, tight dress.

Ben walks the few paces back over and circles me once more. This time, I keep my gaze straight ahead.

"You are complete and utter perfection. Do you know that?"

I nod.

A soft chuckle. "Yes, I suppose you would." I hear him take a long breath behind me and let it out slowly. "When I first saw you, you know what I thought?"

I shake my head.

"I thought, I'd like to ruin that girl."

I can't help the breath that sucks through my lips or the sharp noise it makes. I clench my thighs together and shift slightly to one knee.

"Oh, the girl likes that, does she?"

I have no idea how this works, if I can speak or not, so I just nod again.

Ben circles until he's standing directly in front of me, his erection prominent in the front of his pants that's now level with my face.

"Close your eyes."

I obey.

"Now picture me ruining you."

I do, a tiny whimper escaping my lips at the scenes flashing in my mind's eye.

"Tell me what you see."

I shake my head.

"No?"

"No."

"Why not?"

"I don't want you to do what's in my head. I want to be surprised."

"Oh, that's right. Tired of men not being able to make choices for themselves."

I open my eyes when I feel his fingers cup my chin, tipping my face up to look at him.

"Well, I'm more than capable of making the decisions for us, sweetheart, if that's what you want."

I nod as much as I can with his hand holding my face.

"I will warn you, though, you may not know whether or not you've made a mistake until it's over."

It sounds almost like a threat, but I'm too far gone to even consider what it could possibly mean.

"Do your worst."

Ben licks slowly across his bottom lip, eyes locked on mine. Finally, he releases my chin and takes a step back. "The doors are unlocked. You can leave at any time."

I nod.

"Well, I guess it's time for you to get yourself undressed then, isn't it?"

I blink in surprise at his words, having expected him to stand me up and unzip the long zipper on the back of my dress while he grazed his mouth down my spine.

But that was my fantasy. And we're doing his now.

The rush of excitement almost overtakes the desire pounding between my legs.

Almost, but not quite.

I press my hands into the floor to help me rise, but Ben places a hand on my head.

"I didn't tell you to get up."

I look up at him, making my face the picture of innocent surprise. His lips curl up in a snarl at the sight of me, and the power of my position is suddenly very clear.

I think I'm going to like this.

I fumble a bit to get the high-backed zipper into my hands, having to shift and turn and spin my dress.

Ben just watches me struggle.

When I finally manage to get the thing unzipped, I pull it down and crawl out of it, saying a grateful prayer to my past self for putting on such ridiculous underwear for my drink date with Sally.

I hook my fingers in the waistband of the lavender lace thong and look up at Ben from under my lashes. Asking.

He nods.

I crawl out of my panties and set them on my crumpled dress.

I'm sitting on my heels, legs tucked under me, as Ben starts to walk slowly around me once more.

"Beautiful. So perfect."

I'm dying for him to touch me, but I try my hardest to be patient.

I'm not the one calling the shots here.

His next command is not completely unexpected.

"Take my cock out."

He's standing a foot in front of me, so I crawl the few inches necessary to get my hands on his belt. I go ahead and pull the belt all the way out of the loops and lay it on the ground next to me before starting on his zipper.

Just in case he wants it later.

I don't dare look up at him, but I hear his soft laugh as he watches my deliberate movement with the belt.

His pants fall as soon as I have them unzipped. I pull his boxers down quickly, practically grinding my teeth in anticipation.

When I'm about to get my hands on the prize, however, he takes a half step back.

"Stop."

My hands fall to my sides with a soft thud, and I look up at him. He holds my gaze as he steps out of his pants and boxers, taking the time to fold them and drape them over a chair, adding his own shirt to the pile before walking back over to stand before me, naked and every bit the picture of male perfection. His strong arms lead to chiseled shoulders and pecs. His abs belong on a man twenty years younger, and I feel a rush of respect for the work I know it takes to keep it looking that way. He's textbook perfect. And I'm about to get a crash course.

"Open."

I obey, praying that he can't tell how much I'm salivating for him.

Without laying a hand on me, he slides his tip down my eager, outstretched tongue until he taps the back of my throat and then slides it back out.

I take a deep breath and look up at him, tongue still laid out like a red carpet.

"What are you going to do if you want me to stop?"

I close my mouth and swallow. "I'll just get up and walk over there."

He eyes the bar I'm gesturing to and nods. "Promise?"

I nod.

"Open."

This time, I get both of his hands wrapped around my head when he enters me. His fingers slowly snake into my shoulder-length hair until he's got a death grip on me. Two fistfuls.

He's gentle in my mouth at first, playful even, sliding in and out, allowing me to lick and suck at him as he fills me.

Slowly but surely, however, I feel him working his way further back until he's breaching the top of my throat. I breathe calmly and squeeze my eyes closed as a rush of embarrassment and fear starts to overtake me. Tears hit my cheeks and run hot down to my chin before dripping off and hitting my thighs over and over again.

"Look at you."

His words are a balm—but only a small one.

I know I'm getting what I asked for, but all of a sudden, I'm starting to wonder if I made the right decision by handing this man control.

You may not know if you made a mistake until it's over.

His words play back in my mind, suddenly making a lot more sense.

He doesn't push farther down, but he does push to the same place in my throat over and over. Each time he slides out, the relief is overwhelming, only to have him thrust back in. The up and down emotional roller coaster does strange things to my brain.

"You say it's your first time, but look at you taking my cock like a dirty little slut."

Okay. And now my brain is officially misfiring.

I should not be tilting my head back when he thrusts to remove some of the resistance.

I should not be lifting my butt off my heels in order to force him to slide down farther.

I should not be moaning in pleasure at being called a slut.

But I am.

Oh god, am I.

"That's what you like, huh? Well, you came to the right place, didn't you?"

He pushes in farther than before, and my eyes go wide at the sensation of him breaching my body. My hands are balled up in tight fists and pounding against my thighs, splatting over and over in the pools of my own tears.

He pulls back out, and I suck in a breath.

"Greedy, dirty little whore."

Yup.

I squeeze my eyes closed as he pushes back inside, farther than ever.

It's too much.

I'm just about to pull my body back and retreat to the safety of the bar when he pulls out.

My eyes pop open just in time to see him fist himself and pump his cock as he groans, shooting his hot cum onto my chest. The thick, ropey liquid drips down my breasts and coats my nipples.

I look up and find him watching me.

"I bet you were hoping to get that in your mouth, huh?"

The answer is no, but I say nothing.

"Go clean yourself up."

I gratefully push myself to my feet and hurry to the bathroom, closing the door behind me. I'm worried I look like an absolute mess after that little scene, and I'm not wrong.

My makeup is smeared everywhere, and my hair falls to my shoulders in messy bunches, my usual part barely visible in the disarray.

I turn on the faucet and quickly wet one of the towels, cleaning off my chest and wiping my armpits out, too. Just for good measure.

I take the makeup towel and do the best job I can cleaning up my smeared mascara and lipstick, shaking my head and laughing silently to myself. I so badly wish I had my purse in here so I could have snapped a selfie before cleaning myself up.

A souvenir of this night.

I'm just running my wet fingers through my lost cause of a hairdo when the bathroom door opens.

"You forgot to lock the door."

Ben walks in, naked and glorious with his arms crossed over his chest. With him reflected behind me, it's impossible to miss the giant erection he's still sporting.

I have to admit, I was a teeny bit worried when he came so early in our evening, but it seems to have done nothing to diminish his ability to fuck.

"When I said clean yourself up, I just meant your tits."

I blush and look down, completely overwhelmed by his confident presence and unsure of what to say.

He walks over, unbothered by my now shy demeanor. Taking a fistful of my hair, he undoes all of the hard work I just did. "I did not tell you to fix any of this lovely mess."

"I looked terrible."

"Impossible."

"There's no way you liked me looking like such a mess."

"You liked it."

"Excuse me?"

"Look me in the eye and tell me you didn't like the way you looked when you came in here."

I can't.

"Fine." I let out a breathy laugh. "I kind of wished I had my phone so I could take my picture."

"Well, I can't allow any pictures, but if it makes you feel better, it's a vision I won't forget as long as I live."

"Sorry. I should have left it—"

He silences me with a hand over my mouth. I can taste the salt of his cum on his fingers. "Let's get you messed back up, shall we?"

Rule #3

IT'S SINK OR SWIM

BEN

"I don't need a fucking tour, Avery," I snap at the man next to me, just trying to stop his incessant chatter.

My attitude, as usual, doesn't faze him in the least. "I know, man. I just...you've been gone for over two months, and a lot has changed down here."

I know he's not about to bring up the fact that I spent those two months searching the globe for my son when, in reality, the kid was shacked up right here on Faraday the whole time.

"It looks great." I try to bring us back to safer territory. I don't want another ruined morning thinking about Ainsley and what I'm going to do next.

I want to bask in the afterglow of last night.

That girl—woman, excuse me—was a goddamn delight.

The sight of her falling to her knees before me with that surprised and bashful look on her face. Getting to see the tough act fall to pieces as she practically begged for my next command.

Fucking hell.

None of that was acting.

You can't make that shit up.

I know I have to file the whole experience, and the woman, in the never-happening-again drawer, but I'm not ready to do that just yet.

I'm allowing her to live in a dangerous part of my brain for a dangerously long time.

Longer than I've ever let anyone linger there before.

"Looks like a class is getting ready to start. Do you want to join?"

With a sigh, I leave my daydream and turn to Avery with a glower. "I thought we came down here to work out in the new facility."

"The new group fitness program is a huge part of the grand opening for next week. We could check it out."

"What's the class?"

Avery squints at the schedule. "Pilates."

"Pilates?" I've heard of it, but I'm pretty sure it doesn't involve barbells and heavy reps, so I've never taken a closer look.

We step aside to allow another small group of women to enter the studio, closing the door behind them.

"Yeah. It's like yoga or something."

"I don't do yoga."

"Fran says it's like yoga but harder."

Another group of tall, fit women in pastel leggings and matching sports bras pass us to enter the room.

Once the door closes behind them, I turn back to Avery with an unconvinced look. "How hard could it be, Ave, if these are the people taking the class?"

He laughs and claps me on the shoulder, already reaching for the handle as if I agreed to attend. "Exactly, man. Let's just go in there and kick some Pilates ass, and then we'll get brunch."

He's already halfway through the door, holding it open for me. I huff and follow him into the studio.

The room is gorgeous.

This is what I really came down here to see, and it's worth whatever fluffy class we have to sit through to get to experience it.

When I was here last, this was just framed out studs, awaiting sheetrock. Now it's a glowing white and oak fitness studio, splashed with bright tropical colors in the form of jewel toned workout mats and hanging pendant lights. One full wall is mirrors, and there is a thin wooden bar railing across the opposite wall.

Directly in front of us is a large, two-door closet where women line up to grab mats, resistance bands, and inflatable balls.

What the hell have we gotten ourselves into?

"Doesn't it look great?" Avery is asking from beside me as we wait our turn.

"It does. The space really came together."

The man puffs up like a rooster, pride written across his face. I shake my head and look away. While it's true that this was his little pet project over the last year, I had as much say in all of it as he did.

The last woman ahead of us takes a seafoam green mat from an outstretched hand inside the closet, and we step to the front of the line.

"Okay..." the woman in the closet says, her back to us, as she pulls two more mats out of the shadowy corner. "We're starting to get full, but I think there's still enough—"

She stops dead as she faces us, two fuchsia mats in her arms.

Well, if it isn't Victoria, the lovely, dirty talking, cock-sucking woman from last night.

Her shoulder-length black hair glimmers under the fluorescent lighting, perfectly framing her slender face. Those big green eyes pierce through me with the same intensity I remember from less than twelve hours before.

When she was mine.

"Room for two more." She recovers quickly, although her color doesn't return.

She passes the mats to Avery, not meeting my eyes.

He heads out to find a spot on the floor, not picking up on the energy in this closet, but I stay exactly where I am.

Victoria, to her credit, continues handing me workout equipment like I didn't just give her the shock of her life.

"Bands and…balls." She piles the items into my outstretched arms and then finally looks at me.

Our eyes lock for a long moment.

"Okay, that should be all you need," she says finally.

"That's it?"

"Yup, a mat, a band—"

"No, Vic. I mean, that's all you have to say to me? Not a good morning or anything?"

"I…I wasn't sure you would want me to acknowledge…you know." A blush hits her cheeks, and she looks at the floor once more.

"And what do you want?" I ask directly.

Those emerald eyes, the ones I was just fantasizing about shining up at me from her knees as she takes my cock between those sweet lips, finally meet mine.

I feel the request before I hear it.

"I want my first class at this fancy resort fitness center to go well."

I give a nod and turn to join Avery.

"But we can…we can get coffee after class."

I turn back to her, allowing the surprise from her statement to flash across my face.

"I mean, if you wanted to give me feedback about the class, or whatever."

I don't know why I'm so surprised that the woman who had the balls to pick me up at the bar last night is now asking me out for coffee, but something about her bravery really hits a note.

"Yeah. That seems appropriate."

She flushes a darker shade of red, and I smile at the effect I seem to have on her. And thank the fucking stars the effect she's having on me isn't painted across my cheeks.

Or tenting my workout shorts.

Speaking of which, I need to get the fuck out of here before that happens.

Avery has our two pink mats laid out side by side and is chatting up a whole circle of rich-looking fitness ladies.

"There he is. Did you get our balls?"

I restrain myself from throwing one straight at his head.

"Rebecca and Samantha here were just telling me that this is their third class in the studio. They took spin yesterday and yoga earlier this morning."

"The studio is beautiful," one of the women gushes at me. "We've been looking forward to Pilates, though. It's my favorite class back in the States, and this teacher must be amazing if they hired her to teach here."

My eyes dart to the front of the room where Victoria, dressed in skintight Lycra, is messing with her phone.

A sudden blast of music makes us all jump. Victoria jumps right along with us and then laughs. Once she has the volume down to a reasonable level, she turns to us, her smile bright.

"Welcome, everyone. It's so nice to see so many faces out there for my first class."

The women around us return her greeting.

"Good morning." I follow suit, but it's too late, and my deep voice rings out alone through the studio.

After a brief, but painfully awkward pause, Victoria recovers. "As you know, we are here for a mat Pilates class. Can I see some hands for people who have done Pilates before?"

All the women eagerly raise their hands.

"And first timers?"

Avery raises his hand, and after a moment, I do the same.

"Okay, a couple of newbies. Well, we'll try not to break you."

The women all laugh and exchange knowing looks.

I nearly take a page from my son's book and answer with an eye roll, but I catch myself just in time.

Whatever these half-naked women can do, I can do.

After an hour of trying not to get caught staring at Victoria's ass as she led us through a series of grueling movements, I am fully and completely broken.

I may never walk normally again.

The movements were so tiny, and there was no added weight at all, but here I am, forcing a smile as we wipe down our mats and roll them up to place back in the closet.

I can feel muscles in my core and hip flexors that I didn't even know existed.

I briefly consider the possibility that I might die in my sleep tonight, my poor, aching body succumbing to the pain and throwing in the towel.

"What the fuck did she just do to us, man?" Avery hisses at me as we reach the front of the line to put our mats back in the closet.

"Just keep it together until we get out of here."

He huffs a laugh but says nothing.

I briefly catch Victoria's eye as we slink out the studio door, the intensity of her gaze zapping my last remaining reserve.

Terminally sore and desperately horny.

It's not a combination I have much experience with.

We collapse onto a bench in the locker room, mercifully alone.

"That was some fucked-up shit."

I laugh at the way Avery can sum things up so perfectly. "Yeah."

"I mean, she was like, hold the ball between your knees and tilt your pelvis, and I was like—hell, I'll pretend I'm fucking Franny, but I couldn't even pretend. It was so hard, I could barely even do it."

I shake my head and huff out another laugh.

"And who knew we'd been doing planks wrong all these

years? Jesus, when she came over and tucked my hips, I thought my arms were going to buckle and send me onto my face."

The memory of Victoria putting her hands on Avery is not my favorite one from the class. I know he's a committed man these days, but still. The rush of jealousy and possessiveness I felt in that moment caught me off guard. And I can still feel it hovering just inside my ribcage.

"We've been doing wimp planks our whole lives. And those chicks?" He breaks off, shaking his head. "Those chicks are hardcore. They just did all that shit and didn't even complain once."

"It was a humbling experience."

Avery laughs. "That's all you have to say about it?"

"I'm not going to be able to walk tomorrow."

"That's for sure. Want to grab brunch? I thought I would need to change, but I'm not really all that sweaty. Which is odd considering the fucking ordeal I just went through."

I glance down at my own shirt, which is also free of sweat.

Interesting.

"No, I'm getting coffee with the instructor."

I could not have surprised Avery more if I sucker punched him right in the face.

"You what?"

"Coffee. Pilates teacher. Me."

"Wha—why?"

"She wanted to meet up after class to see if I had any thoughts or suggestions."

"Wait, so she asked you out?"

I nod. "You didn't think I asked her, did you?"

"No, of course not. It's just…I'm not sure what to do with this information."

"You can take it and leave."

Avery laughs, clapping me on the shoulder. "Sure thing, man. Have fun. Be nice, okay? That chick is hot, and no doubt hardcore as fuck if that's her jam, but she's young. Probably…you know…still building confidence in herself. Still figuring life out and whatnot. Be nice."

"I'll be fair."

"Ben, it's not the easiest thing in the world to find a great Pilates teacher willing to move all the way out here."

"I said I'd be fair."

"And I asked you to be nice."

"Fine. I'll be nice."

My tone apparently does nothing to convince him. "Where are you meeting her?"

"So you can surprise us by joining? Nice try."

"I'll bring Fran. We can all talk about the class and what a great job—"

"See you later."

I exit the locker room with him still calling after me.

Rule #4

SEMANTICS

BEN

Just as I walk into the lobby between the men's and women's changing areas, I spot Victoria going into one of the private bathrooms with her bag.

I make it there just in time to catch the door before it closes all the way and wrench it open, slipping inside and pushing it closed behind me.

I click the lock into place before turning to face her.

"What—oh." She visibly relaxes when she sees my face.

I fold my arms over my chest. "Not a resort employee, huh?"

She opens her mouth and then closes it, folding her own arms to cross over her delicious, nearly visible breasts. "Technically, I'm here on a contract. So, no, I'm not a resort employee."

"Semantics."

She just shrugs.

I stalk toward her, and she backs away until there's nowhere left to go.

Once she's pinned against the wall, my arms on either side of her shoulders, I lose the battle against the tent in my shorts. It's all I can do not to lunge my hips forward and press my erection into her.

Not that I'm entirely sure those muscles are still functional.

"So, the very first thing out of your mouth last night was a lie."

She breaks eye contact as her gaze drops to the floor. "I'm sorry," she whispers.

I huff and stand up straight, walking halfway across the small room before turning back to face her, hands on my hips. "Don't ever apologize. It makes you look weak."

Confusion twists her lovely face. "But...you just said...I thought you were mad that I lied to you."

"I'm not mad at you for lying. Hell, I think young women need to lie more. Level the goddamn playing field. But what difference would it make if I was?"

"I don't know, I guess."

"You just automatically apologize anytime someone might be mad at you for something?"

"I...I'm going to go, I think."

"You think? You want to exit the small, locked room where a man twice your size is threatening you, and you're not even going to say it like you mean it? You're asking me permission to leave. Well, I don't grant it."

"I don't need your permission."

"Prove it."

She lunges for the door, but I'm already halfway there. As she passes me, I catch her around the middle and pin her to the closed door, pressing my chest firmly against her back. I wrap one hand tightly in her loose hair and slide the other down one of her thighs.

We just breathe together like that for a long moment before she starts to struggle. I may be sore, but I'm still strong as hell, so I keep her pinned without all that much effort.

"Let me go."

My erection is achingly hard, and I don't try to hide it as I push my hips more firmly into her ass.

I turn her head so I can see the profile of her face, and what I find there nearly sends me to my knees.

It's not tears.

It's not a flushed red face of a woman in distress.

She's got her eyes squeezed closed, bottom lip bit between her teeth.

She looks an awful lot like she did last night when I was filling her up.

"If you want to leave, Victoria, unlock the door."

I shift slightly to the left to make sure her arm is good and free.

I watch her hand reach toward the dead bolt and then ball up in a fist. She brings her fist back and strikes my thigh.

"I said let me go." Her voice is hushed, but full of feeling.

"Reach up and unlock the door, Victoria." I breathe the words into the crook of her neck as I wind my fingers more tightly into her hair. "Then you can leave."

The choice is hers, and she knows it.

I am hardly a man who can get away with assaulting a woman in a public place. There isn't a more recognizable face on this island.

She knows I'll let her leave.

I watch the thoughts pass over her expression without her even needing to open her eyes.

Finally, after a painfully long pause, she gives the tiniest shake of her head. I feel it against my fist more than I see it.

"Your safe word is Bentley. Do you understand?"

She nods quickly and then flinches as the action pulls her hair.

"Say the word out loud right now so that I can be sure you know what it is and what it means."

The pause sucks the breath right out of me. I'm not sure I've ever wanted to hear a single word as much as I want to hear this one.

"Bentley."

"And if you say that word again..." I prompt her, pulling back on her hair so her face comes away from the door, forcing her to face me.

"I can leave."

"That's right."

Fucking hell.

I'm not sure if I wanted her to turn that lock or not. I mean, obviously my cock wanted her to stay, but there's no denying the fact that this complicates things a bit.

And I don't like when things get complicated.

But I can hardly back down now. This little vixen issued me a challenge, and I'm going to have to rise to it, consequences be damned.

I slip my free hand under the tight waistband of her yoga pants. The noise she lets out is halfway between a whimper and a moan that shoots straight to my dick.

I grip the stretchy material and pull down sharply, taking it over the round part of her ass.

And I'll be damned if there isn't a trace of panties under them.

I take a big handful of the soft, bare flesh and squeeze, earning myself a nice little gasp. When my hand slides between her legs, she offers up a full-on moan.

"I should have known you'd be so wet, you little slut."

Her moan turns back to a whimper as I press a finger roughly inside her, adding another before giving her body a few quick thrusts.

"Dripping fucking wet," I murmur, my head still tucked into the crook of her neck, pinning her shoulders against the wall. "You wanted to leave, but that was nothing but another lie."

"I thought..." she starts, barely able to get the words out with her face pressed against the door. I pull back on her hair and turn her head to face me. "I thought it was okay for me to lie."

"Are you apologizing again? Asking for my permission?"

"No. I mean...I don't know."

I release her entirely, pulling my fingers from her warm pussy and dropping my grip on her hair. I take a step back and leave her gasping against the door, pants around her knees.

"Is that all this is? You didn't leave when you had the chance because you thought I'd be mad if you did?"

She turns, the picture of dishevelment, hands raking through her own hair as she tries to form a sentence. "No, I mean. I do want to...I mean, I don't know."

"Victoria," I growl, allowing my displeasure at her indecisiveness to echo against the walls.

Her knees buckle, and she slides her back down the wall until her butt hits the ground. "I don't know why I'm still here. I don't know exactly what I want. But is it so terrible to want to please you?"

And what I want, of course, is for this strong, beautiful, courageous woman to stand up for herself.

But I also want her cowering on the floor in front of me.

I want both things equally, and the war between the two nearly splits my mind in half.

I wish I was a stronger man. The kind who would wipe her tears and fix her hair. Help her to her feet and give her a nice little lecture about stranger danger.

Maybe I even thought I was that man, before the lock slid closed on this bathroom door.

But I know now that I'm not.

"If you want to please me so much, take your clothes off."

Her eyes shoot to mine and go wide for just a moment before she springs into action. Her top comes off first, and my mouth waters at the sight of her beautiful, handful-sized tits, bouncing as she pushes herself to her feet and strips the tight pants down.

"Face the wall again."

She turns and presses her palms flat against the door, her right hand just inches from the dead bolt.

The fact that her escape is so close, and she refuses to take it…well, that does something to me.

"Spread and bend over."

She obeys, sliding her feet apart and then shuffling them back so her arms extend in front of her as she bends at the waist.

The view of her wet, spread pussy, waiting just feet from my cock, is a glorious fucking sight.

"I don't have any condoms."

"That's okay," she says, too quickly.

"It's not fucking okay. Say it."

"It's…that's not okay." She stumbles over the words but manages to get through them.

"Oh, really. You think you get to decide what goes down here, huh?" I know what a low blow I dealt her, but I want to see her crumble. If we're doing this, we're doing it my way.

"I…I mean…I didn't—"

I cross the room in two strides and grip her around her waist at the same time I drive my fingers back inside her. "What did you mean, then?"

"I'm clean."

"And?"

"And you need to tell me right now if you're clean, too."

"How would you know for sure I wasn't lying?"

"I wouldn't."

I start a quick slide of my fingers, in and out of her, as my thumb finds her clit. "So, you're just going to trust me?"

"I'm already trusting you a lot, aren't I?" Her voice is strained. I can hear her trying to steady her breath.

"If you're trying to deny me the orgasm I deserve right now, you better cut that shit out."

She sucks in a loud breath and holds it.

The telltale clench of her core follows quickly behind.

I grip her hip harder and pound into her with my hand as she cries out. Her hands slide helplessly down the slick metal door as she tries to keep herself upright through her orgasm. I strengthen my hold on her middle, keeping her from hitting the ground as I continue to work her pussy.

When she stills, I lower her to her knees, her hands finding the floor in front of her as she slumps forward and pants.

"I was just going to tell you to get on your hands and knees, but you beat me to it."

Her face turns to me, and I get those wide eyes once more. I can't quite read her expression, but once again, she's not running.

"You're going to let me fill you up with my bare cock?"

She nods.

"Say it."

"I trust you to fuck me without a condom. And I trust that you're going to do it right the fuck now."

Oh, this little vixen.

She will be the death of me.

I drop my shorts, my erection springing back up to hit my abs. "Do you want to suck it first?"

She shakes her head no.

I cock my head to the side. "You think you can tell me no right now?"

She nods her head yes.

A slow smile spreads across my face. "Get up on those hands and knees."

Victoria lifts her body back up from where she relaxed on the ground and shifts so her ass is pointed right at me.

The wetness from her orgasm makes her pussy glisten in the fluorescent lighting.

"Fucking hell, girl. I am about to pound you so hard."

She glances back over her shoulder, and I catch a flash of emerald eyes before turning my attention back to the paradise awaiting the tip of my cock.

Fisting myself, I slide the head of my dick up and down her

wet slit. Every inch of her body is pure perfection, from her toned calves and thighs to her adorable, round ass, but these few inches? These are the ones I've been dreaming about.

I nestle my tip at her entrance and prepare to take the plunge.

"Do you want me to fight you?" she asks.

I pause at her words, my cock poised and ready. "Do you want to fight me?"

I'm far more used to contained scenes with carefully agreed upon parameters, but I'm not going to turn this down. Especially when I'm already so far down this rabbit hole.

She nods.

"Say it," I demand.

Instead, she springs to her feet and runs the few paces she can before she hits the wall in the far corner.

I'm right behind her, pinning her flat once more. "You think you're going somewhere?"

"I—" Whatever she's planning to say is muffled as I clasp my hand over her mouth. Her words become cries and little shrieks against her makeshift gag.

With my free hand, I bring the tip of my cock back to where it nearly hit home base just moments before. Victoria thrashes her hips back and forth, but not enough to dislodge me.

I give one hard push and slide to her depths, inhaling the sound of her muffled screaming down to my soul.

I pull out and press back in, wetting myself and preparing to really take her. I don't miss the way her feet slip to the sides and her hips tilt forward just a bit to allow me room to properly fuck her.

I hold tightly to her mouth for leverage as I begin my punishing pace. The room starts to blur as the pleasure from my cock seeps out into the rest of my body. Into my nervous system.

Victoria tilts her head just a bit and bites down hard on my palm, the pain splashing into my ocean of pleasure and turning the whole thing gold. I only grip her tighter, fuck her harder, and before long, her jaws lose their grip.

I release her mouth and reclaim my grip on her hair, pulling her head back as far as her neck will allow and biting down on the soft flesh I find there.

"Look at you, taking me like the fucking slut that you are."

She whimpers, and I bite her again.

"How do you like that?"

Her body thrashes as her fight is renewed by my words, but I'm still not letting go. She's clenched down on me so hard that pumping in and out is a struggle, but it's a challenge I'm happy to rise to.

"So damn tight. Tight and wet, just the way I like it."

"Please…"

"Please what?" I ask, jostling her body with every thrust.

"You're hurting me."

"And?"

"I want more."

I roll my head up to the ceiling and squeeze my eyes closed.

This fucking girl is going to be the death of me.

"I'm hurting you as much as I can in a public fucking restroom."

"More."

I'm giving the girl everything I have. Her neck is forced backward at an odd angle by the grip I have on her hair. I'm practically drawing blood with the grip I have on her hip where my arm wraps around her middle, holding her in place as I impale her with all my strength.

With an impatient snarl that I don't even recognize, I pull her out of the corner and drag her across the room, holding her body close to mine, still inside her.

I push her down by her head onto the small pedestal sink. She spreads her own legs and lifts her hips.

I slide impossibly deeper.

We moan in unison at the new depth.

"Is this what you wanted?"

She nods against my grip, making herself wince at the pull.

"This is what's about to happen." I'm learning the plan myself as the words come out of my mouth in someone else's voice. "I'm going to pull out, and you're going to kneel down while I come on your tits. Got it?"

"Yes," she gasps out as I continue to slam her body into the sink with my thrusts.

"And then I'm going to leave here and go to my house on Merit Island. You're going to get in the car I send to your house and get on the helicopter that will be waiting and come to Merit Island as well. Yes?"

"Yes."

It all sounds so perfect.

Just the thought of this woman, spread for me in my own private space, no one to hear, no one to interrupt, is enough to send me over the edge.

I pull out, and she turns and drops to her knees like the obedient little thing she is.

She squeezes her eyes closed but leaves her mouth hanging open. I almost aim for it, but at the last second force myself to honor the plan.

Watching my hot load hit those peaked nipples is plenty satisfying.

She just kneels there and takes it, her chest rising and falling quickly with her labored breathing.

I pump myself through my orgasm, my vision finally coming back to full clarity as it passes.

And I see the scene before me in the true light.

Shit.

With a sigh, I drop my cock and grab a wad of paper towels. Kneeling down, I clean her chest. Her eyes pop open and watch me as I clean her.

"I'm sorry," I say softly.

"You said never to apologize."

"I said you should never apologize. You have too much to lose."

"And you don't?"

"It's different."

"Tell me."

I look up from her torso and meet her eyes, sitting back on my heels. "I got a little carried away there."

"Yeah, well…"

"No, really. I never should have said or done—"

"I wanted you to."

I shake my head with a sigh. "I'm going to go."

"To your house to wait for me?"

My heart sinks as she recites the plan. "I'm not actually sure that's such a good—"

"It is a good idea."

"Victoria."

"You don't want me anymore?"

I grind my teeth as I retrieve my shorts and pull them on, grabbing for my shirt and heading toward the door. "That's not it. I want you so much."

"Then stop."

I do, hand resting on the handle.

"Just follow the plan."

"Vic—"

"Nope." She's on her feet now, gathering up her clothes. "Whatever that was, it was incredible. We are doing that again. Right away. Bigger. Better. There's something here."

"You are a child."

"I am not a child."

"You are an employee."

"I am not an employee."

"You deserve better."

"I…wait, what does that even mean?"

I shake my head. "I can't give you what you need."

"What I need is one more night of getting railed while I

pretend to try to get away. Can you give me that? Full on. It'll be fun. Do you know what fun is?"

I shake my head slowly.

Victoria pulls her tight pants on and rolls her eyes in frustration. "Well, what we just did, that was fun."

She pulls on her tight pastel sports top.

"It was fun," I say without conviction.

"But?"

"But I just worry."

"Well, you don't have to worry about me. I have literally spent my entire dating career being told by guys that they aren't interested in anything serious and taking whatever meager scraps of time they have to throw at me. I'll be fine."

"I'm sorry, what?" I flashback to all the times Ainsley has brought girls around only to flinch at my referring to them as girlfriends. He would tell me it wasn't anything serious. That they were just hanging out. The thought that those girls were just putting up with his behavior because they thought they didn't deserve anything better turns to bile in my stomach.

I shake my head to clear the image of my son. He's the last person I want to be thinking about when locked in a public restroom with a woman closer to his age who I just completely and utterly violated. "All the more reason for this to end. I don't want to contribute to any ideas you may have about your self-worth being tied to your sexuality."

She laughs. Actually fucking laughs.

And once she starts, she can't seem to stop.

After a few moments of watching her crack up to the point of tears in her eyes, I can't help but start to smile myself.

And then I laugh.

When was the last time I laughed?

"Mr. Suck My Cock Like a Dirty Whore is now worried about making me feel objectified?" She laughs harder than ever.

And, incredibly, so do I. I can't even get it together long enough to respond, so I just shake my head and laugh.

The hormones and adrenaline from my orgasm start to pass and the pain in my core from my hour-long plank session starts to kick in. I hold my stomach and bend forward, trying to take a deep breath and avoid getting a cramp.

"You murdered me in that workout class."

My statement only makes her laugh more. "I know. I did it on purpose."

Tears stream down my face as I laugh. I have to turn away.

I press my palm flat on the cool, white, tiled wall, followed by my forehead. The solid surface has a calming effect, and after a moment, I'm able to breathe again. When I get my shit together, I turn back around to find Victoria standing with her hand on the door handle.

She's flushed red from laughing—and fucking—and looks completely and utterly stunning. It's all I can do not to run across the room and grab her.

I clench my hands into fists and force my feet to remain glued to the spot.

"I'm going to go. I'll be waiting for the car to arrive." She waits for my answer.

All the dopamine from my laugh session fades away as reality sets in. I'm only going to disappoint this spunky, gorgeous, young woman. I may as well get it over with. "I can't make you any promises."

She turns the handle and pulls the door open a crack. "I didn't ask for any."

And then she's gone.

Rule #5

GET AS MUCH DICK AS YOU CAN BEFORE IT ALL GOES TO HELL

VICTORIA

"And he pulls his cock out of my throat and is like—go clean yourself up."

"Oh. My. Fucking. God."

"Yeah. And so I do, but then he's just like, you cleaned up too much, I liked you all dirty, let's mess you up again."

"And he did?"

"Oh, yeah. He definitely did."

I'm giving Sally the rundown of what went down since I last saw her at the hotel bar.

It's quite the tale. By the look on her face, it could be the best story she's ever heard.

"And then he's like, I gotta go, it's best for both of us, blah blah. And I'm like whatever. And then I take the most amazing shower and sleep in that bed, which is seriously the softest bed on the planet."

Her mouth hangs open, waiting for me to go on.

"I came home with just long enough to change into my workout clothes and run to my class."

"Your first class at the new fitness studio. After spending the night getting railed like a porn star."

"Yup. Class setup was going great. I got the lights figured out, thank God. The ladies were coming in, and the room was almost full, and guess who walks through the door?"

"No."

"Yes. It's freaking Ben. And he's with Avery Covington."

"What? Why?"

"Fuck if I know. But they come over, grab mats, and set up for class."

"Did he know you were going to be teaching?"

I shake my head. "No way. When he saw me, I thought he might bolt. But he didn't. They stayed for the whole class. I taught the most punishing class ever." I pause to laugh at the memory of those two strong guys struggling to keep up with my Pilates ladies.

"But that was hours ago. The story isn't over?"

I shake my head. "Not even close. So, after class they bail without saying anything, but then as I head into the private bathroom between the two locker rooms, Ben's right behind me, pushing me in and locking the door behind us."

"No."

I'm blowing her mind, and it's so fun.

"Yup. He's all, I thought you weren't an employee, and I'm all, I'm a contract worker so technically, I'm not. And then he fucked the literal brains out of me right there in the bathroom. At one point, I was like, do you want me to fight you, because I'm crazy or something, and he's like if you want, and so it turned into this whole thing where we pretended he was forcing himself on me like in a movie or something."

"What the actual hell? Are you for real right now?"

"I couldn't make this shit up."

Sally shakes her head, looking a bit ill. "If I could kill you and put your skin on my body, so I could have one night like that, I would do it."

I nod in solemn agreement. "I know."

Sally gets to her feet and shakes her whole body. Then she turns to me, hands on hips. "But you're leaving out, like, the most important part of this whole thing."

I grimace. "I know."

"This man is not just some random guy. He's your ex's dad. So, fucking him is never going to be simple. As a matter of fact, you should give him to me."

I laugh and shake my head. "He's not mine to give. And really, if we're getting all technical, was Ainsley ever really my anything? I mean, he made it pretty clear that we were just casual. Because of the whole *I'm not ready for a relationship* thing all guys do."

"I mean, yes. I get that. But regardless of what that shithead said, you two were something. I mean, you moved here together from Bali."

"Well, he was coming here anyway and suggested that it could be a good place to get a job teaching. Which it was. My job is amazing, even if it's not a permanent gig. So, I wouldn't say that we really moved here together. We just both moved here at the same time, from the same place."

"And spent every night together."

"Yeah, for like two months, until he disappeared last week and showed up on Instagram with some other chick."

"Yeah, that wasn't great."

"I think that's the nail in the coffin of any attempt to call what we had a relationship."

"What would his dad say about that?"

"Ugh. Stop. Can't you just let me enjoy this?"

"I mean, obviously I want you to enjoy it. But it's just not really like you to throw caution to the wind like this. I mean, how long do you think you can keep this a secret? What if Ainsley comes back and sees you together?"

"That's not going to happen."

She looks unconvinced.

"Ben doesn't live here. He lives in New York. He's only here because Ainsley was here. Remember Ains complaining that his dad was flying in to give him a hard time about not going back to college this month? That's why he bailed. He's not coming back as long as his dad's here. And, the reason Ben came is gone, so it's only a matter of time before he leaves too."

"And you want to get as much dick as you can before that happens."

"Exactly."

"Well, you know I support that."

"You are my most supportive friend."

"So, when are you meeting up with him next?"

"He said he's going to send a car to pick me up and take me to a helicopter that's going to take me to another island where he has a house."

"Of course he did. What are you going to wear?"

Rule #6

NAVIGATION IS A LOST ART

VICTORIA

When Sally returns a few hours later, she finds me waiting, all dolled up, on the chair in my room, trying not to cry.

"What on earth happened here?" she asks.

"The car never came. He never called. Or texted." I'm feeling pretty shitty and don't know what to do.

"And you're just sitting here?"

I throw up my arms in exasperation. "What am I supposed to do?"

Sally is not giving into my victim mentality. "Um, something. You can't just sit here and take this. You need to get over there and take his dick."

I shake my head, sinking back into the chair. "He said he'd send a car. He must have changed his mind."

"And just like always, you're going to allow a man to decide what's happening?"

"What's that supposed to mean?"

"Well, this is exactly what happened with Ains. I know you weren't, like, super serious about him, but even if you had been, you would've waited for him to make the first move. As it was, you allowed yourself to exist in limbo for months, even after following the guy across the globe. And you would have continued to do so if he hadn't ended things with a very public post about banging another chick."

"That's one example."

"What about Steve from high school?"

I roll my eyes. "I seriously regret every drunken heart-to-heart sesh with you right now."

"Or Thomas in Bali before you met Ains?"

"Okay, okay. Fine. But what am I supposed to do? If the guy isn't interested in something, no amount of throwing myself at him is going to change that."

"You never know until you try."

"You want me to swim my ass to Merit Island and bang on his door or something?"

"I'll drive you to the beach."

In the end, we both decide it's safer to talk a local snorkel guide into delivering me to Merit Island. The guy warns me that there's only one beach he'll be able to drop me on because of the current tide.

That sounds reasonable. It's a small island, right?

Once I arrive on that beach, however, I'm not quite sure what to do. From the ground, I have exactly zero ability to navigate. I looked at a map before I left, which is lucky considering there's no reception on this rock, but a shit lot of good that does me when I'm standing on a beach with little to no sense of direction. I know the house is on the northeast side of the island. My compass app still works, so I follow it like a pirate.

Other than my handy compass, I'm in no way prepared for a trek across an island. Instead of packing lifesaving essentials like water, sunscreen, bug spray, or even road flares, my tiny day bag contains my favorite DVD, some fun snacks I snagged at the little shop next to my house, and extra underwear.

It's nearly dusk, but still so hot that I'm sweating before I even reach the palms at the edge of the tropical forest. Cursing Sally and her stupid plan every step of the way, I follow the tree line down the beach, hoping to find some kind of path or inroad to get me out of the sun. I've watched too many scary movies in my life to just traipse off into the woods.

Actually, now that I think about it, this whole situation is perfectly stereotypical horror movie heroine behavior.

What the hell am I doing here?

I do find a gravel road that leads into the forest after walking for about ten minutes. I'm grateful to turn inland and get into the shade the trees provide. I only walk for about ten minutes more before a golf cart pulls up beside me.

"You look like you could use a ride."

"Oh, yes. Thank you," I say to the older man driving the cart.

"Hop in," he says. "Where are you headed?"

"I'm trying to get to Ben Adams's house."

The man nods, not looking very surprised.

I suppose there aren't that many places on this tiny island where a lone woman wandering down a dirt road through the jungle in flip-flops could be headed.

"But can you deliver me a little way down from the house? So it looks like I walked the whole way?"

I catch an eyebrow raise and some side eye, but the man refrains from giving me any kind of lecture. He drops me off and points me to a massive house on the beach five hundred yards away or so.

"Gate's unlocked, just push it open."

When I reach the front steps of the house, Ben's standing in the open front door, arms crossed.

"How'd you know I was coming?" I ask.

"Maxwell is my employee."

"Traitor," I mutter under my breath.

"What are you doing here?"

I reach into my bag and pull out the DVD and some of the snacks with a pathetic smile. "Movie night?"

Ben's features remain unmoved. Over his shoulder, however, a smiling face appears.

"Oh, company?" Avery asks, grinning at me.

"No," Ben says.

"Yes," I say. "I just came over to watch a movie."

The silence stretches for a long moment.

"Great," Avery says finally. "I got kicked out of my house because it's girls' night."

"Avery was just leaving," Ben says.

We both look at him in surprise as, in one smooth movement, he pushes Avery out onto the front porch and pulls me into the house, slamming the door behind us.

He slides the dead bolt into place.

"You know, this is my house too, and I have a key. Not to mention the fact that there's like fifteen other doors that I could use," Avery calls through the door.

"Go home," Ben calls over his shoulder without taking his eyes off me.

I smirk at him. "So, movie night?"

"What are you doing here, Victoria?" Ben asks again.

"Well, the car never came."

"I know. I never sent it."

"Well, that was kind of rude. You said you would."

"No, what I said was that I couldn't make you any promises."

"Well, I thought you were talking about some imagined future relationship or something. I didn't know you meant the car."

He crosses his arms across his chest again.

"Do you want me to leave?" I ask, feeling suddenly very foolish for having shown up here.

"No, I don't want you to leave."

Relief pours through me. "Well, you don't look very happy that I'm here."

"It's not that I'm not happy you're here. I just got to thinking about it and decided it would be better for both of us if we just let this be."

"Let it be..."

"Over. Let it rest. It was fun, but I'm not sure it's the right choice for either of us."

"Well, you don't get to make decisions for me. And I disagree." I jot that little line down in a mental notebook to show Sally later. She's going to be so proud.

"I seem to remember you being quite pleased with me making decisions for you."

I feel my cheeks heat as his words conjure up images of our night together. And our morning. "That's different."

"Oh really?"

"Yep."

"Okay, since you're in charge now. What did you have in mind for us this evening?"

The sudden change in his tone and the direction of this conversation takes me a bit by surprise. I scramble to pull the DVD back out of my bag. "Scary movie?"

"Is that a disc?"

"Yeah. You must be old enough to remember DVDs."

"I'm just surprised you are."

"I also brought snacks." I pull the colorful packages out of my bag and hold them up.

Ben's eyebrows go sky high as he examines the loot. "Snacks, huh?"

"Yup. You can't tell me you don't like Combos. Everyone likes Combos."

"I haven't eaten a carb since I was your age."

"You know, if you keep referring to my age so much, I'm going to get the idea that you have something of a younger woman fetish."

Ben lifts his eyebrows, and I can see him holding back a smile. "There's no DVD player in this house, but I'm sure you can find something on one of the streaming channels that will suffice."

And with that, he turns and leads me down a long hallway into a massive living room with vaulted ceilings and enormous windows looking out over the ocean. There's a row of white rimmed French doors that open the room up to the sea breeze.

A set of decadent-looking, cream-colored couches sit in a horseshoe around a low wooden table, with comfy chairs scattered about. The cool tile floor is the color of wet sand, ornamented here and there with long, colorful shag rugs. I can just see into the open kitchen from where I stand, over an island with a row of cushion-topped stools.

"Wow," I say, unable to hold in my awe.

"Yeah, it's really something."

"You guys own this house together?"

"Did your homework, huh?"

"Yeah," I say simply, caught up in the sassy character I get to play around this man. "Did you?"

I don't know why I say it. It's easily the stupidest thing I could've ever said. Why would I suggest he look into my background?

I quickly try to distract him, hoping the idea won't sink in.

"You live here?"

"I live in New York."

"This is your vacation home?"

"Something like that."

"Okay, Mr. Mysterious. Do you like scary movies?"

"I'm not sure I've ever watched one."

My mouth falls open in horror. "Never?"

Ben shrugs, crossing the living room into the open kitchen and heading for the fridge. "Drink?"

"Yes please, what do you have?"

"Most things."

I laugh at the man's inability to elaborate. "I'll have a White Claw."

"I don't have that."

"I'll have whatever you're having then."

I make my way over to the massive television and start fishing around for remotes.

I hear a clink behind me and turn to see Ben setting down two rocks glasses, half full of amber liquid, on the table behind us.

Of course.

"How do you turn this thing on?"

"Just tell it to turn on."

"Television, turn on."

The television turns on.

Wow.

I walk back and settle myself onto the couch, lifting my drink, and taking the tiniest sip of the room-temperature liquor. "Mmm, warm, straight booze."

"You said you wanted what I was having."

I roll my eyes and turn my attention back to the television. "What streaming services do you have?"

"I'm not sure," Ben says.

"You don't watch TV at all?"

"Not really, but the guys do."

"Okay." I turn back to the television. "Television, put on Netflix."

The television obeys.

Perfect. "Television, scary movies."

I scan the screen until I see something I think will be appropriate for a newbie. "Television, Zombieland." I turn to Ben. "Is it safe to assume you've never seen this one?"

"That would be a correct assumption."

"You're going to love it."

Rule #7

YOU MIGHT NEED A LIABILITY WAIVER

BEN

Yet another character meets some sudden, gruesome death, and Victoria jumps a little in her seat and then laughs.

"You like being scared," I observe aloud.

She turns to me, eyes narrowed. "You already knew that."

"What's that supposed to mean?"

"I mean, the little games you like to play."

"I..." I fight down a rush of panic and try to keep my voice level. "During those games you were scared?"

She shrugs. "I mean, I'm not sure fear is the first word I would use to describe it, but it's really overwhelming. It's in the same family of emotions."

"I'm not sure how I feel about that."

She gives me an incredulous look. "You can't tell me that you're shocked to hear that you scared me a little bit."

"That's exactly what I'm telling you. If I thought for a second you were afraid for your life, in any of those situations, I—"

"You what, would've made me sign a liability waiver?"

I laugh. She's got me there. "I mean yes, but no. I don't want you to be in a situation where you need to sign a waiver. You know what I mean."

"I know what you mean. But to answer your question, yeah, I think it's fun to be scared."

I can't think of anything to say so I just grind my teeth and worry about where this conversation is going.

"You look like you're about to cry," she says and not in a soothing way.

She's teasing me, and I can't decide if I like it.

"I'm just concerned."

"Concerned about me becoming a liability?" She rolls her eyes. "Don't worry. I'm not gonna ask you to chase me through the dark house wearing a Jason mask or anything."

I narrow my eyes at her but say nothing.

She balks. "Please tell me you know who Jason is."

"I understand it's some kind of pop-culture reference, but—"

"Oh my god." She turns sharply away from me to face the television. "Television, play Friday the Thirteenth."

I can't make myself turn away from her to face the screen. "I need you to know that you are never in danger with me."

Her head whips toward me. "I know."

"If you're scared, I need you to tell me."

"No."

"What do you mean no?"

"I mean, no. My emotions are my own business. I like the little games we play, and if I decide to let them go far enough that I get a little scared of what's going to happen next, that's my own business."

"That is definitely my business as well."

"Well, I guess you better type up that liability waiver."

"We won't be needing it."

"That's that, huh? You're just gonna walk away because I was honest? Oh, that's right, you prefer it when I lie, don't you? Okay, sorry. Oh wait—don't apologize Victoria, it makes you look weak. Okay, not sorry. Anyway, I was just joking. I'm never scared at all when we're together. When you grab my skull and fuck my throat like a madman, I feel like I'm skipping through a field of wildflowers. That's what all girls think when you do that."

"Cheeky little thing, aren't you?"

She shrugs.

"Okay, fine. You're right. You're allowed to feel scared if you want to. And I'm not going to lie, the idea of scaring you is not completely repulsive to me."

Her eyes narrow. "Oh, now we're getting somewhere."

I shake my head. "I don't know if I want to go to that place."

"Why not? It could be so fun."

The combination of blood rushing to my groin and dread building in my stomach starts to make me feel a little bit crazy. "Let's just watch the movie."

"Of course," she says. "It's just movie night."

I make a mental note to draw up a liability waiver.

For all her big talk, Victoria isn't even awake long enough to see the first blonde-haired, big-bosomed woman get macheted to ribbons by the man in a hockey mask.

I, however, can't take my eyes off the screen.

During the first movie, all my attention was on Victoria, transfixed watching her reactions to the gore and violence on the screen.

But now, with her sleeping peacefully in my lap, I'm able to let myself experience the film.

And it's fucking glorious.

Rule #8

THE GAME IS ON

VICTORIA

I wake up refreshed and happy in an enormous white bed, facing two large, sunny windows overlooking the ocean.

I know I'm in Ben's guest room. And I know I'm here because he refused to let me sleep in his room. What I don't quite know is what I'm going to do next.

I mean, we had a pretty good time last night, watching scary movies, having snacks, and teasing each other. But then I fell asleep, and he tucked me in here. There was no wild, late-night sex in the spooky mansion. No sneaking into anyone's bedroom for a rendezvous. Not even a single kiss.

After our first two encounters, both of which ended with him inside me, I just assumed that's what would happen every time. Since it didn't, I guess he's done with me.

I can hear Sally's voice in my head telling me that I have a choice here too, but it's much harder to conjure up the courage to act when faced with the absolute reality of the situation. We hung out but didn't fuck.

I think I may have been friend-zoned.

Made only worse by the fact that I'm pretty sure we're not friends.

I crawl out of bed and slip my shorts back on, having been put to bed in my tank top and panties. I am momentarily reassured remembering that he, at the very least, saw my fancy underwear.

He saw them and decided not to rip them off my body. Shit.

There goes that little bit of confidence.

I make my way downstairs. The house seems to be empty, but I smell coffee, so I follow my nose to the kitchen. There's a fresh pot, but no one is around. I pour myself a cup and suffer through the first sip of black coffee after failing to locate any cream or sugar in this health nut's kitchen.

Holding my cup, I start to wander through the house. It's airy and open, filled with light, even down the hallways, which all have windows open to the fresh morning air. Brick red and cream tiles line the floors of most of the halls and bedrooms, merging into jewel toned blues and greens in the bathrooms. I shake my head imagining how many hours were spent laying tile in this mausoleum.

I encounter the first sign of life when I reach the far end of the main floor and follow the sounds to a full-on fitness center. Ben is at the weight set in the center, doing deadlifts. I freeze there for a moment, admiring his fine ass before taking a good look around.

To my left is a black modular rack filled with athletic shoes of all sizes and colors. I set my coffee cup on top and start hunting through small-looking pairs until I find some that are just my size. I slip them on with no socks, leaving my flip-flops in a pile by the doorway.

"Good morning," Ben says, finally noticing me as he sets down the bar he was holding and wipes his brow and shoulders with a small towel.

"Morning."

"You found the coffee?"

"Yup. Nice and black, just like punishment."

I earn a small, huffed laugh for my joke and I tuck it into the secret pocket of my shorts for later.

"I'm going to go for a run on the beach. If you don't mind me borrowing these shoes?" I ask.

Ben glances at my feet and shakes his head. "No, those have all just been abandoned here over the years." He starts to walk toward me, and I steel myself to remain cool and collected with his sudden closeness. "Give me ten, and I'll go with you."

A glimmer of excitement shoots through me at the idea that he wants to spend time with me, even if it's just joining me on a run. "Sure you can keep up, old man?"

His narrowed eyes and smirking lips do nothing to calm down the wildfire that ignites in my nervous system.

"You know, if you keep bringing up my age, I might start to think you've got an older man fetish." He twists my words from the night before and tosses them at me.

I don't react in time to catch them, and the full force of his flirtation hits me right in the chest.

"Most girls do," is all I can manage to squeak out.

Ben just raises his eyebrows at me.

I turn and start to escape.

"Wait for me on the patio. I just need to change my shoes."

I run up the stairs to the kitchen and hide behind the wall, eyes squeezed closed, head pressed back, trying to calm myself down.

What is it about this guy that throws me for such a freaking loop? I wasn't so flustered last night when we spent the whole evening practically snuggling on the couch.

But last night I figured we were just in foreplay mode.

Now I have no idea what's going on.

I wait for him on one of the chaise lounges on the patio, enjoying the cool morning breeze from the ocean. The view from this house is absolutely incredible.

"Ready?"

I jump up. "Yeah."

"I usually run north about five miles and then back."

Oh, so just a quick ten mile run along the beach? Sure, no biggie.

"Sounds good to me."

Another eyebrow raise. "Okay then."

He jogs down the steps toward the sandy path to the beach. It's slow going here in the loose sand, and I follow him until we reach the shore. Once we're on wet, packed sand, he veers right, and I come up beside him. We jog along for a few moments, me looking straight ahead, and Ben looking I don't know where because I haven't dared to look over.

His voice shakes me out of my own mind.

"It's a bit different, running on sand. The slight give with each step makes your body work harder to push off each time. If you're not used to it, you'll be feeling your calves tomorrow like never before."

The fitness junkie inside me perks up at the idea of unlocking a new way to target a muscle, but I keep it cool. "Is that a challenge?"

Ben just laughs. He's starting to do that more and more, I notice. "Isn't everything?"

"I suppose," I say, picking up my pace just enough to pull ahead as we head into a narrow strip of beach between the lapping tide and a bed of seagrass. I can feel Ben on my heels.

"You know," he starts, sounding not even a bit winded. I may have met my match after all. "I usually don't like falling behind. But I don't mind this one bit."

His obvious flirtation sends my heart soaring. I toss a smile over my shoulder. "Picking up my rear?"

Another laugh from Ben has me grinning.

After a mile or so of white sand beach, glittering sunshine, and watching birds dive for their breakfast, I'm feeling exhilarated—and a little fatigued.

Am I going to make it through ten miles of this?

Don't get me wrong. On a treadmill, I could bang out ten miles in ninety minutes or less. But on this beach? I can feel my body struggling for purchase with every step.

But I'll be damned if I'm going to let Ben see how hard it is. I've got twenty years on him. I'm not quitting before he does.

I wonder…

"You know, you've been back there an awful long time, Ben. Are you having trouble catching me?" I toss the words over my shoulder, trying to sound as calm as possible.

I hear him laugh. "I didn't realize that was the point of this exercise."

"Well, it could be," I sass over my shoulder.

And then I take off.

I won't be able to sustain this new speed for long, but luckily, Ben's right behind me, matching me step for step. I hadn't exactly thought this plan through—besides the fact that it might involve getting his hands back on my body.

Now I'm gazing furiously side to side and down the beach, looking for a soft looking place for him to take me down.

As if I was in control of that.

His arm takes me completely by surprise, swooping in from the ocean side as I was distracted looking up the beach. It knocks me off balance, and I start to go down. His other arm clasps hands with the first, circling my body as we both hit the sand.

He presses me to my back and settles his hips over mine, one leg on either side of my body. I open my mouth to speak but Ben presses his hand immediately over it, my lips wide against his sandy palm, the taste of the ocean filling my mouth. I struggle, twisting my body back and forth but his strong hands keep me in place.

"We wouldn't have had to go through all this if you would have just stopped running now, would we?"

A heady rush of excitement and desire pulses from my chest to my toes with the way he falls right into this little game.

As if he could read my mind.

"I wouldn't have to chase you down if you would just be a good girl and stay where I tell you to stay."

He's flipping my body over, his hand still cupped tightly over my mouth, his grip lifting my head and keeping my face from planting right in the sand.

"I'm going to let go of your mouth now, but do you know what will happen if you scream?" He speaks the words right into my ear, the rush of hot air sending chills down my spine.

I nod the best I can with my head in his grip.

He releases my mouth, and I suck in a gasp of fresh air. I rest my forehead on the sand in front of me, still struggling to catch my breath. Ben's hands are everywhere, snaking down my body and slipping up the legs of my shorts. His touch sets me on fire, and I wriggle in his grasp, trying to inspire more of it.

"You think you're going to get away from me?"

"I just…" I want to play too, but my mind is slow to catch up. "Didn't think you'd actually chase me."

"I didn't want to," he says at the same time he pulls my shorts down with a sharp tug. The breeze on my now bared ass is a shock to my system. I nearly moan with desire but try to make it sound more like a yelp. "But you had to take off running and ruin the perfectly nice morning we were having."

"I'm sorry," I whimper.

My reward is a firm smack on my ass. I yelp again in surprise.

"What did I tell you about apologizing?"

This man is going to be the death of me.

"Fine, I'm not sorry." I force the words out, reigniting my struggle, actually making an attempt to get free this time.

Ben reacts by using one of his strong hands to pin both of mine to the sand above my head. "I'm not sorry either." His other hand snakes between my legs, and I know damn well what he finds there. My entire slit pulses with anticipation as he drags his fingers through my wetness.

"I'm not sorry one bit." As he speaks the words, he drives his fingers inside me, pumping them in and out as I continue to squirm.

It's lost on no one that all I've managed to do is wiggle my legs wider.

"Little fucking slut," Ben starts, his invasion of my body complete as he adds a thumb to my clit, and what feels like it might be his pinkie right into my asshole. "Always telling me no. Always running away. But always so wet for me."

I can feel his erection rubbing on my ass as he grinds his whole body against mine, fucking me mercilessly with his hand. I squeeze my eyes closed and press my forehead harder into the sand in front of me. There's nothing for me to do here except surrender control.

And come.

I reach my release hard and fast, taking in a mouthful of sand as my mouth flies open. I turn my head to the side and spit as I moan and grind myself against his hand, pulses of pleasure clenching my core and taking away any breath I manage to gasp into my lungs.

"God, your pussy is so tight clenching down on me like that."

Ben's dirty words hit my mind like lightning, unlocking a new wave of pleasure as he continues to pump his hand in and out of my body.

"I'm about to fuck that tight little pussy. Would you like that?"

I'm gasping for breath, still held down tightly by his hips and his arms holding mine overhead. I offer a bit of struggle, but it's halfhearted. "Anyone could see us."

Ben scoffs, pulling his hand out from between my legs and wiping it carelessly on my bare back. "You didn't care much who saw when you ran from me."

He jerks my arms down, so they're held behind my back, my fists clenched tightly right above the swell of my naked ass. Then he hauls me back toward him, so my legs bend, and I'm folded over them, face still pressed into the sand. "Besides, this is my beach. There's no one here to see. No one here to rescue you. I don't know where you thought you were running before. But there's no escape."

His cock slides into me without warning, the full length of him bottoming out on his first thrust. "So fucking wet for me."

It's true.

This is easily the hottest thing that's ever happened to me, and this week has had some close contenders already. There's just something about the deserted beach that takes it up a notch, like I'm a pirate's prisoner or something.

I freaking love it.

"So tight. If I didn't know any better, I'd say you were a virgin."

"Is that what you want?" I manage to get out, turning my head just enough to be heard.

Ben pauses for the briefest moment in his complete and utter domination of my body, and I catch a glimmer of something in his eyes. From this angle, though, it could just be the sunlight.

But then he speaks. "Yeah. I guess so." It's more of a grunted whisper than anything, but I take the cue.

"Yes, I'm a virgin. I was supposed to be saving myself for marriage."

Well, that did the trick. He pounds into me harder than ever. "Too fucking late for that, little virgin. You're all filled up with cock. How do you like it?"

He grips a handful of hair and uses it to pull my head a few inches off the sand. "It's good—"

Oh, no, wait…

"It hurts." I remember my part and call the words out in my best tearful whimper.

"I bet it hurts. Your little pussy is so tight, and my cock is so big. That's why it hurts." He pulls my hair harder, my back arching as my body comes up to meet his. The sting from my scalp brings tears to my eyes, and when he turns my head, the sight of those does something to him.

If he was mean before, now he's more like feral.

"Say it. Tell me why it hurts so bad when I fuck your pussy."

"Be...because your cock is so big," I manage to get out, the complete and utter overwhelmingness of the whole scene threatening to close in on me.

Ben drops his grip on my hair, and I manage to catch my head just before it hits the sand. I close my eyes and rest my face down, happy to have my head back under my own control. From here, I can calm down a bit and focus on the best part of this—the punishing thrusts into my body. His cock really is very big, and it might actually hurt a lot more if he hadn't spent the last few days stretching me to fit him.

The thought of that makes my eyes roll back in my head, eyelids cinched tightly closed. This is so fucking hot. I will never recover.

"No one's ever going to want you now."

The strain in his voice tells me that he's getting close, and I can't help my little smile—that luckily, he can't see. I'm seriously impressed with how deep and fast he fell into this game. For a guy who just last night was telling me we needed a liability waiver for any more rough sex, he sure is violating me in public like an animal.

"Only you."

The words are all wrong, and I wish I could take them back the second I say them. I was trying to play the violated virgin captive, but I realize my mistake the second I utter those words.

But Ben's hips don't even slow down, if anything, he goes at me harder. My knees are starting to sink with his punishing downward thrusts, but I can still feel every inch of his cock slide through my wetness.

He stumbles in his pace, not pulling out before slamming deeper inside me. I can feel his core contract against my ass as he presses himself deeper. I start to think he's going to come silently, but he lets out a strangled moan and takes my hips in both hands, pulling almost all the way out and then slamming back in again. And again.

Playing around in his own wetness in my body.

Just when I think he might use my body until he's completely limp, he finally flops on his back on the beach next to me. "Holy shit."

I laugh softly, carefully uncurling my body and sitting up. I stretch my legs out, shaking them and my arms, before laying on the beach beside him, propped on one elbow. I'm half naked and leaking cum, but I don't even care right now.

"Yeah," I say finally.

My voice shakes Ben out of whatever stupor he went into post orgasm, and he opens his eyes, finding mine as he props himself on both elbows. "What the hell was that all about saving yourself for marriage?" He's got a sly smile on his lips, and it makes me smile back at him.

"I was a rich merchant's daughter who you kidnapped."

Ben lets his body flop back down onto the sand, shaking his head.

"It was an arranged marriage, though, to the corrupt mayor of the town where I grew up, so you actually kinda did me a favor."

Ben just shakes his head again. "I just got off so hard, forcibly deflowering my virgin prisoner on the beach. Right out in the open. What the fuck is wrong with me?"

I scoff. "There's nothing wrong with you. It was fun."

He rolls over to his side and considers me. "You had fun."

It's not a question, but I nod.

After a long moment, he nods too. "Don't get me wrong, I had fun."

"But…"

He sighs. "But I'm supposed to be a role model. I don't know where this behavior is coming from." As if something terrible just occurred to him, he turns to me sharply. "I don't actually do these kinds of things in real life."

I just laugh at his fluster, letting my body flop back onto the sand. "Kidnap virgin townswomen and hold them prisoner on your pirate ship?"

"You know what I mean."

I'm annoyed enough with this line of conversation that I say nothing.

That doesn't fly for long.

"Tell me that you know what I mean."

I roll back over to face him. "I know what you mean, okay? I don't think that you're running around the city accosting innocent girls. This is a game. It's fun. I'm totally good with it. Better than good. I have a safe word. We're safe."

The way my words visibly reassure him makes me feel a bit bad about not offering them sooner. I just thought…

"You know, I thought you were kinda into this stuff. At least, that's how it seemed at the hotel that first night."

"There's a big difference between BDSM scenes at a club and whatever that was."

"Tell me."

Ben pulls his shorts back up and lays on his back, arm over his forehead to shield his eyes from the morning sun. "It's all very controlled. That's what I like about it. I need that kind of control in my life. I need to be in control. Going to those clubs is my way of feeding two birds with one seed. I get off. It's enjoyable, the women are very experienced and professional. And I get to sharpen the skills I need to hold the reins of my life."

Whoa, there's a lot to unpack there.

I decide to grab for the lowest hanging fruit. "Feeding two birds with one seed?" I don't laugh, but even I can hear the laughter in my voice.

Ben doesn't look over. "Yeah, it means to take care of two needs with one action."

Now I'm laughing. "I know what it means, but the saying is kill two birds with one stone."

He rolls his head to the side and smiles at me. "I guess it is, huh? Well, that's what years of putting a kid through yuppie private school will get you. Dumbed down."

His tone turns harsh on the last two words, and my forehead wrinkles in question. There is clearly something there, but I'm not sure if it's my place to ask. I mean, I know for damn sure it's not my place to ask, but will he think it's strange if I don't?

I finally decide to let it go, rolling back in the sand until I'm flat on my back. While that conversation took an interesting turn, I won't say I didn't learn a few things. A bit of Ben's history, and a glimpse into the life he and Ainsley had together.

It's nearly too much.

I know I have to keep it together in order to keep my façade up for Ben, but it's all I can do not to fall into a puddle of my own regrets. Ainsley probably would have grown out of this phase of his, whatever it is, and been the perfect guy to settle down with. If only I could have figured out a way to stick with him. Or, more accurately, gotten him to stick with me. Gotten him to decide that I was the one he wanted, instead of just some girl he hung out with for a while.

Ugh. Even the thought of him right now makes me want to hurl. What a fucking douche.

I roll to my side and consider the man in front of me. His eyes are closed, arm still covering the top half of his face. It does nothing to obscure his good looks, however. The man is a freaking smoke show. Chiseled just how I like, tan, and clean shaven. His chest is covered with a fine layer of dark hair that I'm dying to run my hands through again.

Maybe I don't regret his loser of a son.

Maybe the real regret in this situation is the fact that I'm walking a tightrope over a steaming pit of lies and deception, and it's only a matter of time before I fall in.

Because if there's one thing I know for sure—Mr. I Need to Be in Control of Everything in Life over here isn't going to go for an affair with his son's ex.

So, what am I doing?

Am I really going to push this along as far as I can, even with the inevitable end already in sight?

I mean, obviously, yes.

The sigh I let out as I flop onto my back must be loud, because Ben rolls to face me. "You okay?" he asks.

"Oh, yeah. For sure." I try to keep my voice calm and level, but I probably fail.

He lets out a sigh of his own. "You know, I never should have brought up those other women like that. It seemed like an innocuous thing to discuss at the time, but I can see now how insensitive it was to talk about having sex with other women when I'm here with you."

Um—not what I was expecting him to say, but okay.

"Oh, it's okay. I mean, I asked about the clubs."

"Yes, but there were ways I could have answered without making it seem like I just use professional women as a regular hobby. I'm sure you interpreted that to mean that I think that way of you, and I need you to know that I don't."

Um…

Before I can speak—not that I had anything intelligent to say—he pulls me over, so I'm curled against his body like the small spoon.

"When I told you that I used those clubs for pleasure and control, I hope you know that I meant that in the past tense."

Okay, what the actual fuck is going on right now? Maybe I hit my head when we fell and am hallucinating this?

I turn in his arms until I can see his face. His hair is mussed, and sand is sticking to his sweaty parts. I have to smile at his dishevelment—it's not something I've seen before.

"What do you mean?"

His eyes narrow slightly, and I can almost see his mind churning, coming up with the perfect thing to say. "I just mean that whatever this is between us, it's not like anything I've ever had before." His tone is controlled, as if the machine of his mind is feeding him each word one at a time. "I usually strive for control in all areas of my life. And, while I definitely want to control you and dominate you, it's different. It makes me nervous, but also very interested. I should be backing away from this, but I'm not. Quite the opposite. I kind of want to see where this goes."

He's silent for a long moment, probably waiting for my eloquent speech, but it's not forthcoming.

Finally, his own brow crinkles. "I mean, if you want to."

And I do, certainly. I want this. I want him. I want everything.

But I can't have it.

And prolonging this will only break my heart even more when it all finally comes crashing down.

But do I tell him the truth? Do I tell him we can't do this?

No, no I don't.

"I do," I say quickly, every cell of my being terrified that if I don't claim him, the offer will be rescinded.

"Okay." He places a kiss on my forehead, and I melt. "Well, I'm sure it goes without saying that we need to take it slow." He laughs softly at his own words. "I mean, as slow as we can, having already done all the things we've done. My relationship history doesn't exactly give me a guide for how to navigate something like this."

Uh, yeah. Mine neither.

"Of course. Slow is good."

Oh, sweet treachery.

Rule #9

IT'S PROBABLY NOTHING

BEN

It took me a lot of years to reach private helicopter status, and these days, it's the only way I like to get on and off Merit Island.

I actually cringe at the idea of how this girl must have been ferried over here yesterday when she snuck up to my house.

Woman. Victoria is a woman. Not a girl.

I make a mental note to remove the word girl from my thoughts and vocabulary when it comes to her.

I'm still not quite sure what's going on here, but what I do know is that I couldn't make myself stop if I tried.

And I am nothing if not the master of my own willpower.

She's got some kind of draw that I don't want to ignore. Our time together is…well, it's fun.

When was the last time I had fun?

Never comes to mind, but that can't be right, can it? I mean, I raised an entire child, there must have been fun times.

But when I scan back through my memories of Ains's childhood, the only emotion that rises inside me is fear. I spent his childhood terrified that I would screw him up or let him die and fail to live up to the promise I made to my dying wife.

Take good care of Ainsley, Ben. He loves you so much.

Words I used to write over and over in my dark study at night while he slept in his bedroom. Words I tattooed onto my soul.

And I did take good care of him. I raised him according to the very best advice available on the topic. Gave him every opportunity for education and enrichment. Every opportunity to succeed in life.

Only to have him squander it on a life of—

"What's got your face all twisted like that?"

I smile at Victoria's voice, coming out of the house to join me in the golf cart. "Oh, it's nothing. Just work stuff."

Not that this girl, woman dammit, would care that I more or less failed my job as a parent. She has no idea what a commitment like that does to a person and probably won't know for years.

Oh, to be young and free again.

"Speaking of work, I kinda forgot that I have a spa center meeting coming up at eleven this morning, so do you think we could head out?"

I glance at my watch. Ten thirty. I grind my teeth just a bit at the thought of her carelessly shirking her responsibilities, but then I hear my dentist's voice in my head and relax my jaw. "You might be a few minutes late. I can call ahead and let them know if you—"

"No. No, that's okay," she says, far too quickly. "It's not a huge deal. We're just going over the schedules for the next few weeks and talking about how the opening went. It'll be okay if I'm a few minutes late."

Sounds like a very important meeting to me, but there's nothing I can do about it, so I just drive off toward the helipad as quickly as I can without looking like a madman.

The helicopter lands on Faraday at ten fifty, not that I'm

keeping track.

As we climb out and head toward the waiting golf cart, Victoria pauses and turns to me. "Do you think I could take this one, and you could grab another? I mean, I don't really want to show up at the resort together."

"Of course. Sure. You go." It's only now that I realize I foolishly failed to properly negotiate the terms of our "arrangement" or whatever it is. It makes me feel naked, exposed, and scared to not know the boundaries or rules.

It's exhilarating. The feeling swells in my chest, and I feel my dick start to harden.

What is going on with me?

"But we need to talk soon about what exactly we're going to tell people and who is being told."

Had to go and ruin it, huh, Bentley?

"Oh, sure. I can't do tonight because I have a super early class in the morning. But soon."

"Okay." Letting her leave without a solid plan for when I get to see her again is absolute torture, but what choice do I have? "Have a good day."

She turns as she slides onto the front bench of the cart, next to the driver, and smiles. "Thanks. You, too."

And then she's gone.

Eventually, another taxi comes and takes me to The Sands. I head straight for Sam's office.

"Hey."

He looks up from his desk and smiles. "Morning, Ben. I didn't realize you were still here."

"I've been on Merit…sleeping with one of the resort employees. I'm about to head up to HR to file paperwork. I just thought you should know."

Sam, bless his heart, doesn't let out the laugh that clearly accompanies the smile on his lips as he nods. "Okay. Great. I mean, good for you."

I huff. "It's probably nothing."

Sam crosses his arms and leans back in his chair. "Probably nothing?"

"I just mean..." What do I mean? Why did I even say anything and open this line of questioning? Before I know it, I'm going to be spilling my guts out right here in the office for everyone to see.

No better guy to share them with, though, probably.

I sigh. "I like her. We've had fun these last few days. But she's much too young for me, and she lives here, not in New York."

Sam says nothing, but his eyebrows raise enough for me to know that I've sparked his interest.

Like a damn fool, I fall into the oldest trap in the book and keep talking. "She teaches Pilates in the new spa fitness program, so technically she's a contract worker. I don't know how I got into this. We met at the bar, and she just...I don't know how to describe it."

"She picked you up at a bar?"

I laugh at the sheer ridiculousness of his words. "Yeah. I guess so."

"That's great, Ben. I'm happy for you."

Of course he is.

"I trust you'll do the right thing by the resort, so you've got my full blessing. Go have fun."

I huff out another laugh at this whole situation. "I guess I am having fun."

"If you're sticking around for a while, you should come over for dinner one of these evenings. I've been working hard on the property, and I'd love to have you out to see it."

Sam purchased a fixer-upper when we first moved to the island nearly a decade ago and has been slowly turning it into a inhabitable space. It's been over a year since I visited him out there, so it's far overdue.

"Absolutely, man. Let's make it happen."

HR signs off on my new entanglement without much paperwork due to the fact that she's not actually an employee, and I don't actually work at the resort.

Ten minutes later, I'm left with the entire day ahead of me and no idea how to spend it. I know Ave would tell me to relax and enjoy the weather, but I'm no good at relaxing. I need something to do.

But the only thing I want to do is currently in a staff meeting in the basement of my resort.

It's been an hour. She could be out by now.

That deranged thought only sends me further for a loop. What am I doing here? Chasing this woman around like a puppy dog. I mean, sure, the only thing I want right now is to go find her, but I shouldn't.

I turn my attention to the only other person on the planet who can fully and completely absorb my attention. My son.

Ainsley lets the call go to voicemail, and I slam my phone down on the table at Reef where I came to have an early lunch. I switch to stalking his socials just as my salad arrives.

His last picture was over forty-eight hours ago, and, while it was location tagged, there's no reason to think he's still there. Not even a year ago, I would've taken the bait and flown over there, tearing apart the island for him, but I've learned my lesson enough times not to bother.

He's got a tight group of friends who are apparently bankrolling his globetrotting. God knows I've shut off his credit cards. The kid's ability to keep pursuing this lifestyle, even with all my obstacles and backlash, is truly impressive.

Or it would be impressive if it wasn't so damn infuriating.

I mean, would it be so hard to just go to college? He could get a job that allowed him to travel after graduation. Doctors Without Borders, the Peace Corps, or even a goddamn travel journalist. Anything but this.

To be perfectly honest, I don't even know what he's doing these days, and maybe that's the worst part about it. I need him to go to the college I chose for him, get an approved degree, and then he can travel the world.

I do understand that I have control issues. I watch myself behaving this way and am fully aware of the insanity of it. But that doesn't stop me.

I can let it go when I watch resort employees working in the most inefficient manner possible.

I can keep my mouth shut when my law interns make mistakes and let their supervisors discipline them.

But I cannot stand aside and watch my child ruin his whole life because he doesn't understand the consequences of his actions.

"Hey, man."

Avery slides into the booth across from me.

"Hey."

"How'd movie night go?"

He's acting casual, but I can see the excitement rippling under his calm facade. And I get it. Having a woman over to the house like that isn't just unusual for me, it's unheard of. There have been times in the past when I've brought women from the club to Merit, ones I got along with particularly well, but those arrangements were all just that. Arrangements.

And what the hell is this thing with Victoria?

"It went well."

Avery's eyebrows raise as he tries to stay calm in the face of my intentional evasion.

"And…"

I smirk at him and lean back in my seat. "And what?"

"And you just had a date for…I don't know, the first time ever? Give me something, man."

"I'm going to see her again."

He shakes his head, snorting out a laugh. "Fine, keep it to yourself. I'll find out eventually."

The server stops by our table and takes Avery's order. I'm grateful for the interruption. I wasn't expecting it to be so difficult to talk about what seems to be happening between Victoria and me. Usually, I have no problem offering people the truth, even when that truth is complicated or challenging to admit.

With her though, I want to keep it all to myself. Keep her all to myself.

Interesting development.

"You didn't find Ains, I take it?" Avery cuts into my thoughts with his words, effectively derailing my wandering mind. Back to business.

"No. He took off right before I got here. He's posting on socials, but I have no idea if he's still at any of the places where the pictures were taken. I'm sure it would be pointless to fly over there. I'll probably do it anyway, just to have some kind of action to take."

"Let me go."

I look sharply toward him, our eyes meeting as I try to read his intentions. He knows me too well and glances down at the table.

"Fran and I have a few weeks off between weddings. I'll country hop for a while, pin him down, figure out what's going on. You know that'll go better than if you show up and start reading him the riot act."

I let out a sigh and shake my head. He's right, of course, but it's still challenging for me to let go of control in this situation. If it was any other person offering this, I'd blow them off immediately, but Avery's got a better chance of securing a positive outcome with the kid than I do at this point.

"Okay."

If he's surprised by my sudden relenting, it doesn't show on his face. "Great." He smiles up at the server as she sets down his coffee and croissant.

I can't stop the smile from sneaking onto my face as I recall Victoria showing up at the house with all of her snacks. I actually ate a couple of them, just to stop her from teasing me.

"What's that look for?"

I fix my face and shake my head. "Nothing. Thank you for going to find Ains."

"Yeah, man. It's no problem. What should I do when I find him? I mean, I'll talk to him, of course, figure out what's going on. But what's the desired outcome of all this?"

"He needs to go back to the city and prepare for the new quarter. He's already enrolled. All he needs to do is show up."

Avery is giving me that look he gives when he doesn't quite agree but hasn't decided if fighting me is worth it.

"What?" I demand.

He cocks his head to the side. "That's the only outcome that would be deemed a success?"

My temper flares, but I keep it under control. "He's had a whole year of fucking off to get this out of his system. It's time for him to show some semblance of adult responsibility and start college. I already enrolled him. I even leased an apartment, so he doesn't have to worry about that."

"You choose his major for him, too?"

I scowl over at my best friend. "The first two years are general ed. He'll choose his own major with his guidance counselors when the time comes."

"Oh, and you're just going to let him pick whatever he wants? Do you even know what he does on these trips he takes?"

"Party?"

"His last long stay was in Indonesia where he was working with Aid International to build a school."

"I'm glad to hear he's so fond of schools. There is a very nice one in Boston waiting for him."

Avery grins at me, but I can see the pity in his look. He thinks I'm being unreasonable, driving my son away with my unrelenting stance on his future. And maybe I am, but I don't know what else to do.

"Just get him back to the States, okay? Get him to the estate, and we can work things out."

"I'll do my best," he answers, but I know what that means. Avery accomplishes anything he sets his mind to—just like Ainsley.

It's a damn shame those two don't set their sights a little higher.

Rule #10

DO IT OR DON'T

VICTORIA

I have to be up early for my class, but Sally talks me into dinner and wine with her at our apartment. Dinner is takeout and cheap wine from the little shop down the block from our ground level flat, but it's a lovely little date anyway.

And my stories from the night before are good enough to make both of us forget about any shortcomings in the menu.

"He's, like, into you."

"I mean, that's what I thought too, especially after that shit he said on the beach, but now that I've had some time to think about it, I don't know."

"What's not to know?"

"I mean, sure he said that stuff, but it could have just been the adrenaline from fucking or something."

"I don't think that's a thing."

I let out a sigh. "It's just…it's hard to believe that he could be so interested in me so quickly. And after having not dated anyone in, like, years? Why me?"

Sally shrugs and forces down another slug of her wine, trying not to grimace. "Men always want what they can't have. Maybe he can sense the fact that you've got a big, nasty secret looming over you. Your dark cloud of deception is casting you in the perfect light."

I roll my eyes and take a sip of my own wine. It really is a shame that they can't import some nice pinots or even rosés from the States. I mean, they managed to get our peanut butter and Doritos on their shelves, why not wine?

I make a mental note to find out if the Merit Island house has a wine cellar.

"Our fling has an expiration date, that's for sure," I say finally. It's what I keep reminding myself in my own head, and it feels good to say it out loud. Makes it even more real. Because the worst possible thing I could ever do in this situation is take his kind words to heart and forget what it is we're doing here.

"Well, get it while it's good, I guess." Sally holds her glass up, and we cheers, but my heart isn't in it.

It's one thing to joke with my friend, or even to tell myself in my mind that this is a short-term thing. It's quite another to be faced with the man himself and try to hold onto these thoughts. Try to do anything besides melt into a puddle at his feet. And then he goes and says stuff like, *I kind of want to see where this goes,* and I let myself think that I want that, too.

But then the truth comes crashing down. I already know how this goes. We fuck for a while, I get attached while trying to play it cool and pretend I'm not attached, he leaves, and I pretend I'm okay with it while on the inside I'm devastated.

It's the story of every "relationship" I've had in my short adult life, why would this one be any different?

Oh, maybe because I'm actually lying to him about something super important, which will be an extra spicy layer on the funeral pyre of my heart when this shit finally goes down. He'll not only leave me for someone cooler or older or richer, he'll do it knowing that I'm a deceitful, opportunistic loser who jumped from his son's cock to his with not even a week between them.

"Are you going all doomsday in there again?" Sally asks.

The woman has only known me for a short time, and yet she can already read my mind. I'm so grateful to have her here, especially for this one. I'm going to need extra comforting after the storm that is Ben Adams leaves me decimated.

"Yeah."

"Girl, you gotta either do it or don't do it. You can't do it while also beating yourself up about doing it. Do you need a pros and cons list?"

I laugh darkly. "You mean, do I need to see the reasons why this is totally fucked up, and I'm a huge gold-digging loser written out on paper? Pass."

"Is that really what you think?"

I shrug. "It's what he's going to think when he finds out about Ainsley."

"He's not going to find out about Ainsley unless you get stupid and tell him."

"Yeah, I guess."

"And you're not going to do that, right?"

I shake my head. Just the thought of those words coming out of my mouth is enough to make me feel ill, so I can't imagine actually telling him.

"Then you're fine. Just chill and enjoy this."

I try to remember her advice as I drag myself out of bed at the crack of dawn and get ready for my class.

I mean, this is why I'm here. This teaching gig is a great opportunity for me. After graduating from Pilates training, I only had a few months of subbing classes at the studio in my hometown before I decided to take a trip to Indonesia with some high school friends to help build a school.

It was just the break I needed after my injury, recovery, and my decision not to go back to college.

Dropping out wasn't something I took lightly. I just couldn't see a future for myself in business any longer. Once I experienced the broken healthcare system firsthand and knew that so many injured people who needed help were falling through the cracks, all I wanted to do was get trained in the modality that brought me from flat on my back with a slipped disc to dancing around and jetting off to build a school in Asia.

Pilates changed my life, and I wanted to change other people's lives in the same way. I mean, I still do, of course. I just got a bit sidetracked. First, by the trip of a lifetime to do some volunteering, and second by a handsome face I met while doing the volunteering.

Ben will not be a third derailment for me. I've been through this plenty of times before. Guys come and go. They want you, and then they don't want you anymore. Sure, this one is particularly good, and I want him extra bad, but that doesn't change the reality of the situation. You can't get attached to men because they just leave.

The studio is cool and quiet as I turn on the lights. I'm the first one down here, as usual, and I revel in the peaceful space as I get my class set up.

When the first students start to arrive, I'm more than a little surprised to see Ben among them. I try my best to hide my utter glee, as I walk over to say good morning.

"No Avery this morning?" I keep my voice calm and cool as I offer up the joke as a greeting.

Ben smiles, and my knees go soft. "I think one class was enough for him."

"But not for you?"

"The woman at the front desk told me this was a six-week series. I like to see things through."

I pray to God that my cheeks aren't as flushed as they feel as I retreat back to the front of the room without responding to that particularly leading statement.

I know it's stupid, considering the secret truth of our situation, but just the thought of this handsome, genuine man thinking someone like me is worth seeing through, worth anything, well…it's intoxicating.

I manage to make it through the forty-five-minute class, averting my eyes as much as I can from the handsome as sin, half-naked man in the middle of the room while still fulfilling my role as a responsible teacher.

Ben is strong and lean, far more flexible than I generally see from men his age or with his muscle mass. I wonder if he's done flexibility training before. I wonder if he has a personal trainer. I wonder so, so many things.

I wonder if I'll ever get a chance to ask.

The thing about walking around with a grenade in one hand and the pin in the other is that you just never know when things are going to blow. All you know is that they definitely will.

I wait in the large private bathroom after class for as long as I feel I can get away with it, but the knock never comes.

I finally find him again after resigning myself to heading home alone. He's sitting on a bench just before the stairs that lead up to the resort, typing on his phone.

My heart lurches, but I keep my pace steady, approaching him cool as a damn cucumber.

"Hey, you did great today."

He looks up from the screen and smirks at me. "Thanks."

"This isn't your first Pilates series, is it?"

He stands and approaches me, putting his body right into my space. "It's the first time I've taken Pilates, but plenty of the exercises are familiar from my own trainer's routine."

So, I was right about him having a trainer. Of course I was.

A guy like this has everything.

"You want to grab coffee?" he asks, pocketing his phone.

The invitation is nearly enough to send me to my knees, but no. I definitely don't want to get coffee with the owner of the resort. At the resort.

"I..." I can't figure out what to say, so I drift off, my eyes casting downward.

Ben takes my chin in his hand, a move so intimate that I can't breathe. "You..."

I turn my head to free it from his grasp, and he lets me. "I'm just not sure if getting coffee with the resort owner is the best move for me. I mean, I'm new here, and I really like the fitness center. I'd like to stay a while."

"Got it. Of course."

I meet his eyes and offer a sad smile and a shrug.

"It's not a problem. Go find a cab and have them take you to the helipad. I'll be there soon."

"Oh. Okay." It's what I dreamed he would say, but now that he's said it, I'm not sure how I feel.

"But..." Ben asks, attuned to my thoughts, apparently.

"But I'd like to go home and grab a few things."

"What time would you like to meet me there?"

I glance at the big clock on the wall. "Nine?"

"How about ten? That gives you three hours to prepare."

"Prepare for what?" I squeak out.

Ben steps even closer, leaning down to whisper in my ear. "The possibility that I'm not going to let you leave my island."

He turns and jogs up the stairs without another word.

It takes me a full minute to recover, and when I do, I'm practically giggling with glee. OMG, OMG, OMG. Why, oh, why does this guy have to be so freaking perfect?

I pack a bag and shave every inch of my body, primping and styling the best that I can in ninety degrees with one hundred percent humidity.

When I arrive at the helipad, Ben's already there.

It's a short flight to the island, and an even shorter drive to the house.

I feel like a damn princess, and Ben is doing nothing to dispel that. His arm drapes over my shoulder as he drives the golf cart.

I'm part of the Merit Island royal family, and this man is my king.

For now, anyway.

Just enjoy it while it lasts, Vicki.

"I thought you might be hungry," is Ben's only explanation for the epic picnic laid out on the patio when we arrive at the mansion.

"Oh, I'm definitely hungry." I practically throw myself at the food, heaping my plate with sliced meat and cheese, fruit, soft rolls, and pasta salad.

"Oh, to be able to eat like that again."

I look up from my feast, mouth full of bread. "What?"

Ben chuckles, and I feel myself blush. "I just miss the days when I was your age, and I could eat anything I wanted."

I roll my eyes, even though I know it's only driving his point home even further. "You gotta quit with all the *when I was your age* stuff. You're not that old. Are you?" I have a vague idea of how old this guy is, but I keep forgetting to Google him and find out for sure.

Ben just smiles and shakes his head as he watches me eat. "I'm old enough to wonder what you're doing on Faraday Island teaching Pilates on a three-month contract."

That's enough to halt my hand as it lifts the next bite to my mouth. "What do you mean?"

Ben sits back in his chair and crosses his arms over his chest. I suddenly feel like I'm about to get scolded. And not in a good way.

"I mean, what is it that you're doing with your life? What's your plan for the future?"

Surprise makes my mouth fall open, but I snap it shut quickly. The last thing I need is for this guy to spot the weakness he just uncovered. I take a deep breath and set my sandwich down. "Well, I got my Pilates certification last year in Baltimore," I start.

"Maryland?" Ben cuts in.

I nod.

"That's where you're from?"

I nod again, and he nods, signaling me to go on. I narrow my eyes at the sudden interrogation I find myself in, but I continue. "I got my training hours at the studio, but I need more experience to be able to land a full-time gig in the States, so I took this contract." I'm proud of myself for how succinctly I summed it all up, but my happiness is short-lived.

Ben is not impressed.

"You just threw a dart at the map and landed on Faraday Island of all places?"

Shit, does he know?

I take a deep breath and try to figure out how I can lay the rest of this out without flat out lying, just in case. "No. I had some high school friends who were doing a volunteer trip, and I joined them to get away from my hometown. While I was there, a friend I met mentioned they were heading to Faraday, and I looked into it. The job was there so I applied."

It's not entirely untrue. I mean, when people asked Ainsley who I was, he introduced me as his friend. The heartless bastard.

"Your friend Sally?"

I shake my head but don't offer any more information.

Ben considers me carefully for a long moment but lets it go. "Why Pilates?"

Finally, a subject I can speak to from the heart. "I was injured at work my first year of college. I worked at the coffee shop on campus. It was a silly thing, really. I was lifting a box of chai concentrate onto a shelf, something I did all the time. But for whatever reason, I tweaked my back. I thought it was okay, like it would work itself out, but it only got worse and worse until I couldn't leave my bed. The doctors just gave me pain pills, but they didn't help anything, really. My manager suggested physical therapy and from there I ended up in Reformer Pilates. I went from drugged up and bedridden at twenty-one to perfectly healthy in just a matter of months. I was already on a break from school at that point because I hadn't been able to attend classes or focus with all the drugs, so when the Pilates studio owner suggested that I take the training, I went for it." It's my comeback story, the tale of how I succeeded in healing my own body when all the doctors told me I'd be disabled for life.

The last thing I expect to see on Ben's face is disappointment. When he speaks, my heart sinks even lower.

"You dropped out of college to be an exercise instructor?"

"I dropped out of college because I was incapable of attending due to an injury. While I was on that break, I found a different path. One that lets me help people."

"You could help people as a doctor. Or a physical therapist."

"Or as a Pilates instructor."

"You're not exactly helping rich white women heal themselves at The Sands."

Oh, no you didn't.

My anger flares. "I already told you that I'm gaining the teaching experience necessary to be taken on by a studio back in the States."

Ben is undeterred by my fluster. "Will you go back to college?"

"I don't think that's any of your business." I'm nearly yelling the words, and I finally seem to snap Ben out of whatever prosecutor mode he slipped into.

"I'm sorry. You're right. I just…I have a nineteen-year-old, and I'm struggling with his path. I guess the similarities in your story set me off."

"Your son?" I ask. The moment of truth. If he knows, he'll tell me now.

"Yes, Ainsley. He's been on a bit of a break. A gap year that's turning into two. And I'm trying to get him back on track, but it's proving to be more challenging than I expected."

This is news to me. I thought Ainsley was the golden boy, traveling endlessly with his father's credit cards, not a care in the world. "He doesn't want to go to college?"

"He does," Ben snaps quickly, and then softens and shakes his head with a sigh. "I mean, he'll go. He's just taking a more roundabout way to get there."

"Maybe what he wants in life isn't at college."

"That's not an option. College is where adulthood begins. He can do what he wants with his life after he graduates."

"Can he, though?"

"What do you mean?"

I'm overstepping here, but I can't stop myself. "Do you think this need you feel to control his life is just going to evaporate when they hand him a diploma? Somehow, I don't think that's the case."

Ben lets out another sigh and leans back in his chair. He runs his hand through his hair and suddenly, he just looks exhausted. "I just want the best for him."

I shake my head. "What makes you think you know what's best? It's his life. He's the only one who can know which choices are right for him."

Ben doesn't argue, even though I hit straight at the core of his statement. He just shakes his head. "Young people just don't understand how hard life can be. All I want is for him, for you, for all young people, to just give themselves a chance at a steady, comfortable future. To look at more long-term goals, rather than chasing after instant gratification."

It's my turn to shake my head. "Your rich son is going to be fine no matter what. If you really cared about the future of us 'young people'" —I do air quotes as I try to keep the attitude from overtaking my tone, but it's a lost cause— "You'd be working toward scholarships and programs to help less privileged youth go to college. Not continuing to pay for a seat in class that your son clearly doesn't want."

"You're right. I should probably do that," he relents, looking as tired as ever yet somehow just as handsome. "I just can't let it go. Let him go."

I nod in understanding, even though I don't understand at all. More than anything, I'm just terrified to speak. This conversation is not exactly what I was expecting when I was pretending to be a princess on the helicopter ride over. As a matter of fact, I feel a bit like a child now, waiting for instructions from my father.

Not the sexiest feeling I've ever had.

"Well, you sure know how to make a girl feel like a ridiculous teenager who's throwing away her life." I turn back to my plate. At least the food is good. Maybe I'll head back to the helipad after I'm done eating and hope the pilot takes pity on me.

Ben sighs and crosses his arms. "I'm sorry. I shouldn't have put this on you. That wasn't my intention."

I look up from my plate and narrow my eyes at him. "It wasn't your intention to drag me over here and hold a one-man intervention about my career choices? I'm sorry to inform you that—"

"I know, I know. It got out of hand. I'm just not used to…the women in my world are all very…" He struggles to find words, and I do nothing to help him, making myself a loaded cheese and jam cracker without even glancing up. "Settled. They're all lawyers, for the most part. Or doctors or engineers or consultants."

"That's the kind of woman you like?" The words burn my chest on the way out, but what's the point in not saying them? This isn't a real thing between us for so many reasons. May as well let Ben think it's one of his reasons for the death knell.

"Do you see any of those women here?"

I roll my eyes without looking up. It's a sweet thing to say—or is it? This man is confusing as hell. "Those are the kind of women you respect, though. Not young exercise teachers who dropped out of college."

My eyes dare to dart up from my food, and I find him watching me with such intensity that I have to look away. I kind of thought I was being dismissed here, but once again I'm not sure what's going on.

"With women like that, the women in my world, in the city, I feel even more boxed in than I already do. Like I'm a character in the story of my New York law firm, and they expect me to play a certain part. My life there is already so rigid. I have an ironclad schedule. I have the exact same standing grocery order delivered from Whole Foods each week. I have the same suits made again and again. I just go through the motions of my life like a train on a track. The few times I've been set up with women in that world, all I've been able to see are years and years of the same thing spread out before me. Repeating the same day over and over until I'm dead."

My mouth opens when he finishes his surprising little speech, but I can't think of what to say, so I just suck in a breath and hold his intense gaze. It's not long before I'm rewarded—or punished—with the exact words I hadn't even known I wanted to hear.

"With you, it's different. These last few days, I've felt more than I've felt in years. I'm having fun. I laugh." He laughs softly as if surprised by the words. "I feel wild, like I've been released from my cage. I've never acted like this, never felt like this. And it's you giving me this freedom. I know it is. You have this quiet self-assurance about you. As if you don't care what I think. And you haven't already decided what kind of man I am. You don't have a box for me to fit in that says lawyer or potential husband or anything like that. I feel like I get to watch you create each moment from scratch, and it's fascinating. And terrifying. And intriguing. I can't help but want to be around you. I want what you have for myself, even though I know that's impossible. Forgive my incessant need to shove you inside a box that I understand. Know that it comes from a place of fear on my part.

Fear of what will happen if I stay outside my own box for too long."

The silence that falls is heavy. I can hardly breathe and can't tear my eyes away from my plate. Far too scared to see the expression that goes with an admission like that. After too long of a moment, I do look up and find him watching me. Our eyes dance around each other for a few seconds, speaking volumes without saying a word.

Finally, Ben must resign himself to the fact that I'm not going to respond because his face softens, and he stands, holding out his hand.

"I brought you over today for a reason. Are you finished?" He motions to the feast on the table that I've only just begun to explore.

I look at the table, down at my plate, and then up at him, unsure if what he's got in store for me could possibly be better than this.

He laughs. "The staff will package this all up, and it will be in the fridge for you anytime you want."

I set my plate on the table with a small sigh and stand, taking his hand. As soon as I do, I know I've made the right choice. His warm, strong hand sends shivers through my body, and I have to work to breathe. I can't believe I was just wondering if some silly food would be better than this man's touch—even if he did just say the most terrifyingly lovely things to me and will probably say more. Expect me to say some back.

I certainly have things I'd like to say. About how he makes me feel sexy and in charge. About how much I love teaching him new things about life and sex and exercise. About how I can't close my eyes without seeing the look on his face when I do something that surprises him.

This man is addictive as hell. I'm fully and completely gone for him.

And that's a problem.

But it's a problem for later.

Because right now, this strong, handsome man, who just admitted to having some kind of feelings for me, is leading me by the hand through his giant, beachfront mansion and down a hallway I haven't explored yet.

Rule #11

DUNGEON, YES. DEAD BODIES, NO.

BEN

I shouldn't feel nervous opening this door, but I do. The feelings rise in my chest as we head down the hallway. They form a boulder in my throat as my hand touches down on the knob.

I go through my usual steps to overcome strong feelings.

Identify it, give it a name—it's fear.

Acknowledge that I'm feeling it and why—I'm scared to show this woman this side of myself because I don't know how she's going to react. Usually when I'm bringing women to a place like this, it's with an agreement in place about what's going to happen. This time, it feels more like baring my soul. I have no idea if bringing her here will result in a scene or her running for the hills, but I have to do it.

Okay, all that's left is to express the feeling in a healthy way and move on.

With a deep, relaxing sigh, I pause with the door open a crack and turn to her. "I'm nervous to bring you down here. And that's not something I'm used to feeling."

Her eyes narrow slightly. "I'm excited."

I smile. "I'm glad to hear that. I hope you feel the same way once we're inside."

"Are you about to show me the dungeon where you hide all the dead bodies?"

"Dungeon, yes. Dead bodies, no."

Her eyes narrow again, this time to little slits, and she cocks her head to the side. "Prisoners?"

I shake my head and laugh softly. "I want you to know right now that my bringing you here doesn't mean that I expect anything from you."

"Liar," she correctly calls me out as she pushes past me and opens the door wide herself.

With a deep breath, I step in behind her and flip on the light.

"Holy shit, Ben. This is…"

I wait behind her with bated breath, unable to decide if she's about to proclaim the room incredible, or incredibly terrifying.

I'm quite proud of it myself, if for no other reason than the sheer amount of work it took to put together. There's no next-day delivery on an island like this. Each and every toy, bench, and bondage component came over as my own luggage at some point over the last nine years. It's not a fully stocked dungeon by any means, but I've managed to make myself a nice little play space down here in the windowless room I'd put on the building plans specifically for this purpose.

Not that I've gotten much use out of it.

I won't say that I'm a hardcore practitioner of BDSM. I don't have any interest in full-time D/s or M/s relationships. I simply enjoy the feeling of control in a controlled environment. Nothing calms me down quite as much as a silent, bowed submissive, awaiting my every order. Placing their trust in me to give them what they need.

Or at least nothing used to calm me down as much. If the amount of sleep I've gotten in the last week is any indication, whatever spell this woman has me under might have greater medicinal effects.

With Victoria, it feels more like asserting control over a chaotic situation and forcing it into submission. I've watched plenty of scenes like that in my days attending clubs around the world, but it never occurred to me that it could have the same effect on me as my quiet, meditative, sexual dominance practices.

Bringing the two worlds together down here is my chance to find out.

I'm sure that once I get this woman into my own peaceful, controlled environment, my raging desire for her will mellow into my usual soft longing for everything to go as planned. I'm absolutely sure of it.

I don't know what it would mean for it to go the other direction.

She turns to me, forehead crinkled. "Is this some kind of *Fifty Shades of Grey* thing?"

"I didn't see the film."

"It was a book."

"Oh, okay, well, I didn't read it. Is it about a rich bachelor who brings his gorgeous younger date down to his BDSM room?"

Her face illuminates as she smiles. "Yeah, it is."

I nod, happy to have pleased her, if slightly confused as to what this means for us right now. "Well, I guess it is like that, then. What happens after he brings her down to his dungeon?"

She's wandering further into the room, examining tables and tools and toys, but not touching anything. "He ties her up and stuff." She whirls to face me, a mischievous look lighting up her features. "Is that what you're gonna do to me?"

"Do you want me to tie you up?" It takes my full strength to keep my voice level as I walk toward her.

"Sure."

"And then what should I do? After I tie you up?" My hands finally find her body, and I pull her close to mine, her back pressed against my chest, her ass squeezed in tight to my hardening cock.

"What…what are my options?" she breathes out, melting into me.

Oh, the things I would like to do to this woman.

But alas, we haven't talked about it nearly enough for me to feel comfortable playing yet. At least, not in this room.

"Well, we'll go through a list of options together, and you can say yes or no to all of them. And then when we begin, you won't know which one of your yeses is coming." I slide my hand up to cover her eyes as I speak, pulling her head into the crook of my neck. She gasps softly as she loses her vision but allows me to move her body without putting up a fight.

Her immediate submission docs things to me.

"So…you'll be in complete control," she says softly, pensively.

"That's the idea," I murmur into her neck, excited that she seems to be on board.

The feeling is short-lived.

She pulls from my grasp and turns to face me, hands on her hips.

"But aren't you trying to work on your control issues? I feel like if this *was* a novel, your character would be better served by being the one who gets tied up. The one who has to release control."

A thought I'm not entertaining for even a moment. "Is that what happens in your Fifty Shades novel?"

"No."

"Good. Because that's not what's happening here, either."

"I just think it could be good for you—"

"You are one more word away from a ball-gag."

Her hands fly up in a gesture of surrender. "Okay, okay. I'll be good."

"You are very good. You please me so much. That's what you want, isn't it?"

"I guess?"

I chuckle at her adorable, sassy personality, which refuses to dim, even though I can feel her body reacting to my words.

"You guess you want to please me?"

"I just mean…you're always talking about how much you like being surprised. I don't see how there's any room for surprises here. I mean, for me, yeah. I'll be tied up and probably blindfolded. But you're just going to be going through the motions."

"Your reactions are my surprise. My delight. Every time I touch you, I get to see how it affects you. Every time I surprise you, I get to hear the little noises you make." I spin her suddenly so her back presses to me once more, using one hand to cover her eyes while the other snakes around her throat. She gasps.

"Yes, just like that."

Her gasp sends a jolt of electricity and power through my veins. I want more.

"Okay."

"Okay, what?"

"Okay, you can do all this stuff to me."

I chuckle softly and release her, walking over to a cabinet and pulling out a soft black scarf. "It's not that simple."

I turn back and find her watching me.

"There are forms and rules to go over," I start to explain.

"Ah, Ben's box."

I inhale, smooth and steady, as I let her jab pass through me.

She's trying to rile me, but it's not going to work. Not down here.

"There will come a time during our games down here when you will earn punishment for statements like that."

"Ooh, punishment? And it's my job to pretend that I don't want it?"

I laugh softly and shake my head at her summary of BDSM, an oversimplification, but not entirely incorrect. "That will be part of your role, yes."

"I can do that." Her voice is almost a whisper as I reach for her, using both hands to push her hair back over her shoulders. She shivers slightly from the smallest brush of my hands across her face. I cannot wait to see what she does when my touch is a bit firmer.

"For today, I thought we could just play around a little. Introduce you to being in the room. Nothing heavy, nothing painful or scary. We can talk about all that stuff later."

"Once you have my liability waiver signed?" she whispers as I reach up to tie the black cloth over her eyes.

"Exactly."

I take a step back and take her in now that she can't see me.

She's stunning. The black cloth hides her sharp, wise, green eyes, but I can still see her mind working as her teeth chew softly on her bottom lip. She's dressed simply in a dark green sundress, her feet bare after having abandoned her sandals on the deck, and her toenails painted lavender to match her fingernails. A simple gold bracelet is the only jewelry she wears. I've noticed the same bracelet a few times before and examined it once while she slept. It's a delicate chain that doesn't seem to have a clasp.

She shifts back and forth on her feet. I know from experience that her senses are reaching out as far as they can in all directions, trying to decide where I'm standing. Trying to predict what's coming next. I'm still and quiet a few feet away so she can't find me. It's making her nervous. That's not my goal right now, so I let out an audible breath. Her whole attention turns in my direction.

"Why don't you get down on your knees."

She obeys, tucking her skirt between her thighs and calves as she sits on her heels. Her hands smooth the front as she settles there, looking up to where she's decided I must be.

"You look stunning down there."

"Thank you," she answers without hesitation.

I smile to myself. "For the next little while, I'm going to ask you not to talk unless I ask you a question directly or otherwise ask you to speak."

"Okay."

My smile widens. It's been a while since I scened with anyone so inexperienced. The women at the club I visit in the city are all professionals. "That was you speaking out of turn."

I wait to see if she's going to speak again, but she doesn't. Her mouth twists to the side briefly, and then she relaxes.

"Good girl. I knew you had it in you to obey."

Her forehead crinkles at the word, but she doesn't speak.

I kneel in front of her, so close that my knees touch hers. She leans forward at the sudden contact but doesn't make a move to touch me.

"I'm going to touch your arms and legs now. Is that okay?"

She nods.

"I'm going to need you to speak your consent aloud for me."

She laughs. "Speak, don't speak. Make up your mind."

"Oh, you think sass is a good idea at a time like this, do you? Would you like me to spank you for that disobedience?"

"Sure."

I'm grateful for her blindfold now as a wide grin spreads across my face. It's all I can do not to laugh. I take a deep breath and hold it together. "You like being spanked like a bad girl?"

She shrugs. "It would be a first for me, but it sounds fine. As long as you promise to fuck me afterward."

"I think we should go back to you not speaking."

She raises her hand to her lips and mimes zipping them closed.

"And you just lost the use of those." I pull a second silk tie from my pocket and secure her wrists behind her back.

"Now we're getting somewhere," she says.

I consider scolding her once again for speaking, but I have a feeling she's only doing it to get a rise out of me, so I give her the opposite.

I stand and cross the room to the cabinet once more. I

promised a small dose of low-key play for our first time down here, but I'm suddenly at a loss. I'm so used to feeling in control, letting my intuition guide my next step in situations like this, but it's failing me. As I turn to look back at the woman kneeling in the center of the floor, all I can think about is how I can impress her.

That's the last thing that should be on my mind right now.

I choose a long feather and cross back to where she kneels. I might have to make this a short session and rethink my entire plan for bringing her down here in the future.

I kneel behind her and blow softly on the bare skin of her neck to let her know how close I am. She tenses and then relaxes with a soft sigh. When I touch down on her collarbone with the feather, however, it's a different story.

She squirms away from me, looking back even though I know she can't see a thing under that blindfold. "You are not going to tickle me."

I smile. "And what if I do?"

"I thought you were going to beat me or drip hot wax on me or something. I hate being tickled."

I bring the feather down the back of her bound arm, watching the goose bumps rise with her temper. She shifts further so that she's on her butt, facing me, mouth twisted into an indignant pout.

"You have your safe word if you want me to stop."

I can see the effect my words have on her—it's as if I issued a challenge. I might consider that a reason to stop the scene myself if we were doing any harder play, but I feel safe pushing this limit a bit.

"I'm not going to use my safe word."

"Okay, then." I drag the feather so softly down her calf. She's not expecting it and jumps nearly a foot.

"I won't use my safe word, but I will run."

I pause, considering her words. I have the still, meditative feeling in my chest that scening always brings me, but there's no denying the flare of excitement that grows as the meaning of her statement settles in.

I can't decide which feeling I want more.

"This isn't really a game where one person runs," I say.

"It is if I get up and run."

"I would prefer us to wait until we have some time to talk about boundaries, consent, and hard limits."

"You want consent and limits? Okay. I, Victoria Easton, hereby consent to let Ben Adams use my body, including all my fun holes, mouth, pussy, and ass, in whatever way he sees fit. He can chase me, tackle me, call me names, tie me up, force me to be quiet. Hard limits are starvation, anything involving poop, and doing things in public."

Well, it's hard to argue with that.

My rock-hard cock and gritted teeth certainly agree.

I'm torn between wanting to show respect for the sanctuary I've built down here, to follow the strict rules of the world that has offered me so much personal growth, to honor the time I've spent honing my control both in and out of the dungeon…and giving in to her.

Because, truth be told, even surrounded by every implement of pleasure and pain that I thought I could ever need in life, there's still nothing in the world I want to do more than chase this woman down.

I close my eyes as I hold a mental conference with myself. Try as I might, I find absolutely no compelling arguments for denying myself this.

"If you run…" I start, my voice low and gravely, spoken into her ear much closer than she was expecting. "You better hope I don't catch you."

The moment of heated silence that follows is a living thing between us. Victoria's breathing is audible, and I can almost watch her consider her options.

Then I take them away with one soft swipe of the feather across the back of her knee.

She's on her feet in an instant in an impressive display of strength considering her hands are tightly bound behind her. She runs for a few feet until she meets the wall, smacking straight into it at full speed. I flinch as I watch her nearly fall to her ass as she tries to recover from the blow.

But then, impressively, she's back on the wall, dragging her body across the flat surface, searching for the door she knows is there somewhere.

I watch her with my arms folded, harder and more rabidly turned on than I've ever been in my life.

"What's the hurry, kitten? We were just getting started."

She doesn't let my voice interrupt her work. If anything, she searches more frantically. When her nose grazes across what she knows must be the doorframe, she lets out a small squeak of triumph.

I let my shoes sound loudly on the floor as I walk slowly toward where she's got her back to the door, head bowed in concentration as she tries to use her bound hands to turn the knob.

I lighten my steps and approach silently, leaning down until my mouth is just inches away from her ear. "What makes you so sure I haven't dead bolted it?"

She jumps and lets out an actual shriek at the sound and proximity of my voice. It's freaking music to my ears.

Fun.

This is fun.

There's that word again. It's no coincidence that it's come up yet again when I'm with this woman. She's fun. When I'm with her, I'm fun.

Wasn't I having fun just moments earlier when I was blindfolding her and making her kneel?

It's not the same, though. I know for sure I'm going to have to spend some time thinking about this, but now's not that time.

My little prisoner has gotten the door open and is turning to make her escape down the hallway. I watch her go, letting her get almost to the staircase leading back up to the main floor before I bound after her, taking her down in one swoop.

I get another real, honest-to-god scream for my efforts, the sound is painful, exciting, and gloriously erotic.

"Did you really think you were going to get away from me?"

"Let me go!"

She's thrashing violently in my arms, her back pinned against the tile staircase. I hold her there easily. My position, and the fact that she can't access her arms or vision, makes keeping her pinned barely a challenge.

"You know, I was going to go easy on you. I told you that over and over. We were just going to play a little. But that wasn't good enough for you. You had to go and spoil it by running. Do you know what I'm going to do now?"

"Let me go!" she cries out again, attempting to use her head and teeth to dislodge me.

I laugh, the sound so evil it surprises me. "Nope. That's incorrect."

She's struggled so much that I don't even have to push her dress up, it's already bunched around her waist. Her lacy panties are in full view, and damn if they're not tempting.

Not to mention what waits underneath.

What was it she said in her little speech about consent? And her fun holes. I laugh again at the memory, the sound just as evil as before.

"What's wrong with you?" she demands.

She's starting to tire. I can hear it in her voice and feel it in her struggle.

"What's wrong with me? I'm just trying to have a nice afternoon. You're the one trying to ruin it."

"You're sick."

I slide my hand under her panties and find her glorious wetness waiting for me. My fingers slip inside her with ease. "Really. Would a sick man do this?" I pump her a few times as she struggles—but this time, she's struggling to get my hand to brush up against her clit.

"Yes," she manages to get out, her head hanging back. "That's exactly what a sick man would do."

I reach up and pull the top of her dress down with my other hand, her breasts bouncing free. She screams again and thrashes from side to side, causing them to swing. If I could reach them with my mouth while still holding her like this, those delicious looking nipples would be in a world of trouble.

I'm still pressing my fingers into her, pumping hard, and she's thrashing back and forth, but with a downward pressure that I know is rubbing her just the right way.

My cock is throbbing to be set free to join the fun, but there's no time for that yet. She's on the edge, and I can't decide whether to let her get there.

What kind of punishment would it be if I did?

I stop my movement suddenly, pulling away and using both hands to pull her dress up and over her head, leaving it tangled around her bound arms.

Victoria screams again, but this time in frustration.

She's naked and feral in my arms, her denied orgasm turning to rage on her lips. I spin her so she's kneeling on the step above where I kneel, my arm still tight around her waist. I did promise a spanking earlier, and there's no time like the present.

I lay into her, my palm landing loudly on her ass over and over until her skin is bright pink, and she's wailing.

And then I finally free my cock.

It slides into her drenched core in one hard plunge, and we both gasp at the contact. She's still trying to hold up her end of the game and fight me, but she can barely manage to shift her shoulders back and forth.

She's exhausted and trapped and mine. All mine.

I hold her hip with one hand, the other presses firmly into her back so she stays pinned to the staircase while I fuck the living hell out of her. I'm a madman. Something in me must have snapped because I pound into her body over and over like I'm trying to exorcise a demon.

Sweat slides from my forehead in long drips that land on her back as I pump. "What do you have to say for yourself now?" I growl out as I pull her head up to meet mine by fisting my hand in her hair.

"If you don't make me come," she starts, her voice feral and otherworldly, growling out of her dry mouth in a snarl.

"Oh, she's about to make a threat. I'm so scared."

She goes on as if I hadn't interrupted. "Then I'm going to kill you in your sleep."

The laugh that escapes my lips is the most joyous sound I've ever heard leave my own body—and I once watched the birth of my own son.

I'm so high on whatever it is that's happening right now. So grateful to this woman for the bravery it must be taking her to offer it to me. So incredibly and undeniably happy.

I use her hair to pull her body up until I can hold her upright, squeezed against me with one arm while I continue to fuck her, slipping my other hand down to give her clit a little pinch.

She cries out and forces her hips forward into my hand, grinding against me as best as she can with my cock still impaling her.

I give her what she wants, only because it's also what I want. She comes spectacularly as I fill her and rub her clit, the firm clench of her pussy around me enough to push me over the edge as well.

I bellow out my pleasure as I feel my body empty into hers, pumping into the pulse of our combined orgasms. When I can't hold her any longer, my body gives way, my arms falling to my sides like dead weight.

Victoria tips forward, unable to catch herself with anything but her core strength since her hands are still tied. I muster up the last of my energy to catch her before she hits the stairs and release the silk tie.

She slips the blindfold down and crawls up a few stairs before turning to face me, legs splayed, leaning back on her elbows. Her hair is an absolute mess, but the glow on her skin is radiant, as is her grin. "Okay, then," she says, laughing.

My whole body is bowed from exertion, but I manage to join her in a laugh as I shake my head.

"Now *that* was fun," she whispers.

I just shake my head again. Not in disagreement, more like wonder or fascination.

Victoria reaches out one bare foot and uses it to slap my bicep. I finally look up into her grinning face.

"You okay?" she asks.

I nod, still catching my breath. I'm not sure what my face looks like, but it makes her slide down a few steps until she's on the step above where I kneel, straddling my knees with her thighs. "You need me to call a doctor or something, old man?"

I'm finally able to get a full breath in, and I let it out in a laugh. "I think I'll be okay."

"All right," she says, still looking a little suspicious. "I don't want to break you."

"I was trying to break *you*."

She laughs and uses the handrail to drag herself to her feet, pulling her dress down. "Not going to happen."

I can see the evidence of our orgasms dripping down her inner thighs. "Can't blame me for trying."

She sits back down a few steps up, legs together, looking far too put together after what just went on. I continue to kneel here like a fallen soldier.

"You can't tell me that wasn't more fun than watching me sit in front of you in that silent room."

"It was certainly different."

"It was fun."

I nod. "It was fun."

She's just watching me now, as if she's waiting for me to offer some deep insight, but I have none. My entire understanding of myself and my life is sitting in shambles at my feet, and I need a bit of alone time to pick up the pieces before I'll be able to speak sensibly about them to another person.

"What's next?" I ask, just to distract her.

She cocks her head to the side. "Next, I thought I'd go find the pool. There must be one in this place."

"Oh, of course. It's just out—"

"I'm joking, Ben. There's no way anyone missed the massive pool directly in front of the house."

"Right. Perfect. Well, I'll meet you out there in a few."

She tosses one more concerned glance in my direction before skipping up the stairs and out of view.

I collapse. Straight up collapse onto the hard stone steps. I roll onto my back and groan, every muscle in my body protesting something—what I can't quite tell. All I know is that I feel broken. And, based on my level of fitness, and my self-induced punishing workouts, I have a feeling the break isn't physical.

Rule #12

CONSENT GOES BOTH WAYS

BEN

By the time I make it out to the patio to join Victoria in the pool, she's made herself at home in a giant flamingo floatie with a glass of iced tea. Her little red bikini barely covers any of her luscious body.

"Hey," I say as I stop at the edge of the deep end, watching her.

She sits upright too quickly, almost capsizing her comical little boat.

"Oh, hey," she says, shielding her eyes from the sun with one hand. "I was just about to come find you, make sure you were still alive."

I smile at that. "Yes, you look very concerned."

A sassy smirk flashes across those gorgeous features. "Get in. The water's nice."

"I think I'll take a chaise for now."

I don't have it in me to slip into the cool water right now. I feel like I'm barely keeping it together to the point that even that small change in my body temperature might send me right over the edge.

I settle in the chaise lounge closest to her in the shade and close my eyes. The sound of her paddling her flamingo over to the side of the pool makes me smile.

"Hey, I wanted to say that..." She pauses, and I raise my eyebrows, eyes still closed. "I didn't mean to ruin your thing down there. I've been thinking about it, and I wonder if I should have just, you know, kneeled there and stayed quiet."

I let out a small laugh. "I think it turned out all right."

"I mean, yeah, I agree with that. But it wasn't exactly what you wanted. You brought me down there to show me something that's important to you, and I ruined it by forcing you to play my game instead."

"You can't force me to do anything." It's not an answer, but I'm not sure what to offer her at this moment. Everything I thought I knew about myself is now up for debate. And my mind is reeling. I can barely hear myself think over the racket going on inside my skull.

"Consent goes both ways, you know," she says flatly into the silence that hovers between us.

I turn and place both feet on the ground beside the chaise, bowing my head and clasping my hands together with arms resting on my thighs.

She's right, of course.

Right in that my consent should be just as important as hers. The only problem is, it's not just the change to the scene downstairs that's got me worried. I didn't consent to any of this. To these feelings. To this complete and utter lack of control.

I've never felt so wild, so free, and the feelings of impending doom that accompany those feelings scare the shit out of me.

If I'm not in complete control, if I'm not competent enough to be in charge of even myself—what does that mean for the life I've built for myself? What does it mean for my job? For my son?

I've always felt like the only thing keeping the entire world from going off the rails is my firm grasp on reality and the ability to make the difficult decisions necessary to keep things running smoothly.

But all of a sudden, in one little flash of release, a window opened into another perspective.

While it's true that I've managed to keep a death grip on every single aspect of mine and my son's lives over the years, has it really gotten me what I wanted?

Is the life I'm living the one that I want to live?

Shit. I may have completely lost my mind. Full-on existential crisis. But I don't know how to recover. There's no one to ask for help because I'm the person everyone comes to when they need help.

"Ben, I gotta be honest with you right now, you don't look well."

I look up too quickly, and my head spins. "Oh, I'm fine. Just feeling a bit off kilter, I guess."

Victoria pushes off the side of the pool with one foot and floats toward the center. "Just feeling a bit off kilter, I guess," she mimics in what I guess is how she thinks I sound. It's not a flattering rendition.

I collapse back onto the chaise. All I want is to leap up and start fixing things, but I can't think of a single thing to do. There's nothing out there to fix. What's broken is inside my own mind.

What if I've been doing it wrong my entire life?

At this point, I'm almost positive my son would agree with that. Hell, I can't even get the kid to talk to me anymore. I've been blaming him for that, waiting for him to come around and get on board with the life I've laid out for him.

But if my life is wrong, then the life I chose for him is wrong. Everything's wrong.

I've been fighting with him for so many years, trying to make him see my point of view, but what if he's been right all along?

I can imagine the text message I'd send him. *Hey, Ains, hope you're having fun. Just wanted to let you know that I realized you've been right all along, and we should all just do whatever we want in life. So, enjoy Cambodia or wherever you are, see you around!*

And right now, with my eyes closed against the afternoon sun, next to my enormous pool and my gorgeous beachfront mansion, exhausted from spending the last hour fucking the hell out of a vivacious, smart, funny, twenty-three-year-old fitness instructor, I start to believe the words.

I never actually have to go back to the city, back to my office and regiment. This right here could be my life.

I roll my head to the side and crack my eyes open. Victoria has taken off the bikini and tossed it over the side of the pool. She floats naked on the flamingo, eyes closed, seemingly not a care in the world.

I glance down at my own bare chest, sweat gleaming from the heat of the day, then back up at the gloriously naked woman in my pool.

This is my life. Quite literally.

Is it possible this is the first time I've ever realized that I have any choice in the matter? That I've entertained the idea that I could change the rules and enjoy myself?

I'm going to try. Just a little experiment to see if what I'm feeling right now is something that can be real, rather than just some passing dopamine. Or a stroke.

I'll give it two weeks. Let the office know I'm going to work from here. Let Victoria know that I'm interested in her. Let myself do things that bring me enjoyment.

If at the end of the two weeks, I'm still as happy as I am right now, I might have some big choices to make. If not, I just head back to New York and pick up where I left off.

I've got nothing to lose.

Rule #13

PREPARE FOR THE STORM

VICTORIA

"So, you guys are like, dating."

I roll my eyes. "We're not dating. I don't think."

Sally shakes her head and gives me the same frustrated look she's been giving me all week. "You're just waiting for him to decide and tell you?"

"I mean, sort of, but—"

"You get to decide, Vic. You can't just wait around for men to tell you when you're in a relationship. It's not a good look for you."

"I hear what you're saying, but it's more complicated than that."

"Because of all the lies?"

I flop back on the sofa and groan. "Yeah, Sal. Because of the lies. It sucks. I mean, it seems to be going so well. We hang out, and it's fun, and the sex is wild, and I think I'm actually a good influence on the guy." I know for damn sure he's a good influence on me. I've been finding myself making decisions about my life so calmly and confidently. Small decisions, sure, like where to grab dinner or which insurance company to sign up with when my current travel insurance expires at the end of the month, but decisions none the less. Just a few weeks ago, I would have agonized over them, put them off, or made someone else decide.

"I saw him in shorts yesterday. I just about shit myself," Sally tosses my way with a knowing smile.

I laugh. "He's loosening up. It's fun to see. It's like he's coming out of a shell that he didn't realize he was in."

"And you?"

I cock my head to the side and consider how to put the feeling into words. "It's interesting because he is still really alpha. He likes to be in charge, but I'm definitely calling the shots. Like, in the past, he's always expressed his dominance in very specific, very controlled ways. And with me…"

"He can finally be his wild animal self."

We both laugh, and I nod. "I guess so. I feel like a queen, for sure, especially in that big house. And he always wants me there. It feels good."

Safe is the word I want to use, but I chicken out. I'm not ready to admit that to anyone, not even myself.

"But not good enough to ask him if your relationship is going anywhere."

I shake my head and sigh, the good feelings from the last few minutes draining away. "How long could it last? Until the first major holiday when his kid comes home and finds me there?" I shake my head again. "No. It just is what it is. I may be having fun, but it's not a real relationship. I'm sure he feels the same."

"What makes you think that?"

"He's got a life, one that I'm never going to be a part of. He's literally on vacation. I'm a vacation fling. And—" I hold up my hand to stop her protest. I've heard it all before. "It's okay that I'm a vacation fling because we have a basic incompatibility that will never change."

And by it's okay I mean, it has to be okay. There's no other option for us, even as the time I spend with Ben is starting to feel like…more.

If I tell him about Ainsley, it's over.

If I don't tell him, and he eventually finds out, it's over.

If this whole thing becomes too much of a lie for me to live with…well, then I break it off, and it's over.

The last scenario is the only one that doesn't end in an explosion of drama and humiliation, but I still know it's the least likely.

I don't want to give him up…ever.

The world is going to have to rip him away from me. And I know it will, so I'm just going to let it all play out until I lose my man, my job, and my home all in one moment.

I really should be doing something to mitigate the damage, but I'm not.

Instead, I'm having feelings. And not the usual sort.

Not even I'm stupid enough to call it love, but it's something. Something I've never felt before. It's craving and joy. It's an expansive feeling in my chest that inspires me to be better at my job, my life, and taking care of myself. It's a feeling of freedom, like I could do or be anything.

In that man's presence, I'm invincible.

Ironic that he's the one who's always chasing me.

And the one who's going to take me down.

You're taking yourself down, girl.

It's the truth. I can blame this on anyone I want, but I know it's all me. I'm not only going to smash whatever little life I've got going for me here, as well as my hopes and dreams of somehow keeping this guy forever, but I'm going to crush Ben.

He's really opening up, loosening up. He's not the same uptight, suit-wearing, rule follower I met in that bar. In just a few short weeks, I've started to expect smiles out of the guy. He jokes and laughs and surprises me. He eats carbs for god's sake. Not a lot, mind you, but a little bite here and there.

I feel like an egomaniac taking all the credit for his transformation, but I do deserve some. And I'll deserve one hundred percent of the blame when this slippery slope ends in ruin.

"Do you want to walk down to the store with me? There's supposed to be a storm coming in tonight, and I want to make sure we've got food for tomorrow."

Frowning up at the blue sky through the window, I pull out my phone to check the weather.

But I don't get the chance.

Storm rolling in tonight. Get to Merit early.

A grin starts on my lips and shoots through my whole body like lightning.

Sally laughs. "I'll take that as an *I already have plans to fuck my billionaire vacation fling.*"

I nod over at her sheepishly. "He says to get to the island early because of the storm."

She laughs and rises from the couch, stretching. "Get on over there and get you some, girl. I'll still be here waiting when it's over and you need a friend again."

"Thanks, Sal. And I still need you, you know. I can't have these kinds of conversations with Ben."

"Ones about your feelings?" She laughs. "I know. And that's problematic. But it's nice to be needed, I guess."

Rule #14

YOU CAN RUN, BUT YOU CAN'T HIDE

VICTORIA

The helicopter pilot happily ferries me across the channel, having apparently been given orders to fly me over whenever I want. There's a golf cart with keys waiting at the Merit dock.

When I get to the house, Ben isn't home yet. I make my way up to the guest room where I stayed the first night. The one I guess I'm officially claiming as my own. I don't know that I actually need a room here, but it feels good to know there's somewhere private I can go and close the door.

I have the strangest feeling when I'm here. It's like I know he wants me here, but at the same time, I could ruin it all with one word.

And then be trapped on this island. At Ben's mercy.

Is the possible danger of it contributing to my desire for the guy? I mean, I do like scary movies.

I leave my stuff in the bedroom, even though I'm pretty determined to make my way into Ben's elusive bedroom tonight and wander back downstairs. The dusky sky is starting to darken, and the wind has picked up considerably. The large glass doors off the living room are scattered with rain drops.

"There you are."

I jump a foot as the voice comes from right behind me. Ben laughs and takes me by the shoulders from behind, dragging his lips from my shoulder to my collarbone and up my neck.

I shiver as his warm breath dances across my skin.

"Cold?" he asks, noticing, of course. This man doesn't miss much.

"No."

"Hot?"

I smile at him in our reflection in the glass doors. "This is going to be my first island storm."

Ben's grip on my shoulders tightens, and he pulls me to him sharply. "I like the idea of being your first anything," he growls into my ear.

"You can be the first guy to ever make me dinner and eat it in front of a scary movie during a storm."

His gruff laugh echoes through my bones from where his mouth is still connected to my skin.

Then he releases me and walks off toward the kitchen. "I don't think the house got stocked up, you're going to have to deal with my food."

I follow him, hand on hips, grinning. "Torture food?"

"If by torture you mean healthy, then yes."

I let out a dramatic sigh. "I guess I'll survive."

Ben manages to whip up some not terrible looking salads with grilled chicken and arugula. He even found a sweet potato to roast for the side, so I'm happy.

We settle on the couch with our bowls.

"As for storm horror, I think we're deciding between a truly gruesome and violent movie about some bad dudes who do really bad shit to two girls and then have revenge taken on them by the girl's parents and a loosely based Agatha Christie-like movie about a bunch of rich kids who hole up in a mansion to ride out a hurricane and die one by one."

"Did you just give away the ending?"

I laugh. "It's the plot of most horror movies. Everyone dies except for one. Sometimes two or three."

"Which movie's better?"

I crinkle my nose and shrug. "No movie is really better than any other. It's just a matter of taste. The first one, the violent one, has higher ratings, but the kind of people who would choose that movie are going to rate it high. The second one seems to have a broader appeal based on the premise, so a wider variety of people will try watching it. And some of them will hate it. So, lower overall rating."

"When you say bad dudes doing really bad shit to a couple of girls, you mean…"

"Yeah."

"Maybe not that one."

I nod, happy with his choice. Bodies will make for a more fun evening, I'm sure. "The hurricane film will be perfect for tonight." I freeze, remote in hand, and turn to him, my mouth wide in horror. "Wait, you don't think there will be a hurricane here tonight, do you?"

Ben smiles kindly and shakes his head. "It's not hurricane season. We're going to get high winds and some rain, but the house is built to withstand it. We have a generator as well for when we lose power."

"When?"

Another smile, this one slightly more evil. "Scared?"

"No. Of course not."

"We're safe out here. Faraday tends to fare a bit worse in storms like this because the storm drain system clogs easily, and the sewer system is pretty shallow due to the underground coral and rock."

"But we're okay out here."

He pulls me to his side and kisses the top of my head in a move so sweet that I nearly panic. "I'll keep you safe."

I order the television to turn on so I don't have to respond.

We finish our dinner in the first twenty minutes of the movie, which is lucky considering the high gore level that hits about forty minutes in. It's deliciously bloody and violent, each spoiled rich kid meeting their death in a different, highly creative way.

The hurricane rages outside the house they're holed up in, preventing anyone from leaving. Our own storm is raging as well, lashing against the windows and making me jump just as often as the scares on screen.

Ben has pulled me closer and closer throughout the movie, so by the time the credits roll, and the power finally flashes out, I'm pretty much in his lap.

I let out a little scream as the room goes dark. Then I giggle. This is so much fun.

"Don't be scared. I'll protect you."

His lips land on mine, and I really do feel safe here in his arms. I open and let him enter me, his tongue smoothing over my teeth and the inside of my mouth. He's taller than me, pressing down while holding tightly to my waist as I sit on his lap. He's so naturally powerful, so effortlessly in control, it's an instant turn-on.

I want his power overtaking me.

I try to pull away, but he only relinquishes my mouth, keeping the rest of my body close. "Where do you think you're going?"

"I want to go look at the storm."

It's too dark to see his expression, but after a moment, he lets me go. I hear him following me over to the glass doors. He presses me to the cool glass with the full weight of his body and bites down on the meat of my shoulder.

I watch the wind thrash the palms on the trail to the beach, the dark ocean wild with whitecaps. The porch is relatively protected, the staff having put away the furniture and lashed down the pool cover. All that's left out there are the terracotta-colored tile and a built-in cement table, a few feet from the door, collecting rainwater on its wide, smooth surface.

"There's nowhere for you to run."

His words send chills through my already cooled body, followed quickly by a hot rush of excitement. "I can think of a few places to hide in this giant house."

"Not ones where I wouldn't find you."

"Care to place a wager on that?"

Ben's hand moves swiftly from my shoulder, down across my stomach and straight into my shorts. He pushes roughly past my underwear and presses his fingers inside me.

It's slick enough down there to swallow him whole.

"I'll bet that no matter where you try to hide, I'll smell you."

I can't help but grin to myself at his words. I like the sound of this game very much.

"What do you get if you win?"

"You'll have to wait and find out."

"I'm not sure that's a bet I'm willing to take." I'm playing coy. Obviously, I'm going to let this man do whatever he wants to me.

His soft laugh hits my neck in a wave of hot breath. "You already have, lover. You're stuck here with me." He spins me so quickly that I gasp, the sound catching on my breath as his hand catches my neck and presses my back to the door by my throat. "So, you can either submit to me now…"

Even in the darkness, I can see how hooded his eyes are. If I was to reach down, I know I'd find his cock hard enough to drive through my stomach.

"Or you can run."

We stay locked in a heated stare for a long moment before Ben releases me and steps back. I stand frozen against the glass doors, unsure of my next move.

He takes another step back.

I glance toward the staircase that leads up to the bedrooms. No, too confined. It would be so easy to find me up there.

I look to the stairs leading down. More wide-open space, and I could possibly move hiding places if he got too close.

I bite my lip with uncertainty.

"Are we playing a game?" I'm stalling now, still nervous about heading off into the dark house alone but also wanting to build up the moment. It's deliciously tense and nerve-racking.

"If you run, we are."

Oh god. Okay.

"Is it a scary game?"

I watch as his head turns to the left and then to the right in the dark room before coming back to the center and pinning me with his gaze. "Looks pretty scary to me."

"Do you…do you remember my safe word?" The last word squeaks out of me, my confidence draining as I start to embody my role in this little game of ours.

I'm the scared one. And I'm starting to feel it.

Ben laughs darkly. "Do you remember your safe word?"

I nod.

He crosses his arms over his chest and takes another step back. "I'm going to close my eyes and count to ten."

Like a sexy, twisted game of hide and seek.

I'm so into it, my thighs clench together at just the thought of being chased and caught.

"One."

With a deep breath, I run.

I head to the stairs leading up first, taking three of them with heavy footfalls before retracing my steps quietly and coming back to the main room.

"Two."

I glance up at his word and find that he's turned to face me. I can just make out his hands covering his eyes, the image of him standing there, silhouetted against the storm-lashed windows makes the perfect horror movie scene.

I run toward the kitchen and then back to the glass doors, dragging my hand across the pane and causing him to turn in my direction once more.

"Three."

I run in a circle around the living room, barely avoiding crashing into end tables and discarded flip-flops. I make my way up a few stairs again before stopping dead and tiptoeing back down, across the living room, and to the stairs leading to the lower level.

"Four."

I glance up as I creep downward, my last glimpse of Ben before slipping out of sight down the stairs is his back. He's still facing the stairs leading up.

I think I got him.

I creep the rest of the way down to the lower level and glance nervously around in the dark.

"Five."

His voice echoing through the house makes me jump slightly. Is it louder than it was before? Does he know I'm further away?

I'm only partially familiar with the layout of this floor. Other than the gym and the hallway that leads off the main room to the bathroom, I don't know what's down here.

Ben does, though.

He's definitely got the upper hand.

"Six."

Shit. I've gotta make a move.

I decide to stick with what I know, making my way down the hallway across from the exterior doors toward the bathroom. Once inside, I creep into the shower as quietly as I can, pulling the curtain closed and crouching down. I'm on the side closest to the door, figuring I might be able to escape if he comes in here.

"Seven."

Fuck! He's definitely on the lower level with me. I thought I tricked him into thinking I went upstairs, but I guess not.

"Eight."

I hold my breath. I don't want to get caught right away, but I'm not exactly sure why.

As soon as he catches me, the game gets even better, but there's something about the thrill of crouching here in this cold, hard bathtub that has my heart racing. I never want this game to end.

"Nine."

He hasn't come down the hallway toward the bathroom. Maybe he thinks I went into the gym or hid in one of the closets in the main living space.

I wait anxiously for the last number…and whatever's going to happen next.

It doesn't come.

I count to ten in my head over and over as I breathe in and out as silently as I can. I must have counted to at least a hundred by now.

Maybe he went back upstairs?

I'm just starting to wonder if I'm going to spend the night in this cold, hard bathtub, and wishing I'd found a closet full of blankets or something to hide in, when I think I hear something.

My senses kick into high gear as I remain frozen in place, trying to listen as hard as I can.

I don't hear anything else. It was probably the storm.

With a sudden whoosh, the curtain flies open at the far end of the tub.

"I told you I could smell you, lover."

I'm on my feet without thinking, the prehistoric animal in my brain running the show. I manage to escape Ben's grasp as he reaches for me, and I make it out the door—but just barely.

I don't get two steps into the hallway before he's got a strong hand on my shoulder, pushing me against the wall.

"Why are you running?" Ben asks in his calm, terrifying serial killer voice at the same time I scream, "Let me go!"

The contrast of our two levels of calmness is distinct. Every scary movie I've ever watched has had a scene just like this, and the woman being chased—or caught as it so happens—acts just like I'm acting.

I know I should remain calm and think this through, but I don't seem to have that ability any longer.

All I can do is try to escape.

I drop to my knees, hoping to dislodge his arm from my shoulder.

It's the wrong move.

Once I'm in a ball on the floor, Ben covers me with his much larger body like paper covering rock.

"You thought you could get away. I'm going to have to punish you now."

I want the punishment—whatever it is. I want it so bad my clit is throbbing between my legs. I'm surprised we can't both hear it screaming for his touch.

But, unfortunately for my poor pussy, I also want to win.

I go limp in his grasp and make him drag me to my feet, supporting my full weight as we head toward the stairs. It doesn't even seem to faze him to be lugging a hundred and forty pounds of dead weight with one arm.

Hell, he probably does something similar at CrossFit.

My hope is that he's going to set me down somewhere, and I'll be able to make my escape.

I don't have to wait very long.

When we get into the living room, he strips my tank top off, leaving only the white lace bralette underneath. The white fabric seems to glow in the low light.

"My pretty little prisoner."

I continue to say nothing, give him nothing. He tosses me on the couch and comes to stand over me, his legs wide, his hands on the back of the couch as he leans over.

"I was hoping you'd put up more of a fight, but I guess your surrender is pretty sweet, too."

He stands up and looks around the room. I see my chance and take it.

Shuffling to my hands and knees, I scurry sideways toward the far end of the couch. My sudden movement must have taken him by surprise because he's slow in reaching for me.

I almost make it off the couch, but at the last second, he catches one of my ankles, turning my leap to freedom into more of a nosedive into the tile.

I catch myself with my hands on the firm ground and kick at him blindly, trying to free my leg. For a moment he catches my other leg as well, but pretty soon, my violent kicking connects. I can't see where I hit him, but there's a muffled grunt, and he releases me.

I don't take a second to think about whether or not he's hurt —something I might need to examine later—before getting my feet underneath me and running.

Ben must not be badly hurt because he's on me in seconds.

In my blind panic and rush of joy at freedom, I just run and don't consider where I'm running. I hit the glass of the patio door with one hand and cry out. Not a second later, Ben is at my back, grabbing that hand and pulling it behind my back, pressing my whole body into the cold glass.

For a moment, we're quiet and still, both watching the storm outside.

It's magnificent in its power. The palms are thrashing down in the yard, and the sea is roiling. Rain pounds down on the patio in sheets, pooling on every surface. As we watch, a bright flash of lighting lights up the sky above the ocean.

I take the opportunity to scream, more for fun than anything else, and revel in the feeling of Ben's hand clamping quickly over my mouth.

"You know, I brought you to this house so you'd be safe from the storm. I'm not feeling a lot of gratitude right now."

I struggle against his hands, one still firmly over my mouth, the other keeping me pinned to the glass with one arm behind my back. His hips grind into mine, and his erection is hard and obvious. My eyes roll back in my head momentarily at the thought of that hard cock taking me against the stormy window at the climax of our little game.

But, once again, Ben surprises me.

He lets go of the arm behind my back, leaving my body effectively held in place by his. I can't see where he's reaching, I only know it's for something that's not me.

Suddenly, Ben pulls me back an inch and opens the door right in front of me. A blast of cool, wet air hits me right in the face. I don't have time to even think about what's happening before he's shoved me outside.

And closed the door behind me.

After being pinned in confinement for so long, blood rushes into my limbs, and I gasp in a full breath, looking around wildly.

It's raining so hard that I'm already soaked. It's not particularly cold, but it could not be wetter, and the wind is strong against my side, forcing me to focus on staying upright.

Ben is standing on the other side of the glass, arms crossed over his chest.

Smiling.

That motherfucker.

I love this game so much I could laugh out loud. Instead, I throw myself at the glass door and pound with both fists, screaming at him to let me in.

He barely even reacts, simply cocking his head to one side and cupping his hand around one ear as if to hear me better.

I know the asshole can hear me just fine. "Let me in, you crazy bastard!"

Another flash of lightning lights up the world around me, and I scream louder than ever, looking frantically behind me as if the light was creeping up on the patio to get me.

When I turn back to the glass, I scream once more. Ben is now standing with his forehead pressed against the glass, leaning over so he's eye to eye with me.

"Let me in!" I scream.

"You know the password," he responds calmly, his voice perfectly audible even at his normal level.

"You're crazy," I yell back.

Ben shrugs, keeping eye contact.

Another flash of lightning makes me jump and spin around.

I need to get a grasp on my surroundings here so I can decide my next move. I'm not safe wording out. I'm just not.

I need to think rationally about this.

Ben must think I'm safe here on the patio, or he never would have shoved me out that door. He's far too concerned with consent and possible litigation to put me in actual danger.

I decide to lean into that.

I turn around and face him just as the sky lights up once more, the brilliant electric white and blue reflected in his eyes. I hold that gaze and take a deep breath.

And then I turn and start to walk away.

I hear the door behind me open immediately and try to break into a run, but the puddle of water I happen to be standing in at that moment foils that plan. I go down hard on one knee and both hands, scrambling to get myself back up.

Ben's behind me with both arms around my waist, capturing me and lifting my body as I flail and kick, screaming at him to let me go.

I make it as hard for him as I possibly can, but I'm no match for his strength as he drags me back up the patio and presses me over the stone table. The surface is slightly dipped in the center, meaning it's completely filled with water at this point. More water pounds down from the sky as the wind continues to try to throw us sideways.

Ben is unmovable behind me, hips pressing mine to the table. He captures my hands even as I swing them wildly to try to prevent it.

I'm disappointed at how easy it was for him to take me down. I hope that if I knew the stakes were higher, I would have done a better job at fighting back. But it's hard to say. When actually faced with this kind of situation, the whole thing is a lot harder than I ever imagined it would be. It moves too quickly for rational thought, and my instincts are apparently not up to par.

Ben shifts one hand to hold both of my wrists at the small of my back and fists his other hand in my soaking wet mess of hair. "Quite the predicament you've gotten yourself into now, isn't it?"

I struggle against him, even though it's pointless.

Ben uses his grip in my hair to press my face down into the puddle of water on the surface of the table. I hold my breath and clench my eyes and mouth closed.

Finally, he pulls me back up, sputtering and coughing.

"I'm going to give you one more chance to do the right thing here, lover," Ben says, leaning down so his face is parallel to mine.

He wants me to safe word out so we can go back inside. But that would mean he won the game. There's no way.

"Fuck. You." I spit the words into his face.

He smiles. "Yes, that's the idea."

His face disappears from my view as he stands back up. His grip on my hair relaxes, and I feel my shorts and underwear pulled roughly down to my knees.

"Shall we see how wet you are for me, lover?"

He laughs softly at his own joke as the rain continues to drench us. I feel my legs pushed roughly apart, and his hand enters me without warning.

I gasp and squeeze my eyes closed, trying my hardest not to come at the first bit of the contact that I've been dying for.

"So fucking wet. Inside and out."

"Let me go." It's a pathetic attempt, and Ben doesn't even bother to respond.

The next thing I feel is his hard, swollen tip driving into my entrance. He has to push my legs further apart to get the angle he needs to press his enormous, hard cock further into my body, but I'm a puppet in his hands. With a few firm presses, he seats himself inside me.

"Fuck, you feel so good."

I'm teetering on the edge of orgasm once more, his harsh entrance having rubbed my clit just the right way. He continues that sweet, rough rub as he slides out and shoves himself back in.

It's brutal and terrifying, cold and chaotic, but it also might be the best thing I've ever felt. I'm a prisoner to this man, but free as a bird in my own mind. The confinement allows me to let go for a moment and just be.

Ben is slowly sliding his tip up and down my inner walls, still pressing my hands to my lower back.

"If I let these arms go, are you going to use them to hit me?" he asks gruffly, not pausing in his thrusts.

"Probably," I manage to get out.

He lets them go anyway, and I swing them wildly, or as wildly as I can pressed face down on the wet table. They've gone to sleep, making my attempt even more pathetic.

Ben laughs darkly, easily avoiding my attack.

I'm so blind with pleasure, excitement, and the utter darkness that I don't see his next move coming.

With one quick motion, he grabs my hair once more and lowers my face back into the inch deep puddle of water on the table. I didn't have a chance to hold my breath, but my body tries anyway, and a little bit of water gets sucked in. I cough and thrash, but Ben holds me there.

"I never knew coughing could be so fucking erotic. Do you want to know how good it feels on my cock when you cough like that?"

I use every ounce of strength I have left to stop coughing, to calm myself down, but it's no use. Ben uses my hair to pull my head up and then dips my face into the water once more. I cough and spit uncontrollably as soon as he lifts me again.

"Fuck, lover. You trying to make me fill you up with my cum?"

It's not exactly what I had in mind, but the words don't induce panic like they might with anyone else. I trust this guy to not want an accidental pregnancy just as badly as me.

I trust him a lot.

"Fuck you," I sputter, my voice a hoarse whisper.

"So you keep saying." Ben releases my hair, and I barely catch my own head before it hits the concrete table. He's got both my hips in his grip now, pounding into me with punishing thrusts.

If this is my punishment, hell, I'll take it all night.

"If you don't come for me, I'm leaving you out here."

I almost laugh despite my very non-funny circumstances. I've been on the verge of an orgasm since the second this game started.

If he wants me to come, I'm happy to oblige.

I arch my back slightly, shifting his angle just enough. He nearly cries out with pleasure, and the thrusts get harder.

I suck in a breath and hold it, trusting him to keep rubbing my body just like that.

The sky lights up electric blue and brilliant golden white as I come. I try to keep my eyes open to see it, but they clench shut against the waves of pleasure overtaking my senses.

My arms are propping me up, and I arch into the feeling even further, making Ben give me what I need to keep the feeling going.

"God, your pussy gets so fucking tight when you come. You're gonna make me come, is that what you want?"

"Yes." It's the first agreeable thing I've said in nearly an hour, but the orgasm sucked all the fight out of me. It was like the whole game was building to this moment, priming me with the right chemicals and just enough tension to make it explosive.

And it still is. Somehow, I'm still clenched down and spasming when I feel Ben empty himself inside me. His cool, wet body folds over mine as he continues to thrust through his pleasure, moaning unintelligible things into my shoulder blades.

When we finally still, we remain like that for too long, my body turning to ice as he presses me into the wet table, the water continuing to fall from the sky in never-ending sheets.

"Ben."

My word breaks the spell, and he's upright in an instant, falling out of me and pulling my body to his. He turns me so my chest is to his, wrapping me in his arms and kissing the top of my head—a little move I've been trying my hardest to stop thinking about every second of every day.

Fat chance I'll ever forget it now.

I can't speak, can barely move my legs to take a step, which becomes apparent when I stumble trying to walk. Ben scoops me into his arms and carries me back into the house without a word, up the stairs and to the end of the hall, to the room I've been waiting to see.

He places me on a pale green sofa and covers me with a soft blanket.

"We only have the hot water in the tank, so I'm going to fill the tub. You okay out here for a few minutes?"

I nod stupidly in the pitch dark before I remember. "Yeah, I'm okay."

When he comes back for me, I'm nearly asleep. I let him lift me once more and moan in pleasure and pain as he lowers me into the warm tub. I guess all the adrenaline was keeping me warm before because the heat of the bath makes my whole body break out in tingles.

Ben has lit candles around the room and kneels next to the tub in the warm golden glow. His arms dip beneath the water to help me adjust my position until I'm reclining comfortably in the massive clawfoot.

"Bet you wish you'd gotten those release waivers signed now, huh?" I manage to get out around my chattering teeth.

He scoffs a bit, but I know I'm right.

"You make me crazy," is his soft answer. The words are not unkind, quite the opposite. He says the word crazy like someone else might say the word love.

Not me, of course. I'd never, ever, ever say that.

I close my eyes as Ben washes my entire body with a soft cloth from his kneeling position beside the tub. I keep telling myself that this is normal behavior for a guy who I'm sleeping with. It's not strange or sweet or loving at all.

I know I'm starting to drift off, but I feel safe enough to allow it.

Safe. Not loved. Just safe.

Rule #15

WHEN IT RAINS, IT POURS

BEN

The last thing I want to do is wake Victoria, sleeping like an angel in my bed, especially with the news I have.

With a sigh, I finally sit next to her on the bed and run my hand up her arm. She inhales and smiles, her eyes opening and finding mine immediately. Her smile brightens and what was a tiny feeling in my chest just moments before balloons into an emotion so big and bright that it threatens to suffocate me.

"Morning," she says, beating me to it.

I manage to swallow down some of the feeling and smile down at her. "Good morning, beautiful."

Something changed between us last night. I'm not sure if it was the intensity of the game or the way she placed her trust in me so fully, but I woke up this morning a different person. One who sees different things as possible in life. One who just might want different things.

Unfortunately for my hopeful heart, the island also woke up different this morning.

"Why don't you grab some clothes and come down for a cup

of coffee. There's a situation on Faraday that we need to talk about."

Her eyes go wide. "The storm? Is everyone okay?"

I nod. "The people are okay. The roads and many of the houses, however, didn't fare very well."

"The Sands?"

I nod again. "The Sands is fine. It's built to withstand hurricanes, so a little tropical storm won't take it down."

"Okay," she says, pulling off the blanket and reaching for her shorts.

The sight of her naked in my bed is sending alarm signals through every synapse in my brain. *Don't let her leave.* I want nothing more than to tackle her down and take her right here and now.

But now's not the time. I haven't even told her the worst part about the storm damage yet.

I fix her a cup of coffee and bring it into the living room, sinking down onto the sofa next to her. She's frowning down at her phone.

"Phone's still out," she says, tossing the thing to the side to accept the steaming cup.

"Yeah, someone came over this morning to let me know about the damage to this island. Once again, Merit fared much better than Faraday in this one. The main road to town is pretty washed out, only the four-wheel drive carts can pass at this point. The island will have that stabilized soon, though. The real damage happened to the houses along the road, mostly in neighborhoods on the west end. The storm drains clogged early, and then filled completely, and the flooding was pretty severe."

"Wait, the west end? That's where my house is."

I nod. I already know, but I'm dreading giving her bad news. Another brand new feeling for me. When have I ever struggled so much to share a hard truth? Never, that's when.

"Your house took on a lot of water. Sally's at the resort now, as are at least twenty other employees whose houses flooded.

Sam and Dom are trying to figure out how to squeeze people into staff housing for the time being, but there's not a lot of room to spare."

Victoria's eyes go from surprise to concern to shock to sadness all in one moment. I watch her process the news, feeling more grateful than ever that she was safe with me here. I want her safe with me forever.

I won't analyze that now.

"There's room here," she says after a moment, drawing my attention away from my concerning thoughts and back to the present moment.

"There will always be a room here for you, of course. You can stay as long as you need."

Victoria's on her feet, setting her coffee down on the table. "There's room for everyone, Ben. How many bedrooms are in this place? And couches and pullouts? You can easily offer shelter to twenty homeless employees until something else can be worked out."

She's right, technically, and I feel like a complete dick for not even thinking of it myself. But even as the solution gets more perfect the longer I think about it, the more I don't want it to happen. I want my house, and this woman, all to myself. What will happen to our little love affair, and our games, if the house fills with employees?

But alas, now that the idea has been broached, there's no going back. Honestly, I'm surprised the guys haven't started shipping refugees over here already.

I nod, holding in my own reservations and disappointment. "That's a great idea. We have plenty of room. Let's get ready and head over to The Sands to get everything figured out."

The helicopters are grounded until they can be checked after the storm, so we're on a speedboat heading to Faraday. I pull Victoria close to me as the tiny vessel crashes over wave after wave, enjoying our last few moments of peace and privacy before our world is overrun with prying eyes.

The island looks bad. Really bad. The road from the dock to the resort has been cleared of palms and is passable, but just the sheer amount of plant matter piled on either side has me concerned. If it looks like this on the east side of the island, the sloped side where water drains right into the ocean, the flat, lowland west side must be a complete mess.

I know we'll have to make it over to Victoria's house soon enough, but for now, we head straight to The Sands.

The scene looks like something out of a disaster movie. People sit in varying stages of disarray on every chair and surface in the lobby area. They look tired and uncertain, but there's a lightness to the air as well, as if they've already been well taken care of.

I guess having somewhere so welcoming to retreat when your house floods is a comfort most flood victims don't enjoy. Everyone has coffee, people are eating and smiling.

Sally finds Victoria as soon as she walks in.

"Oh, there you are. I was so worried about you off on that little island. It didn't blow away, I see." She has Victoria squeezed tightly in her arms and a pang of jealousy hits me before I can stop it.

I shake it off and head to the front desk, where Sam and Dom are conferring with the local police chief.

"Morning," I say, and the three men look up at me.

Sam smiles and claps me on the back. "Hey, there. Thanks for making it over so fast."

I frown at the small slight, as if this place, this island, wasn't as important to me as it is to them. As if I wouldn't come. Sure, I've been a bit distracted over the last couple of weeks, but I'm still as much of an owner as any of them. "Of course. Where do we stand?"

"The west side is going to take weeks to dry out, although the water is already receding, which is a good sign. The airstrip and the port both survived without any damage, and the road is already close to being passable. The crew started working as soon as the rain stopped. They've been out there for hours. We're taking over food and water every hour or so."

I nod. "And the housing situation?"

"We've got six rooms open here with two beds each, and three checkouts today, so we can put up a good chunk of the homeless employees here at the resort," Sam says, but doesn't look happy about it.

"But…" I prompt.

"But we've also got check-ins. None today, but starting tomorrow, and quite a few this weekend. For tonight, we can house everyone, but starting tomorrow, we need another solution."

"We can take them to Merit," I say.

Sam and Dom both look at me with appraising eyes. They must have considered this as an option but decided not to be the ones to bring it up.

"It's a great solution," I say, suddenly feeling the need to defend myself.

"It's a good solution, but not a great one," Dom chimes in. "Ferrying employees back and forth to work will be a logistical nightmare."

"The Richardsons have their hotel sitting empty right now, and they've offered to rent it to us in the past for events. I'm going to get on the phone with them and see if we can take it over for the next few months as employee housing. But for now, taking the twenty people who have nowhere to go but the hotel lobby and getting them settled on Merit is the best plan we have," Sam says, nodding to me in agreement.

"We can get a couple of the local guides to run boat shuttles a few times a day. It won't be perfect, but we'll make it work," I say. "Do people need time to go to their houses and get things, or should we start taking them down to the docks now?"

Dom narrows his eyes at me. "There's one employee who wasn't on Faraday last night and probably needs to head home and see if there's anything there she wants to salvage."

It's a challenge, issued head-on, and I don't back down. "Indeed. I'll take her over there now and then we'll head down to the docks in an hour. She knows the road well enough to drive people from the dock to the house, and we'll have Max driving as well. With two boats and three carts, we should be able to pull this off fairly quickly."

As I lay the plan out, the logistics do actually seem pretty simple. It's the unusual feelings coloring my thoughts that guarantee things are going to be more complicated.

Rule #16

WELCOME TO CAMP MERIT

VICTORIA

"It was crazy, Vic. One minute we were watching the storm, the next the water was coming into the house. We went next door to Paul's top-floor apartment and stayed the night there with like ten other people. This morning, I went back, and the water was still almost knee deep. The furniture, the kitchen, everything is going to be garbage."

Her eyes brim with tears as she recounts her harrowing night, and my own tears roll down my cheeks. Sure, it's just a short term, furnished rental, but it was home to us.

"I'm sorry I wasn't there." It's true. As much as I would hate to give up my night with Ben, playing scary games in the storm, I would have traded it all to have been there for my friend as shit went down. "I'm going to head to the house now and see if there's anything I can grab. Then everyone is coming to stay at the Merit house."

Her eyes go wide. "Really?"

I smile, glancing around at her raised voice. "Yeah, but don't say anything yet, okay? I don't know exactly what the plan is." I glance over at the three owners, huddled together with the police chief, talking solemnly.

"Well, that's a bright spot in this whole mess. I'm finally going to get to witness you two lovebirds in action." My eyes go wide, and she breaks into giggles. "Not that kind of action!"

I can't help but laugh with her, but the humor soon turns to lead in my gut. I grab Sally by the shoulder and pull her further into a corner. "Sally, it can't be like that, okay? People can't find out. I don't know who knows about Ainsley, but he wasn't exactly subtle about who he was sleeping with, and there are at least a handful of people in this lobby who we partied with."

"Hmm, yeah." Sally glances around and then grimaces back at me. "Your secret is safe with me."

I inhale a long breath and sigh. I can trust her not to say anything. But convincing Ben might be another story. Luckily, I have his sense of propriety and his concern over litigation working in my favor.

Perfect, Vic, you know the man well enough to successfully manipulate him. Well played.

It's a depressing thought, especially after the closeness I've been feeling to him, but I don't have a choice. Yesterday, the man was only holding my heart, and the most fun sex I've ever had, over me. Now that my home has been destroyed, he's holding my safety and security as well.

"Victoria."

I jump and turn at Ben's voice right behind me.

"We can head over to your house and grab a few things. We'll probably need to take a few other employees with us as well."

He glances at Sally, and I smile. "She knows."

Ben relaxes visibly and nods. "Great, why don't you come along. We have two open seats if there's anyone else who wants to grab things from your neighborhood. Sam and Dom are letting their employees know the plan now. Starting in an hour, we'll be ferrying everyone to Merit on a couple of tour boats. Max will be able to drive people from the dock, but we'll need you to drive a cart as well, Vic, if that's okay. Not many people know the way."

"Oh, of course. Sure, I can do that."

"Great. Meet me out at the cart in ten. And if you find two neighbors, bring them along."

And he heads off toward the offices.

"Does he know that you guys are in a secret relationship?" Sally hisses into my ear.

I groan and close my eyes. "Kind of? I mean, he doesn't want to cause a scandal by dating an employee, so we've kept it pretty quiet, but I'm not sure how serious he is about the whole relationship thing secret."

"And of course you haven't talked about it because that would be too easy, and now a bunch of employees are coming to live in the mansion with you two. This is better than reality TV."

I groan and squeeze my eyes closed. "I'm going to have to tell him that we need to keep it between us."

"But what reason could you possibly have for wanting that? I mean, besides the truth, which you obviously aren't going to tell him."

I shake my head. "I don't know. I'll think of something."

I'm still dreading the conversation when we head out to the cart with Paul and his roommate Jack. Their apartment was safe, but they want to check on the older lady who lives below them.

"All right, load up," Ben says like a total dad.

I grin and start to slide in beside him before I catch myself. "You know what? Paul, you have the longest legs, why don't you take the front."

He thanks me, and we all pile in. Ben tosses me a glance that I read as conspiratorial, and I nearly melt into a puddle right there in the backseat. Maybe I won't have to have an awkward conversation with him after all. He seems to get it.

The house is a complete loss. I can barely breathe as we pull onto our block, the four-wheel drive golf cart moving slowly through the still muddy street. The water line on the side of the house is obvious due to the color of the dirt street, and it's high.

I grind my teeth trying to remember what exactly I have in the bottom drawers of my dresser. Hopefully, nothing that can't be washed.

"You said there's an old woman living in that apartment?" Ben asks Paul, looking dubiously at the obviously washed-out ground floor apartment.

"We moved her upstairs with us last night and that's where we left her when we headed to The Sands this morning. She should be okay up there. We didn't get any water or damage."

"But the power's still out," Ben grumbles. "It's going to get hot."

Paul nods. "The locals here are pretty tough. This was a bad storm, but not the first by any means. It wasn't even a hurricane."

He and Jack head toward their building and Sally slides out, walking straight through the unlocked door to our house. I remain frozen in my seat.

"I brought some plastic bags from the resort. We can load up anything you want to take back to Merit to wash," Ben offers helpfully, and I manage a small smile, dragging myself out of the cart and following him toward the door.

When I get to the doorway, however, I freeze.

The scene is nearly unbearable.

Mud is caked two feet up all the furniture, and the ground is a soggy mess. The smell of ocean and damp and dirt is so strong, I have to bring my arm to my face to block it out. Then I squeeze my eyes closed, wanting to block out the rest of it as well.

"You okay?" Ben asks from beside me.

I crack my eyes open and peer up at his concerned face. Then I shake my head. He pulls me into an embrace.

"This looks really bad right now, but it will all get cleaned up."

I shake my head against his chest. "It's so bad."

Ben pulls away slightly and tilts my chin up to look at him. "We'll load up all your stuff and bring it over to Merit. Get it washed. Anything that can't be washed can be replaced. I'll make sure of that."

I shake my head again, tears pricking at the corners of my eyes. "It's not just me..." I break off again, a tear rolling down my cheek. "It's everyone. The lady next door has to live here. All of the employees who work here full-time, they lost everything. Some of them bought houses in this neighborhood, what are they going to do now? I just showed up with a suitcase planning to stay for three months. Nothing I have here even matters. But there are so many people who need help." My heart is breaking, and I'm on the verge of breaking down.

Ben takes me by my shoulders and presses his forehead to mine. "We're going to help everyone. We're the ones who can help, so we will. Right now, we've got twenty displaced resort employees heading down to the dock, about to get on boats to go to our house. When they all get there, they're going to need you to help them—show them their rooms, make them coffee, listen to their stories about the storm, and offer comfort. You're in the best position to help right now. Do you think you can do that?"

I nod, my tears forgotten. He's right. I don't have to wallow in sadness for these people. I can help.

Sally and I load up the bags Ben brought and carry them out to the trunk of the golf cart. Paul joins us, backpack on his back.

"Jack's going to stay here, but I gave our neighbor my room. Do you mind if I grab a room on Merit for now?"

"That's fine. There should be plenty of space for everyone, although I don't think anyone's going to be getting their own room," Ben replies, climbing back into the cart.

"It's no problem."

But it just might be a problem.

I do actually have my own room. One that already has my stuff in it. Am I going to need to share that with a few other ladies? Will Ben want me to move into his room? What will I tell everyone? What will I tell him?

Besides Sally, I'm not close to anyone who works at the resort. The only people I interact with are a handful of other fitness instructors. Luckily, those weren't the people partying with Ainsley and I in the weeks before my job started. Before he bailed.

But Paul was one of those people, and the people he works with were too. How many of them are going to be on Merit with us?

"Are you freaking out right now?" Sally whispers beside me as we bump down the muddy road. "I can practically feel the nerves radiating off of you."

"Yeah," I say simply, in no mood to get into this in the back of the golf cart.

"It's going to be fine," she says dismissively, offering a side hug.

I stiffen in her grasp, suddenly angry at her flippant remark. "What makes you think that?"

She backs away, clearly surprised by my hiss of a comment. "I don't know. Things usually are?"

I roll my eyes and flop back in my seat. I'm stressed about this situation, upset about my house, and completely at the mercy of fate and the whims of other people. It's not a great feeling, but it's also not a good time to be alienating my only ally.

"I'm sorry. I'm just…this has been a lot. It still is. I need some kind of plan."

Sally nuzzles back into me, clearly not at all put off by my mood. "We'll think of something. Let's talk more on the boat."

The scene at the dock makes me forget some of my worries. It's a straight up refugee site, complete with haggard, dirty people sitting in groups on and around piles of their wet, filthy belongings.

Unlike a real refugee site, however, most of the people are in pretty high spirits. The mood is almost festive as people clamber onto the two small snorkel boats that showed up for the job. These are people who know they're going to be taken care of. People who, even though they lost some things, know those things can be replaced.

I help some women from the café load their bags, and then Sally and I load ours. I lose sight of Ben as we're corralled into seats on one of the boats.

When we get to Merit, he's already on shore, directing people to wait in groups to be taken by golf cart to the house. When he spots me, he waves.

"Victoria, you still good to drive?"

I nod and head over to him.

"It's going to be slow going, as people have a lot of stuff, so we won't be able to take as many people at a time as usual. There's shade down here, though, and Max already brought down a cooler of drinks, so everyone should be fine."

"Some people look less fine than others. Let's get them loaded up first."

Ben follows my gaze around the crowd. It's easy to spot them —the ones wandering forlornly with all their belongings in their arms, not mingling with any of the groups. He nods.

"Great. Here's the key to the green cart. Get as many as you can on each trip. Max's wife Petunia is waiting at the house to greet people and get them settled in the main room. When everyone's there we can start putting people in rooms."

"Okay," I reply simply, not giving into the burning desire to step close enough for him to pull me to his body.

Instead, I turn and head in the direction of the lime green and black golf cart that Ben usually drives to and from the house. It'll be my first time driving this cart, but not my first time driving one at all.

As I'm loading my bags into the trunk and preparing to round up a few passengers, Paul comes over.

"Ooh, you got the keys, huh?"

I try not to let my sigh explode out of me. I guess I've been waiting for this exact interaction for hours now. "Yup. I know the way."

"Do you, now?" he asks, just as curious as I would be in his position.

"Yup," I say, allowing too much of my annoyance out with the word. I should be diffusing the situation, but I haven't had enough time to figure out how. Sally and I were not able to formulate the perfect plan on the packed, bumpy boat ride over. "I'm taking the most haggard-looking people first, and that's not you, but if you want to help load, that would be great."

He keeps me pinned there under narrowed eyes for a long moment before softening. "Yeah, okay." He tosses a look over his shoulder at two older women huddled together next to a palm tree. "I think Britt and Susan from housekeeping could probably go first."

I offer a tight-lipped smile and a nod. "Thanks."

Paul helps the women load their things into the cart before heading off to help Ben and Max load their passengers as well. I sigh as I watch him go. It's not that he's a bad guy, it's just that he knows too much.

It takes three trips with all the carts to get everyone and their belongings to the house. When I finally cross the threshold, I'm hot and tired and grimy from the road dust sticking to my sweaty skin. All I want is to throw myself into the pool, but there's a lot of work to do first.

Petunia has been doing a great job of getting people into the house's many indoor and outdoor showers as soon as they arrive, so most people sitting around the living room look clean and refreshed. I can see a couple of local women carting off bags of wet, soiled clothes and remember Ben telling me they'd rallied up an army to help with washing.

Maybe this won't be so bad after all.

I decide to head up and shower after all—not feeling like much of a leader when I'm dirtier and smellier than the people I should be helping.

When I come back down the stairs into the main room, clean with wet hair and fresh clothes, Ben is speaking to the room. He's standing right at the foot of the stairs, so everyone watches me come down.

He pauses in his speech as I come up behind him and smiles over at me. I must be bright fucking red with the entire room dead silent and staring at me, so I just duck my head and hurry to the back of the crowd where Sally is waiting, trying not to laugh at my complete and utter failure.

"Like I was saying," Ben goes on, "we have enough beds if people can share, but there are plenty of sofas, hammocks, and floor pads so no one has to share a bed if they don't want to."

Snickers break out in the crowd. I flush once more, thinking everyone has turned to look at me, but when I look up, I don't find a single stare. People are elbowing each other and grinning among themselves.

I'm completely overreacting. This is going to be fine.

"I'm going to be taking people around to get situated. Women first, to get them settled where they're comfortable, then the guys can fill in around them and take whatever rooms and beds are still free. Victoria," I freeze at the sound of my name echoing through the room as every face now turns to me, "knows the house pretty well, so she's a good person to ask if you can't find bedding, towels, toiletries, or a shower. We have plenty of extra stuff here, so make yourselves at home."

I offer what I hope is a calm, welcoming smile to the sea of curious eyes still pinned on me.

"We heard back from Sandy and Phil Richardson who own The Flamingo Hotel on the east side, and they're going to send the caretakers over to open that property for us to use for employee housing as long as we need it. There are enough rooms for everyone, and they should be ready tomorrow. So, we're all roommates for tonight only. It's more of a slumber party. We're going to start grilling and preparing a big meal, but there are snacks and fruit laid out in the kitchen already if you're hungry. Filtered water machines are in the kitchen and out by the pool. If one of those is running low, just let me, Max, Petunia, or Victoria know, and we can get them switched out."

He looks right at me then, his piercing eyes sending a shockwave through my entire body. "Did I forget anything?"

I'm torn right in half with indecision. Part of me wants to just smile and shake my head, try to play off the fact that I practically live here and share a bed with this man. But the other part of me wants to rise to the occasion that he's offering. Be the hostess he clearly sees me to be.

Unfortunately, only one of my warring sides has the longevity of my relationship in mind.

I shake my head and say nothing.

After a beat, Ben nods. "Okay then. Ladies, let's get you situated."

Women start rising to their feet and crowding around Ben as he talks about the bedroom situations on the main floor and lower floor of the house. He doesn't mention the upper floor, where his bedroom is. And mine.

They traipse off down the stairs to the much larger lower floor, and I start to head into the kitchen, but I'm stopped by Paul.

"You don't want to head off with the ladies and get a room? You never know who you'll get stuck sleeping next to if you don't."

I step away so he has to take his hand off my shoulder. "Oh, that's okay. I'll just take whatever's left over."

"Very generous of you. You know—"

"There you are." Sally comes up behind Paul and slips her arm through his, turning him to face her. She presses her body against his as she whispers loudly in his ear. "I just scored a private room with a queen bed. Want to be my bedmate?"

Paul's focus shifts to Sally without another glance in my direction. "Hell, yeah."

As she leads him toward the stairs, she tosses a wink and a grin over her shoulder.

Taking one for the team, Sal.

The woman has my eternal gratitude, but I know she's getting something out of the deal as well. Paul's been the object of her attention ever since I've known her. Maybe this was what it took for her to finally make that first move.

I only get a second's respite before trouble comes my way once more. Ben's walking toward me, in the same room where he had me pinned to the floor as he fucked me not eighteen hours ago. What are the odds that he's going to walk over and pull me into his arms in front of all these people?

Once again, though, I get lucky.

"I think we got everyone situated with a spot to sleep tonight. I'm about to kick on the grill and help Max with food. Do you want to lead the way out to the pool? People might like hanging out there more than just sitting around the living room."

"Yeah, for sure. I'll start corralling people that way." And even though the smartest thing to do right now would be to run off and do my task, far away from this man, I don't move.

Neither does Ben. He stays just where he stands, about a foot away from me. I can feel the magnetic energy rising from his skin, pulling me toward his body.

I take a step back. Ben smiles knowingly.

"You okay?" he asks.

I nod too quickly. "Yeah, I just…you know…"

The smile turns to a little smirk, and he nods. "I do. I'm glad we're on the same page."

My knees go weak as relief rushes through my body, hot and cold and effervescent.

It's short-lived, however. Fifty percent of my worries are now gone, but the other fifty percent? Those are still milling around us, snacking on pineapple and cracking beers.

Any one of the people in this house could know about me and Ainsley. Some unknown percentage definitely does.

Will one of them open their mouths at the wrong moment and ruin everything?

It should be me.

Yeah, yeah, annoying voice in my head. I get it. I should tell him.

But I'm sure as fuck not doing it today.

"You didn't put anyone in my—I mean, the room where I... you know..." I hesitate to say the words *my room* aloud, even though I'm pretty sure no one is listening.

"I didn't put anyone in the entire upstairs. There's a door at the top of the stairs that can be closed and locked. My room and yours are private."

The thought of that locking door has me wanting to run. Wanting to slam it closed and cower behind it while Ben pounds on it and yells. I can feel the heat rush to my cheeks and between my legs.

When I look up, I'm almost certain Ben is thinking the same thing. His eyes are dark, and the faintest hint of a snarl curls his upper lip.

I gotta get out of here.

"Okay. Pool, food, movie." I'm just spitting words into the silence now, trying to break up some of the sexual tension.

"Bed," Ben replies.

"Bed?" I squeak.

"Pool. Food. Movie. Bed." He lists the items off one at a time, his voice falling to a whisper when he gets to bed.

"Right. Yeah. Okay." I turn and head quickly into the crowded living room without another glance back.

"Hey everyone, I'm going to go take the cover off the pool, if anyone wants to join. There's a basket of loaner suits, all washed, some brand new, if anyone didn't bring one. I'll bring the sunscreen basket out as well, although the umbrellas do a pretty good job this time of day. If you want to stay inside, that's fine, too. There's another deck off the living room downstairs that's fully covered, with hammocks and chairs." I'm so flustered by my interaction with Ben that I don't realize my incredibly stupid mistake until the words are out of my mouth. How am I going to explain knowing so much about the inner workings of the pool and the house? It was one thing to know the way up the road, but this? This is bad.

I can hear Ben laughing softly behind me as he turns to head out the patio doors.

Dread sinks through my chest, but I have no choice but to push on. "Come with me if you want to swim." And I make my escape.

Rule #17

LUCKY YOU'RE NOT UNDER OATH

BEN

The house hasn't been this full since…well, since ever. One of the plans for building this giant house on a neighboring island was to have a place to get away and host parties and events without having them connected to the resort. That never really panned out. Turns out it's much easier to host events at the resort itself, and we don't have a lot of friends.

Except for Avery, of course, but even he tends toward The Sands these days. The Merit Island house has more or less become my private second residence. It's just as well, I suppose, as I was the one who paid for most of it. And I wouldn't consider myself upset about how it all turned out. After a few months of my city life, complete with the commute, the firm, courtroom battles, and constant cell service, I'm more than ready for some time completely alone on what sometimes feels like a deserted island.

But that's all different now. The thought of spending another night alone in this house gives me feelings that I'm not entirely prepared to face.

I don't want to be alone. I want Victoria here with me.

It's probably for the best that we've got twenty interlopers for the night. I keep catching myself almost saying things I don't actually know if I want to say.

I mean, my mouth wants to say them.

Stay. Come back to New York with me. I'm catching feelings for you.

But my mind has issued a gag order.

I load up my arms with pans of meat from the cooler we brought with us from The Sands and back through the glass patio doors to where Max is getting the grill ready.

"It's not often we get to feed a crowd over here," he says good naturedly, helping me to set the pans down on the wide concrete ledge surrounding the patio.

"I was just thinking the same thing. You know, I bet we haven't had a party here since Halloween the first year The Sands was open."

"Usually, it's just you inviting Petunia and I over for dinner."

I catch the teasing tone and smile. Of course, Max, our resident old sage, would have figured out exactly what's going on with me. "Sorry I haven't reached out this trip. I've been a bit tied up."

Max's eyebrows raise nearly a foot as he grins at me.

If I was the blushing type, I might just have been right now.

"She's a lovely woman," he says simply, apparently deciding not to call out my inadvertent innuendo.

"Yes. It was unexpected."

"These things usually are."

I watch him load the hot grills with chicken thighs and consider whether I want to elaborate. I'm not really a feelings-sharing kind of person, but it would be foolish to turn down such a great opportunity for advice.

God knows I need it.

"The most unexpected part is how deeply connected I feel to her already. I seem to be growing attached."

Max looks up at me and cocks his head to the side. He's no longer grinning, but the amusement is still there. "You say that like it's a jail sentence."

I shrug, taking the empty pan and handing him another. "She's not exactly what I would have imagined for myself. Hell, she's who I would have imagined for Ains."

"You're concerned about the age difference."

"Yes, of course. And how that age difference brings with it a difference in...I don't know what to call it. Developmental stage? Season of life? She's barely old enough to have graduated college, which she didn't by the way. She's looking at her possibilities in life for the first time. I'm at the other end of that spectrum, turned back to face her, and it's hard not to want to offer advice or guidance all the time."

"Is she coming to you for advice or guidance?"

I laugh. "Oh, no. She's got it all figured out."

"But you know better," Max says, not looking up.

He doesn't have to. I know just what the old man's face is doing right now—holding back a smile. "I've been around a lot longer and know the pitfalls of certain decisions."

"Do you?"

"Yes. Well, not the decisions she's facing, but similar ones. I know what happens when you decide to drop out of college."

"Because you dropped out of college, and it went poorly for you." It's not a question, but it might as well be. My defenses are all online and ready to fire.

"No, you know damn well that's not what happened. And I see what you're getting at, but I've seen a lot of people in very bad situations, and those situations could have been avoided if they made different decisions in life."

Max sets the still half-full pan of meat down and turns to face me. "Mr. Adams, you're lucky you're not under oath right now."

I grin and shake my head. Max is a huge fan of courtroom dramas and likes to pull this card.

He goes on. "You can only speak to your own life experiences. And if you're going to stand there and tell me that the people you defend on a daily basis from charges of fraud, tax evasion, and embezzlement didn't all graduate from college, I'm going to have to call you a liar. Not one of them makes bad decisions out of a lack of education."

I cross my arms over my chest and look out over the ocean. The tide is receding, and the gulls are diving into the wet sand, hunting. I don't want to have this argument. I don't want to have to defend my values or personal ideals. But I started it, so I guess I don't have a choice.

"It's not only about my personal experience. There is data to support—"

"No, no, no. There's data to support whatever you decide is correct. You say people must go to college to be successful, I say Bill Gates. You say..." he waits for the answer he knows I'm going to provide.

I sigh. "That's a special case—"

Max cuts me off by laughing. "A special case indeed. I say Oprah, you say..."

"Another isolated case of—"

"You first decide what is true in life, Ben. Then you surround yourself with the evidence of that truth, so you don't have to be wrong. You build the case for your own personal worldview one day at a time. You believe college is necessary for success and a good life, so your world is filled with evidence of that. I believe that happiness is the necessary ingredient for success and a good life, so my world is filled with evidence for that. Who's right? Who's wrong?" He throws up his hands in a gesture of exasperated surrender.

I just shake my head. I get what he's saying, but... "Only one of us would win in court."

"As long as life is about you winning and everyone else losing, you will always find yourself at an impasse with those around you."

Well, shit. I definitely should've skipped this conversation. The last thing I need right now is another existential crisis on my hands.

Max recognizes my lack of response for the failure that it is and takes pity on me. "I would welcome you to open up your mind to the possibility of other truths. When you encounter the nice woman who makes your coffee, you tip her extra because you feel bad that her life turned out the way it did, am I right?"

I nod, wishing I could run away.

"But there is another truth possible. And that truth is that you would only accept her being happy in her job if she's working toward a degree to get a better job. She cannot possibly be living a good, happy life unless her goal is to be rich and powerful and successful like you." Max turns the tongs at me, and I have to take a step back to avoid getting jabbed in the chest. "But you aren't happy, Ben. Do you see the irony of that?"

Goddamn motherfucking shit.

"You know, under New York law, I could probably sue you for such statements."

Max just laughs and turns his full attention back to the grill, done with me. "You just keep fighting, Mr. Adams. Fight to the death for something you don't even want."

I don't have any response to that, so I'm grateful when Petunia walks up and interrupts. "Ben, you're looking a little pale. Do you need to lie down?"

I shake my head. "No, your asshole husband just invalidated my entire life. So, I'm processing."

She laughs. "Yes, he'll do that."

"I think I'll go check on the pool situation, if you two can handle the grill."

"Of course, dear," Petunia says, giving my arm a comforting pat.

"We'll be handing out food to people based on SAT scores," Max calls after me. I don't bother to turn and respond to his goading. "So why don't you get them lined up in order. Highest scores at the front of the line."

I just shake my head and keep walking, smiling softly to myself.

The man made his point, and it's not the first time. It's just, usually when we have this conversation, we're talking about my son, and I have exactly zero inches of leeway to consider other viewpoints when it comes to Ainsley.

Victoria, however, presents a very interesting conundrum. On the one hand, I think I know what's best for her. On the other, I obviously don't know what's best for her.

My brain is breaking in half.

Could I really live a life with someone who is actively making choices that I disagree with?

When it comes to my son, the answer is no. I've made the decisions for him, and I expect him to follow through because I know what's best.

But with Victoria, she's an adult. Her own person. She gets to make her own decisions and build her life the way she wants.

But Ainsley is also an adult. And his own person. But he's also kind of my person.

The last thing I need right now is a complete meltdown, but I feel it coming.

"Hey," I call to a kid sitting on a lounger next to a cooler. "Pass me one of those."

The kid—no, not kid. Actually, a fully grown adult man and my employee, cracks a beer and passes it to me with a grin. I pound it and crush the can between my hands in a move I haven't done since college.

"Hell, yeah, man." The guy reaches up for a high five.

After an awkward pause where his hand hangs in the air, he returns it to his side and turns back to the bikini-clad woman beside him.

I have to draw the line somewhere and apparently high fives are where I'm making my stand.

I shake off the interaction and focus on the cooling, calming feeling of the ice-cold alcohol hitting my system. Then I dive into the pool.

It doesn't have the refreshing effect I was looking for. The cool water hits me like a splash of reality, banishing the warmth of my comfort zone and forcing me to confront the brisk truth.

I may have lived my entire life incorrectly.

I stay under the water, mourning my wasted years, as long as I possibly can. When I finally surface, I'm gasping for air.

Gasping for my sense of balance and stability to be restored.

Grasping for my usual lifeline of rules and order.

But it's just not there.

I'm a changed man. I can't go back to how I used to see the world. I don't know what this means for me. For my career. For my son. But I do know one thing for sure.

I'm not going to let my own petty rules and ideas about life ruin my chances with this woman. I can see it so clearly now, and while I'm not entirely sure how to fix everything that's wrong with me, I know how to take the first step forward.

I spin in the water until I find her, sitting on a chaise lounge in the shade, still in her shorts and tank, talking to a group of women I recognize from the fitness center at The Sands. I swim over to the edge of the pool and hang there, watching her.

It doesn't take long for her to look my way. She smiles at me and then looks self-consciously around at the other women.

I try not to take it personally. She's been this way ever since the employees arrived at the house, and I can't really blame her. We've had the whole world to ourselves for weeks. The intrusion is painful.

But it is a little bit odd that she's so averse to anyone knowing about us spending time together. Not that I feel ready to tell the world, but still. It's clear from her behavior that she wants to keep us a secret.

I just don't understand why.

"You ladies coming in for a swim?" I call, cringing at how much of a creeper I sound like.

They're all looking at me now, wearing familiar smiles. I see them on the faces of women everywhere I go. I know that sounds conceited, and it probably is, but it's the truth. I'm a very eligible bachelor, and many women out there are trying to catch my eye.

But only one has. And she doesn't seem interested in anyone knowing about us.

As much as I want to question her about it, this isn't the time or place. All I can do is respect her choice and follow her lead.

Look at me, learning and growing. I deserve a damn medal.

"I'm about to jump in, make room for me?" one of the women calls back, obviously flirting. I smile at her as politely as I can.

"I think I'm going to stay out," is the answer from the only woman I care about. "In case someone needs help or something. And lunch is coming up, so I want to help with that."

I pull myself athletically up the side of the pool and stand dripping on the terracotta concrete. I can feel every set of female eyes on my body, but I don't look away from Victoria.

"That's a good plan. I should get dried off and help too."

I walk toward the towel caddy and grab myself a fresh, folded, beach towel. As I'm drying my hair, I can hear the chatter from the group of ladies.

"…when he takes that suit off…"

"I'd dry him off…"

I smile to myself at the comments, spoken close enough to me, and in loud enough whispers, that I know they don't mind being overheard. But the only woman I want to hear isn't chiming in.

When I glance over, she's looking down at her phone, not paying attention to the women around her who are tossing glances in my direction.

I'm not typically a self-conscious guy.

But I just had my entire life thrown into disarray by a Caribbean wise guy, so I'm already feeling a bit out of sorts.

I'm so up in my head right now, I know I need to step away, rather than causing problems with Victoria by making a scene. Without another look in her direction, I head back toward the patio where Max is grilling.

"How are you doing?" he calls as I pass him on the way to the patio doors.

"Terrible, thanks," I call over my shoulder.

I hear him laugh as I enter the house. "Just let it all go," he calls.

Fat chance of that.

Rule #18

YOU ALREADY KNOW HOW IT ENDS

VICTORIA

This day just keeps getting harder and harder.

I mean, it's one thing to lose my house and be forced to share my beautiful mansion hideaway with a bunch of people who could spill my secret at any moment.

But I just started my period.

And did I prepare for this by stopping at the shop in town to get supplies? Of course not.

Not that I'm not grateful. I am so, so grateful. The last thing I want is to…I'm not going to say it. I'm not even brave enough to think the P word right now. Nothing would get me kicked out of this house, and my imaginary perfect relationship, faster than failing to prevent myself from getting pregnant. Even I, at twenty-three, have been around the dating scene long enough to know that.

But still. I'm kicking myself for not being prepared. Sure, I felt a bit sore and crampy the last couple of days, but I've been fucked in the most wild and crazy ways, so I just assumed it was part of the deal.

"Sally," I hiss, pulling her into the bathroom with me. "Do you have any tampons?"

Her eyes go wide. Then she grimaces apologetically. "No, but I'll ask around. Terrible timing. It's not like we can just run out to the store."

"I know. And I have a limited number of clean underwear here. Not to mention it won't be my own sheets I'm ruining."

Another look of pity from my friend. "Let me go ask around."

I nod. "I'm going to start looking in all the bathroom cabinets. There's like six bathrooms in this house, one of them has to have stuff, right?"

Wrong.

With a giant ball of toilet paper wedged between my legs, I search every bathroom in the house and come up with nothing. But Sally comes back, thank God, with options.

"Okay, I got these from some of the employees." She produces a fair pile of various sizes of tampons. "And Petunia, the housekeeper lady, overheard me asking and went to her house and got these." With a triumphant smile, Sally produces a package of pads that look like they were purchased in the eighties.

Beggars can't be choosers, though, am I right?

"Fantastic. This is great. Thank you."

Sally gives me a hug and leaves me to get situated. When I'm feeling confident enough to go out in public, I bundle all the rest of the supplies into a towel and hug it to my chest. I don't know how, but I need to get this stuff up to my room.

Of course, the first person I meet when I emerge from the bathroom is Ben.

His eyes go straight to the brightly striped towel bundle in my arms. "What's that?"

"Don't make me tell you," I respond.

He starts to laugh, but my face must tell him I'm not joking. "Okay..."

"Just go cause a distraction that will let me go upstairs."

His eyebrows shoot up, but he nods and heads in the direction of the television, on the opposite side of the living room as the stairs I need to sneak up.

"Hey, everyone, if I can have your attention…"

I don't wait to hear what kind of announcement he's thought up, making a beeline for the safety of my room. Once I'm there, I don't want to leave, but I know people will start wondering where I am, so I quickly stash my treasure and change my shorts and panties.

I'm pretty sure I made it back down without anyone noticing, but Paul follows me into the kitchen.

"Did you change again? Do you have a drawer here or something?"

I whirl at the sound of his voice and prepare to fight. Calmly, of course. Not to raise suspicion. "What? No. But I do have most of my worldly belongings in a bag because, you know, the freaking flood."

His hands go up in surrender. "Sorry. Didn't mean to offend you. I was just curious. You seem to know this house so well. And you know Mr. Adams like an old friend. I guess I just didn't realize you and Ains were so close."

And there it is. It takes all my physical restraint to keep my head from swinging wildly from side to side to make sure there wasn't anyone around to overhear that. Instead, I focus right on the threat in front of me. "It's not like—"

"And don't worry, I figured out where you're sleeping, but I won't tell."

My mouth drops open, and I snap it shut, trying to make my brain function through the horror of his statement well enough to form words.

He just laughs at my obvious upset. "I said I won't tell. Honestly, it's on them if they're too dumb to figure it out. I mean, this is Ainsley's dad's house. Of course he has a room here, and of course he'd let you—"

"You're going to be pleased at the movie choice," Ben interrupts, walking into the kitchen smiling, as if my whole house of cards wasn't collapsing down around me.

He stops short when he sees Paul. A quick glance between the two of us tells him all he needs to know.

And he saves me.

"Sally's out there asking for you," he says to Paul with a nod of his head in the direction of the living room. "Everyone's getting settled in for a movie."

"Oh, yeah. Okay. Thanks," Paul says to him with a smile. He tosses a wink at me and heads off to find his bedmate.

"You okay?" Ben asks once we're alone.

I shrug. Then I force a smile. "Yeah."

"Liar."

I shrug again, at a loss for what to say.

"That guy bothering you?" Ben's voice carries a note of concern now. Anger even.

"No, he just..."

"He figured it out?"

With a huge sigh, I offer a resigned nod. It's another freaking lie, but it's a lie that hopefully will get me through tonight.

"Do you want me to have a talk with him?" Ben asks, and my eyes go wide.

"No. No, no. That's okay. It's okay. He's just been wondering where I was going to sleep. He was concerned earlier when I didn't go with the other girls to get rooms, and he just let me know that he figured out I was sleeping upstairs."

There. Not a total lie. It's actually the truth in a sense.

When I look up from my feet, Ben is giving me the strangest look. "Would it be so bad if everyone knew?"

I close my eyes at his words, unable to prevent my feelings from overtaking me. I can't worry about how I must look to him right now. This is all officially too much.

This kind, generous, fun, sexy man likes me. Really likes me.

Wants me. He's plowing forward as if this thing between us is real. He wants it to be real.

I want it to be real, too. So badly I could cry.

I might actually cry.

This is a familiar stage of dating for me. After weeks or days of doing my best to be lovely and fun and cool, there comes a point when the guy decides he either wants me, or he "isn't looking for a relationship right now." And that's when it either becomes real, or I learn that it's just a casual thing.

That's how it's always gone for me. They get to decide while I wait patiently to be proclaimed good enough for a relationship or only good enough for sex.

This time, though...I wasn't hoping for this moment. I've been dreading it. I should have gotten out in front of it and told him from the first second that there was no chance of a relationship between us.

In my defense, I didn't actually think we would get to this place. I never thought he would consider me relationship material, even as I dreamed about it all being real.

I've been watching it get more and more real. I should have been telling him it wasn't. I should have been avoiding this moment. But I wasn't. Because I wanted it.

Because it is real.

Even though it's not.

"Victoria."

Ben lays his hand on my shoulder, and I open my eyes to look up at him. The concern is still there, mixed with something I might call fear. Possibly even disappointment.

That's all I'm going to be to him. A disappointment.

If he finds out the truth, I will have let him down. Betrayed him.

If he doesn't, I'm still going to disappoint him by failing to be able to give him what he wants. What he's clearly asking for.

"This has been a really hard day. Let's not make it any harder right now, okay? Whatever's going on, can we keep it until tomorrow when these people go to the hotel, and we get our house back?" His voice is gentle now, like he's coaxing a scared animal out of a corner.

I nod, and he smiles at me. "There was a vote, and they chose Nightmare on Elm Street."

I smile back, even though I want to cry. He's right. We need to get through this night, and then maybe I'll be able to make myself do what needs to be done. Maybe I'll walk away from this.

"That's my favorite."

He smiles again, taking a deep breath and exhaling in a huff, looking around. I know he wants to hug me. I want him to hug me.

But he doesn't.

"Let's head in there and get seats. Petunia brought over some caramel popcorn that looks like it's been in their emergency storm stash since the nineties."

I smile at his joke, softening at his obvious attempt to lighten the mood.

"After the movie, we'll encourage everyone to get some rest. Then we can be alone. Okay?"

I nod.

"You head in there. I'm going to grab some drinks and be there in a few."

I nod again and turn to walk into the living room. Everyone has brought blankets and pillows, creating a nest on the living room floor. It really does feel like a slumber party.

I raise my eyebrows at Sally as she beckons me over to where she and Paul have curled up with their backs to the sofa. I shake my head and put my hand on my lower belly, as if getting my period is an excuse for not joining them. She returns a sympathetic glance and smiles at me when I settle myself into a large cushy chair that is miraculously still free.

Ben has pulled the drapes over the windows, creating a dim atmosphere even though the sun has barely set. I catch him out of the corner of my eye, settling on one of the high-backed chairs at the bar adjacent to the kitchen. He's behind me, but far enough to the side that I can see him.

I spend the whole movie, which I've seen so many times I have it memorized, watching him. He laughs, and grimaces, and shakes his head, and rolls his eyes. He's so expressive, especially when he thinks no one is watching. He's so much more than the suit-wearing corporate defense attorney he plays in real life. He's everything. He's perfect.

And he wants to be mine.

I'm grateful for the darkness now as the tears that have been threatening for hours finally start to fall. I'm completely and utterly wrecked over this. It's going to end horribly, and it's all my fault. I was the one who lied and is continuing to lie every second of every day with this man. I am the one who sat by and let the guy fall for me, knowing full well what was going on. Knowing that it could never be real.

I've been telling myself it didn't matter. That the guy would never actually want me. And that still could be the truth. I mean, sure he wants me now, on this island, but he said himself that I'm nothing like the women he knows back in the city.

"Do you see any of those women here now?"

A fresh wave of tears run silently down my face as I remember that conversation. It was the one that gave me the first indication that there might be something here besides just sex. It was also when he let me know he disapproved of all my life choices.

So, there's that.

And maybe that's the crux of the problem. We're too different. I'm a college dropout, exercise instructor, and a liar. Ben is a rich lawyer, father, and the most eligible bachelor in all of New York. What the hell would he want with me?

The thought is supposed to make me feel better, but it only makes the tears worse.

I cry through most of the movie, managing to get my act

together toward the end so my face will have a chance to de-puff before the lights come on.

I wish I could have enjoyed it with everyone. The classic film was billed as horror when it came out, but these days it's considered a comedy by many people. There was laughter and shrieks from the whole room in all the right parts. Under different circumstances, this could have been a lot of fun.

As the credits roll and lamps start to click on, most people gather up their blankets and pillows and head off to their various sleeping spots. It might be barely after eight, but people are exhausted from the ordeal of the day. I know I am.

I wait until most everyone is gone, Sally and Paul sneak off together, both of them tossing me a knowing smile and a wink, but for very different reasons.

Finally, when there are only a few stragglers, I gather myself up and slip up the stairs. I'm just finished changing when I hear the thud and click of the heavy door at the top of the stairs closing and the lock sliding into place.

My heart aches anew for the fun kidnapping games we could play with a door like that, but alas. It's not going to happen. If I try to drag this thing between us out longer just so I can have another round of scary sex, it will only sink the dagger into the heart of my self-respect. What I have left of it, anyway.

Ben comes straight to my room and leans in the doorway. "That was quite a day, huh?"

I nod from where I sit on my bed. Hell, it probably is Ainsley's bed. The thought hadn't occurred to me until Paul said something, but it made sense that Ben would give the room closest to his own to his son. Ainsley must have been just a kid when they built this house.

I close my eyes as fresh tears threaten. I don't open them when I feel Ben sit down beside me.

"You must be exhausted." He pulls my body to his for the first time since this whole nightmare started, and I can't stand the wave of relief it brings. It feels so good, so right. But it's all wrong.

I try to pull away, but he keeps me there. "We're going to get it all figured out, okay? Between the four of us guys, we can rebuild the island, and that's what we're going to do. It's going to take time, but there's nothing to worry about. Everyone will be taken care of. All the houses will get fixed."

Bless his heart, he thinks I'm upset about the flood. I mean, I am, but some soggy clothes and a ruined apartment pale in comparison to the real monster I'm facing.

The thought of walking away from this man.

I pull away and look up at him, cherishing the way his eyes crinkle at me as he smiles. It's a secret, kind smile. One that I only see when he's looking at me. "I'm okay. Just really tired."

He nods and lets me escape from his arms. I lay down and pull the blanket over me. "I think I'll sleep in here tonight." I force the words out quickly before I can say what I really want to say—take me to your bed and make me forget all my problems.

Ben narrows his eyes at me. "You sure you're not going to be too scared to sleep alone? I mean, that movie was pretty scary."

I laugh. "It was not."

"I was terrified," Ben says, and I laugh again, rolling my eyes. "Terrified that people like that are allowed to have children. I mean, those parents could have prevented that whole massacre if they had listened to a single word coming out of their children's mouths. They should have been put in jail for child neglect and endangerment."

I smile up at him, my worries momentarily forgotten as I enjoy this perfect moment. "Spoken like an old man."

Ben shrugs. "I call it like I see it."

"You're not worried that a phantom serial killer is going to haunt your dreams when you fall asleep?" I ask, not being serious, but wanting to keep him here longer.

He shakes his head. "I'm more worried that the cold place beside me in bed is going to haunt me."

Oh, if he only knew the terrible foreshadowing he just added to the tragic story of us.

"It's just one night," I say.

Ben growls a bit and bares his teeth. "One night I could have with you."

"And what are you going to do if I say no and stay in my own bed?"

He raises his eyebrows, considering me. "I guess you'll just have to find out." He tucks the blankets around me comically tight, and I wiggle to free myself. "You could just come with me now and save yourself the trouble."

I would, I really would. But there's the issue of the bloody mess I have waiting between my legs. I shake my head defiantly.

"Okay," he says, getting to his feet and crossing his arms over his chest. "But don't blame me if you don't like the consequences of this decision."

I don't like any of the consequences I know will arise from my terrible, terrible decisions, but I say nothing.

"Sleep tight," he says ominously, switching off the light and closing the door behind him.

Rule #19

THE UNIVERSE MIGHT ACTUALLY BE PUNISHING YOU

VICTORIA

I wake with a start when someone clamps a hand over my mouth. There's another hand on my chest, and as my awareness expands, I can tell that the same person has knees on either side of my hips. They're on top of me as I lay on my back in bed.

My first instinct is to scream, and I try, but the sound is muffled almost completely by the hand over my mouth. I try to thrash, but the heavy weight on top of me keeps me on my back, completely immobile.

"Shhh." A deep, low voice growls in my ear. "This is only a dream."

Ben.

Of course.

My heart leaps in my chest, and I smile behind the hand clamped tightly over my mouth. The adrenaline is still pumping, but I'm over the shock of being woken up like this.

Now I'm ready to play.

Oh, wait.

No, I'm not.

Damn period!

I should have told him the truth about why I stayed in my own bed earlier, but now it's too late. He's holding me down forcefully with his hand on my mouth, hips pinned, as he struggles with one hand to get my shorts down.

I buckle at the core and scream once more. In the moonlight from my open window, I can just make out a smile streak across Ben's face at my reaction.

I may have found the perfect man.

Why, oh, why does it have to be like this? Why can't this be someone I can keep forever?

I manage to buck enough to stop him from getting the shorts over my butt, curling at my core and thrashing. His hand moves up to the soft tank I put on to sleep in, probably deciding it's an easier place to start.

And I want this. So bad. When we watched that movie with everyone earlier, I definitely thought about what a great game it would make—the phantom of a deceased serial killer coming through my dreams to accost me in the night.

And now it's happening. If I just relax a bit, he'll get me stripped naked and—

Nope.

It's much too soon in this whole honeymoon phase for him to find what's waiting in my shorts tonight.

I shake off the sadness that erupts at the thought that we'll never get to the place where I can comfortably talk about this kind of thing. We'll never get out of this honeymoon phase at all.

I don't have time to wallow right now. I need to stop this.

As he pulls my shirt higher, freeing my breasts to the cool night air, I see my chance. He's going to have to release my mouth for at least a second to get the garment over my head and when he does…

"Bentley!"

The word echoes out too loud in the otherwise silent house.

Ben freezes for a long moment, his hand still gripping my shirt which is halfway over my head, his other hand holding down one of my wild arms.

And then he retreats. It happens so fast I almost don't know what's going on. One second, he was a heavy weight on top of me, the next he's got his feet on the floor, backing away a few steps.

I struggle to catch my breath, aching with the sudden loss of his touch.

"Are you okay? I'm sorry, I thought that would be fun." Ben speaks gently, but I can hear the concern in his voice. He doesn't come close enough to touch me.

"Yeah. I'm fine. I'm sorry. I just…" I trail off, curling to my side to face him where he stands motionless a foot from my bed. I don't know what to say. I feel like a total fool.

"You don't have to explain yourself, Victoria. It's okay. That's why we have a safe word, so you can use it if you need to stop. I shouldn't have assumed…I just thought…"

He's scared now, scared that he's crossed some kind of line with his behavior. I could let him think that and protect my little secret, but that's the last thing I want to do.

I'm not a complete monster after all.

"I'm on my period." Silence falls after my statement, and I sit up, straining to make out his face in the dark. "It just started, I feel like crap, and I didn't have the stuff I needed, so I have some stuff that's not the best, and I just didn't want you to…you know…"

Another beat of silence, and then Ben laughs. It's soft at first but gains strength as the moment stretches on. Pretty soon, I find myself laughing along with him. It's a madness that overtakes me, seeping in through my mouth and spreading through my body. I laugh until I have tears running down my cheeks.

I reach for Ben's legs and pull his body to mine. He drops to his knees and rests his arms on my knees as I sit with my legs hanging off the bed.

"I should have just told you. It was stupid, but I didn't think…I mean…" I can't think of a single excuse for my behavior other than being completely ridiculous, so I trail off.

"You know," Ben starts, looking up at me from where his head rests on my knees. "I was married for years. I pulled my child from my wife's vagina. I'm intimately familiar with the workings of the female reproductive system."

"Gross." It's all I can think of, and just the word alone, spoken aloud, gets us both started laughing again.

After a moment, Ben climbs back to his feet and pulls me up to stand with him, holding me close in an embrace. "Why don't you let me draw you a bath. It'll make you feel better. I have some painkillers if you need them. And my bed is bigger, and it's cooler in there, so you'll sleep better."

It's the middle of the night, and I'm exhausted, but I nod against his chest. What's one more night of lost sleep when I'm not sure how many I have left with this man?

"That sounds nice."

He leaves me there to run the bath, and I sneak into my own bathroom, changing my tampon and doing my best to get myself looking presentable. When I sneak through his dim room toward the glowing door of his bathroom, I can hear the water running.

I pause in the doorway and watch him quietly for a moment. He's kneeling at the side of the large clawfoot tub, adding Epsom salts and essential oils to the hot water like a goddamn saint.

When I take a step into the room, he turns and smiles up at me. "Water's ready."

Rule #20

KEEP THE SECRET—JUST A BIT LONGER...

BEN

I stand back and watch her slip into the tub full of bubbles.

It's completely ridiculous, such a lavish bath in the middle of the night when what would probably be best for her is a good night's sleep, but I couldn't help myself. The need to take care of her is strong, burning in my chest like an ember.

I know she feels it too. She's letting me play the part of a doting partner like it's exactly what she wants me to do.

And maybe it is.

This whole day, I've been so caught up in worry about why she's acting like she barely knows me around all the resort employees. All I wanted was to do something to reinforce the connection between us.

I thought that would be a midnight game of Freddy Krueger.

I'm really glad it turned out to be a moment when I can show her how well I can take care of her. She knows we have fun in the bedroom. Maybe she's waiting to see if there's anything more to this.

It scares me far more than any horror movie game of chase to admit it, but I think there is. It's time I showed her my true intentions. Now that I've finally figured out what they are.

"How's the temperature in there?"

"Hmm," Victoria says, eyes closed and head leaning back against the bath pillow I draped over the side. "It's great. Want to join me?"

I smile even though she can't see me. "I'm going to sit this one out."

Her eyes crack open at that, little slits of green shining out at me from the tub. "Did I scare you, using my safe word?"

I shake my head honestly. "No. I'm happy to know that you'll use it when you need to. Even if I wish that you told me the truth to begin with."

"I thought you wanted me to lie."

I crack another smile. "There are situations that demand both, I guess."

Her eyes close again and a flash of shadow passes across her face. I can't quite place the expression, so I plow on, selfishly wanting her smile back. "I brought in this brand-new loofah, do you want to sit forward and let me rub your back?"

She obeys, but her eyes stay closed, and she still looks like she's about to cry. It's clearly terrible timing, but I can't stop myself. "You know, we can keep this thing between us a secret if that's what you want. But I wouldn't mind—"

"Just for a bit longer?" she interrupts me, eyes opening and boring into me, so serious it takes my breath away.

"Of course."

"I just...I just want it to be just us for a bit longer. Other people are going to complicate things."

True enough, I suppose. "That's fine. This evening, this whole day, was just a little awkward. I wish we would have talked about it ahead of time so we could be on the same page."

"I'm sorry."

"Don't apologize. That's not on you. If it's on anyone, it's me."

Her eyes crack open once more. "Why would it be your fault?"

Because I'm the adult? The boss? The owner of the resort? The one with the job and the house and the power? Even as I think the words, I know damn well none of them are true. This woman holds just as much power, just as much autonomy in this as I do. Maybe even more. She's a free bird, facing a life with so many options in it that my mind boggles to think of them all.

And she seems to be choosing me. She just isn't ready to tell the world yet.

That's fine, I can wait.

"I'm always the boss." I start rubbing my hand over her back, dragging the soft cloth over her smooth, wet skin. "I'm always the decision maker. No matter where I go, or what I'm doing, there's always a line of people waiting for me to tell them the next step. I guess I just get used to having that weight on me and assume it's there all the time."

"That sounds exhausting."

"It can be. But it can also feel really good. When you feel in control of everything around you, things feel safe. I don't have to worry about what's going to happen next, I already decided and told my team how to handle it. It's like I write the scenes and watch them play out."

"That can't be true, though. You can't control all of life like that."

I let out a sigh, using the cloth to bring more hot water up her back and over her shoulders. "It's true for the most part because I keep my world very small. I only enter into situations I can control. I always do the same things, predictable things, so they turn out how I expect."

"But The Sands?"

I laugh softly. "Yeah, that was a total shitshow for the first couple of years. But honestly, the guys talked me into that. It's not something I would have chosen."

"But you're happy you did?"

"It's been a great growth experience for me. And I built this house, which I love, so that was a huge plus." I pause, unsure whether or not I should say the next words.

Ah, fuck it.

"And I got to meet you, which would never have happened otherwise."

Victoria laughs softly, but I can't see her face. "A decade of struggling through owning an island resort just so you could enjoy a vacation fling with some girl?"

I hold my tongue for a long moment, trying not to step in something I'll regret.

She's clearly fishing for my feelings, and I want to give them to her, but I also don't want to come on too strong. I mean, she's not exactly given me much to reassure me she won't freak out and run if I suggest that this thing between us get serious. "The universe moves in mysterious ways."

She turns to me then, eyes open, with an incredulous grin her face. "You did not just say that." She laughs and rolls her eyes. "Not even two minutes ago you said that you controlled the entire world, and everything went just as planned, and now you're telling me that you believe in fate and the universe?"

I shrug. "Things change."

"What things?"

"Well, me, for one. Sure, I've kept my life small and predictable, but look at me now? I'm changing right before my own eyes. And it's you who's helping me. Two months ago, I would have never believed any of this. I would have predicted that I'd be the one writing a check for flood clean up, not the one on the ground, ferrying people across the channel and grilling them chicken."

"You do realize you didn't actually do either of those things."

I grin and flick a drop of water at her. "You know what I mean. I'm here. I'm doing the messy parts. I'm in a situation that's completely out of my control. All day today, I had to look to you for cues on how I should act. That's never happened. Everyone always looks to me."

"What are you saying?"

"I'm saying that I think this thing between us is good for me. I think you're good for me."

She doesn't respond, and I panic a little. "I know it's soon."

"It's really soon."

"I know. And I'm not suggesting you move to New York with me or anything like that. I just want you to know that I'm here. I'm here for this. I'm not going to just leave."

There. I hadn't known what the words would be before I said them, but I think that sounds perfect. Low pressure but letting her know that she's not going to show up here one day and find out I've flown back to New York for work or something.

"Okay," she says finally, but it's not the response I was hoping for. It's not the self-assured tone I'm used to hearing from her. Once again, I'm fairly certain she's on the verge of tears.

Must be hormones.

"Let's get you to bed."

I help her out of the tub and dry her body as she stands on the soft bathmat. I tuck her into her side of the bed and place a kiss on her forehead. She's asleep before I even undress.

Rule #21

IF IT AIN'T BROKE, DON'T FIX IT

BEN

The next day is a whirlwind of activity, getting everyone fed and back over to Faraday where they can settle into their new temporary homes at The Flamingo. It's a bit farther from The Sands than most people's houses were, which will require some kind of company sponsored shuttle service, but it's a hell of a lot easier than ferrying them across the channel. Everyone gets their own room, which makes them happy, and we're able to bring the entire Flamingo staff back on to manage the property while we rent it, which makes me very happy.

It's not often that I find myself in a situation that money can't solve, but since purchasing The Sands, I've been in plenty of them. Money only goes so far in a place like this. It doesn't matter how many new houses or construction crews you can afford. If the crews and materials and sewer infrastructures don't exist, you're shit out of luck. I'm glad we can at least provide jobs for a dozen or so more islanders during this difficult time.

By the time Victoria and I make it back to Merit, we're both so exhausted we fall straight into bed.

And wake up together. And go to bed and wake up. Again and again.

It's normal and crazy and unexpected and totally, completely right.

We haven't talked about "us" again since the night of the flood, but I'm feeling more at peace than I have in a long time. Something about this is just…comfortable.

A few days ago, I heard back from Avery that he found Ainsley, but not that they're on their way to New York yet. I'm grateful for that on both counts. As much as I want to get the kid settled in school, I'm not ready to leave. I told Victoria that I'd stick around, and I'm not sure if we've reached a place yet where she's going to agree to come with me.

Avery told me he found him in Indonesia, helping out with a sandbagging project on the shores of a flooding river. I don't say a single thing about how much his help could be used on this island, where the residents are still trying to put their lives back together after the storm. Not a word…which is highly unlike me.

He's making a decision. And I guess that's fine.

I would be lying if I didn't have a small bit of worry in the back of my mind about how he's going to react to my new girlfriend.

Girlfriend? *I sound like a fucking teenager.*

She's much closer to his age than mine. I want to think that he'll just be happy for me, but am I prepared if that's not how it goes? I don't want to choose. And I don't want to think about how it will go if I'm forced to.

Victoria and I are still mostly keeping our relationship on the down low. I go to her class three times a week, which continues to kick my ass, and anyone who knows either of us well knows we're shacked up out here. But that isn't very many people.

Honestly, I like it this way. I get to be myself around her, without worrying about what others think. I know Victoria feels the same. The goofy, bossy, wild side of her that I get to see when we're alone in the house is very different from the Victoria she shows in the fitness center.

At first, it felt so important to get to a place where we could tell the world. But now? I couldn't care less. I have what I want. Victoria seems to be getting what she wants. And it's enough. No need to announce our happiness to others.

Time, however, is creeping ever closer to a deadline I won't be able to ignore. There's a court date I'm required to be present at, a case my firm has been working on for over a year. But even as I consider leaving, I'm starting to feel more and more confident that she's going to agree to come with me.

The timing is close to perfect. Her class contract will be wrapping up before too long. Her friends are settled and safe, moving back into their homes as they get dried out and cleaned up. It's almost like it's meant to be.

Meant to be, huh?

Sometimes I even surprise myself with how much of a romantic I'm becoming. This girl just does something to me.

Something I like.

Sure, I may be in an unconventional, mostly secret relationship with a woman young enough to be my child. Sure, I may exhaust myself almost every night of the week pretending to savage her in some creative new way. But I'm having fun. For possibly the first time ever.

I wake up in the morning with her on my mind. I hardly worry about Ainsley at all anymore, which in itself is miraculous. I know he's still working at his volunteer position, and that Avery's with him.

And that's just fine.

College will be there when he gets done.

Seriously, who the hell am I?

Rule #22

YOU HAVE NO ONE TO BLAME BUT YOURSELF

VICTORIA

"Don't forget your leftovers," Ben calls as I follow him out of the little restaurant on the beach.

"Oh, yeah," I say, hurrying back to the table to snag the snack bundle Katy, the proprietor, made for me out of all the little tidbits we had left and, if history has taught me anything, a bit extra.

"Thanks, Katy," I call over my shoulder as I reach the doorway.

The woman smiles and waves.

Ben's waiting for me just outside the building and slides his hand across my bare midriff as I approach him, pulling me in close to his side as we make our way back to the golf cart.

It's madness that I'm allowing this sort of behavior in public on this tiny island, where anyone walking by could be holding the bomb that blows my entire life apart, but it's a hard train to stop.

The closer we get, the more the man seems to need to touch me all the time. The more he touches me, the more I crave his warm hands on my skin. And even though I know every public display of affection is another round of deadly roulette, it's stopped feeling that way all the time. I guess I've just gotten used to it.

Gotten used to the feeling of impending dread that follows you around at all times? That's pretty fucked up.

Somehow, it just happened. The more time we spend together and nothing terrible happens, the more I'm able to convince myself that it'll never happen.

And we spend nearly all of our time together now. Hanging out on Merit, bumming around Saubry, cruising the sunset in chartered yachts.

He leans down to kiss me as he tucks me into the passenger seat. His lips are warm and salty, his essence rendering me immobile for a moment, even as I try to fight off this power he seems to have over me. The power to turn me from the smart, sensible woman I used to be into the flushed, needy woman I always seem to become in his presence.

Madness.

Ben looks over from the driver's seat of the golf cart. "What time is your class tomorrow?"

I look back at him with raised eyebrows. "Seven. And you should know that. It's your class, too."

We're not even apart when I go to work, as Ben has taken to attending all my classes. I get a bit of alone time when I'm setting up and breaking down the room. Ben waits up at Reef or talks with Sam or whatever he does.

I know I should feel more concerned about the way our relationship seems to be developing.

The last few weeks have been fun but also pretty nerve-racking. I'm living in a straw hut, praying that there isn't a hurricane.

I should get myself out before the inevitable storm, but I can't.

I mean, I won't.

I'm going down with this ship, for better or worse.

Ben hasn't said a word about his feelings since that night in the tub, but I know he's catching some. I sure am.

I can't bring myself to broach the topic, even as the questions burn their way through my thoughts day and night. This thing between us is starting to feel real.

Even if it can't go anywhere.

It's so fucked-up. You're leading yourself straight into heartbreak.

But it's more complicated than that. At least, I think it is. I mean, I know I'm a lying piece of shit who doesn't deserve the guy next to me. Somehow, though, my brain has managed to talk me into believing that maybe he'll see it differently. Maybe we can get through this after all.

Either way, the sand is ticking through the hourglass, and I can feel the pressure.

The time will come when someone tells Ben the truth, and I want that person to be me. I owe him that much after what an absolute gentleman he's been.

Don't cry, Victoria.

Instead, I try to drag the fantasy out of my mind and into the real world by saying something really, really stupid.

"Does it bother you that our relationship is still secret?"

"Do you want it to be less secret?" he asks, glancing over at me from the road.

I search his tone for any indication of whether that's what he wants, but he's not giving anything away.

So, naturally, I panic. "Not necessarily, I mean, it's not secret, really, everyone knows, right?"

I can feel his eyes on me, but I don't look over.

"Something going on?" he asks.

"No, sorry. I just…it's been…" I don't know how to put my feelings into words without actually telling him what I'm feeling.

"Yeah, I guess I know what you mean. It's been like that for me, too. And yes, everyone I know around here knows, but it still feels very private. I've been enjoying having you to myself out here, even with all this chaos. But if we need to make some changes for you to be more comfortable, just let me know."

"No," I say quickly. "No, it's okay."

The cart stops right in the middle of the road, and Ben turns fully to face me on the bench seat. "What we have going on here is important to me, Vic. It's something. We don't do a lot of talking about the future, but we should start."

And there it is. Everything I've ever wanted, wrapped up like a rock in paper, smashing through my windows with a note that reads haha.

"Like, the future of us?" I squeak out.

"Yeah. I know it sounds crazy," Ben adds quickly as I open my mouth to protest. "Maybe it is crazy. But these last few weeks, I've felt crazy—in the best possible way. You've opened me up, and I don't know how I would ever go back to business as usual. It's like I don't even know that guy from before. And that has a lot to do with you."

"Ben..." I can't meet his eyes as I struggle to find the words to put Pandora back in her freaking box.

But I know the only thing I can offer here is the truth.

"No, not here. Let's get back to the house, get cleaned up a bit, and then have a real conversation," he says quickly, responding to something he must see in my face. I try to suck it up and put my smile back on, but I can't seem to do it.

"Ben, you don't understand." I'd rather just get out of the cart here and make my way back to the dock on foot. If we're driving back to the house to have a serious discussion about our future, there's no way it ends well.

"Victoria, I understand you might have some reservations, but I know you feel what I feel. I don't want to do this in the cart. Let me take you home, tell you the ideas I have for how we can make this work. You're welcome to argue but just know that I get my way for a living, and it's very difficult to out-debate me."

I could win the argument with a few simple words.

I'm your son's ex.

But, of course, I don't.

"Okay." And it's true. If he thinks he can take me "home" and convince me that this thing between us is real, I'm going to let him. I want it to be real. I want him. I want everything.

And it sounds like that's what he wants too. He doesn't quite realize how convincing my arguments are going to be for why it'll never work, but if he's going to fight for us, so am I.

When we finally pull up to the house on Merit, there's another golf cart in the drive.

"That's Avery. I'll get rid of him. You go grab a shower, okay?"

I nod and accept his kiss, watching him jog up the front steps.

I make my way around the side of the house and through the door leading to the side steps up to my room. The shower is life changing, much like Ben thinks the next hour of my life will be.

I have so much hope. I don't know where it's all coming from, but it's there.

He wants me.

He might love me.

I sure as fuck love him. I love him so hard it's burning through my skin.

This conversation is going to be difficult, but what I've learned from Ben is that I can do difficult things. I can be a leader. I can make decisions.

I'm making one now.

I'm going to fight for us.

I'm going to tell the truth and fight for us.

I find Ben in his office, reading glasses on as he sits in his swivel chair and reads something on his phone. He glances up and smiles as I enter wearing a white silk chemise that he bought me.

"I hope you don't think you're working right now." I know

we planned to have a big talk, but if it starts with sex, it might actually work in my favor. Hence, the negligée.

Ben's eyes graze down my body with desire, but then his attention shifts behind me.

I turn to look and immediately squeeze my eyes closed, regretting each and every one of my life decisions.

"What is going on here?" Ainsley asks from the doorway.

"Oh, Ains." Ben is climbing to his feet, taking me by the shoulder and trying to turn me around. I'm as immovable as a statue. "This is who I wanted you to meet."

"Oh, we've met." The humor in his voice guts me like a fish. I'm splayed out on the tiles for the gulls to pick through. I still don't look up.

Ben's grip on my shoulder loosens, but he doesn't let go. "You've met? Victoria?"

I look up then and meet his eyes. The look there is cautious but not yet devastated.

Give it a second, buddy. It gets better.

"Please for the love of God, tell me this is some kind of fucked up threesome thing. I knew you were kinky, Vic, but I had no idea you were into—"

"That's enough." Ben cuts him off. He looks back down at me, but my eyes are downcast, my entire essence seems to have retreated back inside, rendering me incapable of movement or speech. "Ainsley, give us a second. Close the door and don't wait outside. I'll come find you in a few minutes."

Ainsley gives a low whistle, and I hear the door close.

Ben finally lets go of my arm as he collapses back into his chair, covering his face with both hands. I take a step back.

I watch from the corner of my vision as he drops his hands to his knees and cocks his head at me. "This isn't exactly the way I expected our big talk to start."

The memory of the cart ride back from the dock, when Ben all but told me he wanted to talk about a future with me, comes flooding in, bringing with it a wave of hot tears. They roll down my cheeks and into the corners of my mouth. I don't move to wipe them away.

"I can see that you're having a hard time, so I'm going to take a stab at what's going on here. If I get something wrong, you let me know, okay?"

I don't move to even draw a breath. Let me die here.

"You were involved with Ainsley. He took off or you broke up or something, and then you got involved with me, knowing I was his father, and decided not to mention it to me. Is that a correct summary?"

His cold, businesslike tone sends chills down my spine.

The last thing I ever wanted was to have this conversation, but my body is refusing to fall over dead, so it looks like I have no other choice. "Ben..."

"Just a yes or no will be fine."

"No."

"No, that's not what went on here, or no, you don't wish to answer with a yes or no?"

"Both."

"Okay. Well, you seem to only be capable of speaking one word at a time."

"It wasn't like that." I snap out of my trance, all my survival instincts back online. I have to save this. "Okay, maybe it was at first, but then I got to know you, and you were, are, so wonderful. I know I should have told you, but it got too hard, and I didn't think—"

"You didn't think I'd stick around and continue fucking my son's ex-girlfriend?"

"Ben, don't—"

"Stop. Just, just give me a second, okay?"

I suck in a deep breath to prevent myself from speaking again. After my near paralysis only moments before, all I want to do now is talk.

Instead, I drop to my knees.

Ben doesn't even look at me.

"I think you should go," he says finally, still not looking at me.

My eyes shoot up to his face. "What? No."

"Fine," he says, starting to stand. "I'll go."

"No," I cry out, grabbing at his pants and trying to pull him back into his chair. "No, no, no." I'm on my feet now, following him toward the door, having failed to keep him from walking away.

I get there first and stand with my back pressed to the cool wood. "No."

Ben folds his arms across his chest and finally meets my eyes. I know mine are red and wet with tears. Ben's are bone dry, his gaze cold as ice.

"Let me explain."

"I think I understand."

"Clearly you don't if you want to leave. I can explain better. More." I'm grasping for words as I watch his face remain unmoved. "You…you can't be mad at me for lying. You told me I should lie."

It's a low blow, but I don't have many weapons left.

He sighs and shakes his head. "I'm not mad at you for lying. I get it. You saw something you wanted and did what you had to do to get it. I'm impressed. Possibly even a bit flattered."

"But?"

He scoffs out a laugh. "But, if you actually knew one goddamn thing about me, you would know that I can't be in a relationship with my son's ex-girlfriend." He shouts the last two words, and I flinch.

I've never been really, truly scared of Ben before, but I'm scared now. I'm terrified of what comes next.

"I have one responsibility in this life, and it's to be a good role model to my son."

It's over. I've lost.

But I hold my ground.

"Please, Victoria. After everything we've been through,

please don't make me physically remove you from this room. Please, for the love of God, just go."

My mouth drops open, but no sound comes out. I close it and tear my eyes away from him. I squeeze them shut, trying to burn his image into my mind because I know it's the last time I'll ever see him.

I bow my head and leave the room without a word.

Ainsley, the motherfucker, is waiting right outside the door. "Damn, Vicki, I never—"

"Don't, Ains. Please." I don't look up to see the smug expression on his face as I continue down the hallway.

Something in my tone must give away some of my feelings, however, because he catches my hand as I try to pass him and pulls me to a stop. I'm too weak to fight.

"I'm sorry. I was a jerk, I don't know what's going on here, but—"

He lets me pull my hand from his, and I continue down the hallway, not waiting to hear the rest.

Rule #23

YOU SHOULD HAVE KNOWN BETTER

BEN

I'm still in my chair, hands folded, eyes trained on my desk when I hear Ainsley enter my office. I should have known he wouldn't follow my directions to go far from here and wait for me to come to him.

The kid does what he wants. Something I've always been equal parts annoyed and impressed by. Even in the face of my relentlessly controlling nature, he still makes his own choices. And he doesn't even lie to me about them. He tells me the truth and accepts my criticism.

The air gets sucked from my lungs when I think about what a great kid he was and what a great person he is, and how harshly I've been criticizing him. He flies around the world, helping to sandbag rivers and build schools. Sure, I would prefer him to have an education, but how incredibly short-sighted of me to think that's the only thing that matters in this world.

I've spent my life safe in my castle, behind my desk, writing checks to charity aid organizations and patting myself on the back for it. Ainsley wants to actually help people. And maybe it's because I got to actually help people with my own two hands for the first time in my life that I'm seeing it differently. Or maybe it's because I got to witness firsthand how much a person can relax and blossom when allowed to just be themselves.

And it was fucking with me. I blossomed. Because someone allowed me to be fully and completely myself.

And now she's gone.

Leaving behind a trail of wreckage and betrayal.

That's true enough. I feel like a complete wreck right now, so bad that I nearly consider betraying the promise I made to my dying wife all those years ago.

Take good care of Ainsley, okay?

"You alright, Dad?"

I shake my head but don't look up. Then, I change my mind.

I meet his eye and nod. "Yeah, bud. I'm okay."

He's looking at me like he doesn't believe me, but I don't offer any defense. I don't have any left.

Ainsley comes to sit in one of the leather chairs facing my desk and folds his arms. "This was quite a surprise."

I feel the blood rush to my face and am finally able to put a name to the horrible feeling that's been gutting me alive for the last twenty minutes.

Embarrassment. Maybe even shame.

"For me, too."

"You didn't know that she and I…like, dated?"

"No."

"Yeah. We met in Indonesia, and she came to Faraday with me to take that teaching position. You sure you're okay? You kinda look like you're going to barf."

"It's something I'm considering."

"It's totally fine, Dad. I mean, it was never serious between us. We were more like friends the whole time."

When I still can't manage to contribute to the conversation, Ainsley goes on.

"I'm a little surprised you went for her, though. I didn't realize younger women were your type. I mean, I guess I don't know what your type is. You've never dated anyone as far as I know."

No one that I brought home to the house, anyway. One of the pillars of *taking good care of Ainsley* was not parading a string of women through his childhood. I see now that all I succeeded in was failing to model how a proper, loving relationship could work. He just thought I was alone all those years. What a role model I turned out to be.

"Okay, well, I can see that you need a minute, so I'm going to go get settled."

"Take a different room. One downstairs."

"Excuse me?"

"Victoria's been staying upstairs, in the room across from mine. Don't go up there. And don't bother her."

Ainsley laughs softly. "All right. I'll be nice. What's going to happen now? Surely the three of us aren't going to live here like one big, happy family."

Another laugh from him draws my glare up from the desk and straight into his eyes. His smile fades.

"I'm leaving. I have to go back to the city anyway. It might as well be today. It's better that way."

"Wait, you're just going to leave?"

"You should come with me."

"I just got here, Dad. And besides, I promised Ave I'd help out at Sam's house this week. I guess he's still dealing with some flood damage. He's been staying at the resort."

Another wave of shame washes over me like the tide. I got so caught up in my own shit that I failed to even check in with Sam about his house. I know damn well his property is on the west end of the island. "Is everything okay over there? With Sam's property?"

"We'll get it sorted. Ave and I are going to dig out the back patio and install new legs on one of the outbuildings. I haven't been over to see the damage yet, so I can't say what else needs to be done."

Damn it. I shouldn't leave. But I have to. "Use your credit card to pay for anything that needs to be done over there, okay? Don't worry about the charges."

Ainsley, bless his heart, stays quiet instead of pointing out the fact that no amount of money could replace the goodwill of my showing up over there to help. That I'm doing exactly what I always do—running back to safety and throwing money at difficult situations.

"I would stay if I could. I'll stop and talk to Sam on my way to the mainland."

"Sure."

"Will you just go downstairs and let me have a few minutes to get my things together and talk to Victoria?"

"Sure, Dad."

I listen to the door close behind him. The last thing I want to do is walk out of this room, but I don't have a choice. I've been in some seriously difficult courtroom situations before, but none of it prepared me for what I'm about to do.

I climb the stairs like a man on death row.

The soft slap on the tile draws my attention down, and I smile to myself as I notice my bare feet. I shake my head, thinking of all the times I lectured Ainsley about going barefoot, even in the house. It's too dangerous, not good for his arches. At home, I have a dedicated pair of orthopedic house shoes. And here I am, walking around my house completely barefoot. I know if I looked at the soles of my feet, they'd be dirty.

I reach the top of the stairs and walk straight to Victoria's door. I can hear her behind the closed door, crying softly and shuffling around. She's probably packing. I don't know where she plans on going, but it's understandable that she wants to get out of here. I'm having the same reaction.

Not an hour ago, I was about to propose extending this thing between us indefinitely. Offer her a place in my home. And now? Nothing has ever seemed so impossible.

This isn't even about forgiveness. Hell, I forgive her. Honestly, I do. I could overlook the whole deception, the months of lies straight to my face. Of sitting with me while I talked about my son and my struggles with him. She looked me straight in the eye and kept her secret.

I forgive all that.

But it doesn't change anything.

With a deep breath, I make my decision. I know the consequences are going to gut me, but I'm used to being the strong one. I can take it.

Rule #24

THERE'S NO SUCH THING AS COINCIDENCE

VICTORIA

The knock on my door comes both too soon and painfully late. I feel like I've been shut in here forever, but I'm also not ready to be thrown out on my ass.

It's too late for worries like those, however. Whatever he's got to say, whatever the consequences of this are going to be, I have to take them. I have to stand tall and walk into the next chapter of my life. One that doesn't include the man I want so badly.

I inhale long and slow, exhale even slower. "Come in."

"Hey."

My eyes shoot to the door and away again just as quickly. I busy myself stuffing clothes in my bag.

Ainsley.

"You can stop packing."

I do stop due to the sheer shock his words bring. "Why?"

"You don't need to pack and run away. He's gone."

Cold dread sinks through my body as I absorb his words and what they mean. "What?"

"He left. A few minutes ago. He's headed back to the city. I'm about to hop a boat to Faraday, so you don't need to leave if you don't want to. I mean, the house will just be empty. You can stay as long as you want."

"He's...he's not coming back?" Shame be damned. I can't keep the tears from my eyes or my voice.

"I don't think so, Vicki. He had some kind of work thing that was going to take him back soon anyway, so he just took off early."

I slump against the bed from where I sit on the floor, facing the window. Facing away from Ainsley. I hear him climb on the bed and lay down. When I glance up, his face is looking right at mine.

"Vicki—"

Just the soft tone of his voice is enough to make me ill. This is what my life is going to be like now. People finding out what I've done and lecturing me. "I don't want to talk about this."

"Yeah, well, it sounds like you two have done a lot of not talking about things, and that got you into a pretty big mess, didn't it?"

He's not wrong. "Yeah."

"So, let's talk." He flops onto his back to face the ceiling. "I took off like an asshole, and you shacked up with my dad."

I roll my eyes and start to stand up, but he catches me and pulls me to a seat on the bed next to him. "I'm sorry, I'm sorry. I won't be a jerk. It's just a lot to process."

"I know."

"You knew, though, the whole time. Right? You must have."

"Yeah, I knew."

"So…"

I heave out a huge sigh. I guess I'm going to have to get into this eventually. "It started so stupid. I was pissed about a picture you posted with another girl and decided to tell him what a dick you were."

"But he charmed you instead."

"I mean, yeah."

He shrugs. "I get it. He's a charming guy. My whole life, women have tried to get him to pay attention to them, but he never did. He was so focused on me."

"After a while, I just couldn't walk away from him."

"But you couldn't tell him the truth, obviously, or he would have bailed. So, you just went along, knowing eventually this exact thing would happen?"

I shrug, unwilling to claim the stupid plan as my own, but unable to deny the truth of it.

"That's kinda fucked up. But I get it."

I look at him then, really look for the first time since he came into the room. It's only been a couple of months since I saw him last, but he looks so different. His hair is shorter and more kempt. His skin has a deep, golden tan with a sunburn across his nose.

What strikes me more than anything, though, is how young he looks. So very, very young.

Young and stupid.

Just like me.

"Well, it's over now," I say, resigned to my fate.

"I don't think so," Ainsley replies in his familiar dismissive tone.

"What do you mean? I lied to the guy for months about something really important. He just got on a plane to fly halfway around the globe instead of saying goodbye. That sounds pretty over to me."

"I mean, it's over if you want it to be, sure. But he's a changed man. I've been seeing signs of it for weeks. It's why I came back, really. I was worried he was dying of cancer or something."

I wait, unable to breathe. Ainsley flashes me an evil smile. He knows just what his words are doing to me.

Finally, he pulls his phone from his pocket. "Check out this text convo."

I wait while he scrolls for what seems like forever.

"So, this is from him back in September. This would have been right about the time we were preparing to leave Indonesia."

You haven't answered my texts so I'm assuming that means you don't need a phone anymore. Maybe I should cut off service and save myself the expense.

Ainsley laughs and scrolls again. "Here's one of my personal favorites."

Ainsley Adams, I don't know where you are, but I do know that you failed once again to show up for the new semester. I paid a fortune for that seat, and you wasted it. You could have fed a whole village of hungry children with the money you just wasted on whatever fucking off you're doing now. COME HOME.

"So, anyway, that's how it's gone for the last year since I bailed on Harvard and started traveling the world."

"What do you reply to these?" I ask.

"Oh, I just say I love you or Merry Christmas or something snarky like that. It doesn't really matter what I say. The only thing that would satisfy him is to do what he says." He turns back to his phone and starts scrolling once more. "Or that's how it used to be. Look at this text I got a few weeks ago." He holds the phone out for me to take.

I got to see the most amazing sunset from Merit last night. The incoming storm clouds lit up with gold and pink. It reminded me of that trip we took to MOMA back in your freshman year. You remember those paintings? I guess they're probably back in Rome now. Maybe we can go see them there sometime.

I look up from the screen and narrow my eyes at him.

"Keep scrolling."

So, I do.

Yeah, dad, that sounds fun. We should definitely do that.

Still on Merit, can you believe that? Enjoying what might be my first real vacation. Hope you're having fun.

Did you know that the little island off the east coast of Merit is actually a coral formation? It has hundreds of tunnels and caves that divers explore. I've never thought about getting certified before, but it's a possibility for next season.

Have you ever been to Katy's Crab Shack in Saubry? I just had the best dinner of my life. Ate the whole thing with my hands, but it was worth it.

Ave told me he found you doing some work for people who need help with rising water. I'm still a little disappointed that you aren't here, but I'm proud of you for helping.

I reach the last of Ben's texts in the thread and read it with tears brimming in my eyes.

You know, son, I think I might have been wrong all these years. I've been so focused on work and material success that I failed to ever take into consideration how you feel about your life and what would make you happy. I'm sorry about that. Let's talk soon.

I glance up at Ainsley and find a knowing look there. "You can see why I thought he had a brain tumor. The man has never once in his life admitted he was wrong."

I toss the phone at him and stand, walking over to the window. "I don't see what this has to do with me."

"Are you kidding me? It has everything to do with you. You guys got together right after I left, and since then, he's been morphing from T-Rex Control Freak Dad into a human being who wants to get to know me. You expect me to believe that's a coincidence?"

"Maybe not, but it doesn't mean he's going to forgive me. I lied. I deceived him."

"That's not why he left. He respects people going after what they want in unorthodox ways. You may have surprised him, and embarrassed him, but this doesn't have to be the end."

I sink down to the floor with my back to the wall, the curtains blowing in the breeze above my head. "I don't know if I can do it. I don't know how to do it. He said it was over. He left. And you think I can just…what? Go to New York and demand that he give me another chance?"

Ainsley sits up, pocketing his phone and fixing me with a sly smile. "I'll make you a deal."

Rule #25

NO MAN IS AN ISLAND

BEN

It doesn't take long to go from my decision outside Victoria's door to bumping toward the dock in the green golf cart.

There's not a lot of crossover between my life in the States and my life on this island, so once I pack up my few toiletries and electronics, I'm out the door.

The helicopter is waiting for me as usual, the pilot coming out of the small, metal-paneled aviation office strapping on his helmet as I park.

"Where's the lady?" he asks, the first dagger in my side coming much sooner than expected.

"Just me today," I answer, keeping my face and voice emotionless.

It's a damn good thing I spent years perfecting this poker face. I'm going to need it. I'm a tornado of feelings right now, and the last thing I need is for anyone to pick up on that. Not until I get my steel walls back in place.

The walls Victoria shattered.

My first stop on Faraday probably isn't the best choice

considering my uncharacteristically fragile emotional state, but I don't have a lot of choice. These guys have all shown up for me over the years, in their own ways, and I'll be damned if I'm not going to return the favor.

Sam's house is close to The Sands, but down a narrow, coral sand road through the jungle that makes for slow going. He bought this property the first year we owned the resort, wanting to have a place to fix up and make his own.

We tried to talk him out of it, me especially. We had just acquired a ghost resort on an island in the middle of nowhere. It seemed like plenty of project for any man. But Sam wasn't going to be deterred. He wanted to make a home for himself, and I guess he saw it in this run-down acre of near swamp land, with its three one-room shacks and dilapidated outbuildings.

I was perfectly aware at the time that purchasing anything nicer would have required taking on yet another loan from one of us guys. And, while we would have been happy to hand over the money, it's understandable that Sam didn't think that was a great option.

We've all got something to prove in life, and for Sam, that amounts to showing everyone, us guys especially, that he can stand on his own two feet after being the recipient of handouts from our families for most of his life.

I can't even imagine how I would have turned out if I was in the same position. My independence and pride weigh heavy on my shoulders. I would've ended up in jail or worse. Not Sam. He grew up to be the kind, gracious manager that absentee investors can only dream of. He's everyone's favorite person, something that's painfully obvious when all of us guys are out together.

I turn the final corner onto his property and park next to one of the many carts already there. I know Ainsley isn't here yet because I just left him at the house, but I can see Dom and Ave's vehicles, as well as a dozen others I don't recognize.

This many people turned up on a random Wednesday afternoon to help Sam dig out his flooded yard and rebuild his outbuilding.

I doubt this many people would come to my funeral.

I shake off the thought, cursing my mind for lowering itself to such base concerns and plaster on a calm but sympathetic face when I come down to the crowd of guys hard at work in Sam's yard.

He spots me right away and waves, wiping sweat from his face with his dirty tee before walking over. "Hey, man. I didn't know you were coming by."

My brow furrows as I nod and glance around once more at the men hard at work. I wish I'd stopped by to help, not just to say goodbye, but I suppose it's better than nothing. "Yeah. I was headed to the water taxi and thought I'd stop by and see how things are going here."

"Heading home?"

I nod, bristling slightly as Dom joins us, followed closely by Ave. "I gotta get back for a trial starting next week." It feels like my own trial is about to begin.

"Where's the girl?" Ave chimes in. "I thought I was going to see her bags in your cart when you finally dragged yourself off that island."

"Yeah, well." I glance down and shake my head. I have no idea what I would even say to explain what just went down on Merit, but I suppose they'll hear it from Ains soon enough. "I did, too. But that's not how it worked out."

"How did it work out?" Sam asks in his characteristic friendly, open manner. Like anything I said in return would be just fine. Little does he know how wrong he is this time.

"It just didn't."

Dom clears his throat, and I purposely look away instead of toward him. If that guy thinks he can bully information out of me, he's dead wrong.

"Reina told me she's been seeing you two around town and that you looked an awful lot like a couple."

I shrug. "It was just a little island fling. Back to reality."

"You never brought her over to meet us," Ave says, his voice full of the teasing I would expect from him. "First girlfriend you've had, and we missed the entire relationship? Lame."

"I'll introduce you to the next one, okay?"

They're all quiet, watching me. I've got to get out of here. "I thought it was something, but it turned out I was wrong. Surely you guys can all understand not wanting to air your dirty laundry all over the island."

"It's not all over the island, Ben. It's us," Sam says.

"I have it on good authority that you two were shacked up at Katy's earlier today. Reina said you were smiling so much she almost didn't recognize you. And now you're running off to the mainland with your scowl back in place. Something happened," Dom accuses.

Damn this tiny island. Nowhere to hide.

All the more reason to get back to the city, where literally no one gives a shit what you're doing.

"Yeah, something happened. But I don't really want to talk about it. It's no big deal. We hung out, it's over, end of story."

"Would this something have anything to do with Ains coming home?"

I whip my head to Avery so fast the world blurs. "How the fuck do you know that? What did he tell you?"

Ave's mouth drops open as his eyes narrow. I look away quickly, realizing my mistake, only to find narrowed eyes from the other two as well.

I shake my head. "It's not what you think."

"You're not running away from the first good thing you've found since Breanna died the second your adult son shows up? Because that's what it looks like to me," Ave calls me out.

Dom crosses his arms and cocks his head to the side. I'm not brave enough to look at Sam and risk the kind, understanding face I'm sure he's wearing.

"Coincidence," I offer, convincing no one.

"Ains wants you to be happy, you know. If you found someone you want to be with," he holds up a hand when I start to interrupt. "Even if that woman is a bit younger than you, he would be supportive."

"You don't understand." Not that I'm about to help them with that problem.

"We understand perfectly, man," Dom says. "We were there when Breanna passed. We know you took the responsibility of making sure Ainsley turned out all right seriously. We know that's kept you alone all these years."

"We've always given you your space with all that. I mean, you seemed to find some comfort at the club in New York. And we were all supportive when you started bringing some of that stuff over to the Merit house," Ave adds. "But it never felt like something you wanted to talk about, so we gave you space."

Boiling hot shame rises from my gut and overtakes my mind, turning the whole world gray. "You guys talk about this? You talk about me?"

How could I not have known this?

"We care about you, Ben. You closed off when Breanna died, and we've all had to accept that there are parts of you that you didn't want to share anymore. But that doesn't mean we don't wonder what's going on in your life. That we don't want you to find happiness," Sam offers calmly.

"I'm happy," I retort, hearing the anger in my voice. I shake my head. Fuck.

"That's what you've always told us, and we believed you."

"Until a few weeks ago," Dom adds.

"What do you mean?"

He shrugs. "We got used to cautious, overprotective, play by the rules Ben since Ains was a kid. We thought that was the new normal for you. That was single dad Ben. But either you outgrew that stage suddenly, or that girl shook something loose in you because the last few weeks you've been a lot like your old self again."

"Well, I hope you enjoyed it. It's back to business as usual. Boring, mean Ben who you lot have apparently just been tolerating all these years."

"That's not what he meant at all," Ave says, laying hand on my shoulder. It's all I can do not to step back and shake him off. These guys are doing what they do best—homing in on the truth.

But today, I don't want them to find it.

"We love you and want you around just the way you are, buddy. But we've all seen how losing your wife and raising your son alone weighed on you. We wondered as he got older if you would relax a bit when he graduated high school, but you only doubled down on making your life all about him by chasing him around the world. We're going to support you no matter what, but maybe this little vacation fling, or whatever it was, can be a first step for you to consider some ways you could start living for yourself. Making a life for yourself. Your son is an adult. You may be able to keep him under your influence through college, although that doesn't seem like it's working out. Either way, you're going to have to let him live his own life soon enough."

I do take that step back now, letting Ave's hand fall away. My eyes are on my flip-flops, and I shake my head. I was so prepared to defend my little secret with these guys, but it turns out they rooted right to the heart of the problem. And it has nothing to do with Victoria or her exes.

For the second time in the last few weeks, I'm forced to consider the possibility that the only real problem in my life is my unwillingness to let go. Let go of my late wife and the life we were going to build together. Let go of needing my son to follow in my footsteps, the only path I can lead him down where I'll know all the secrets and pitfalls ahead of time and can guide him.

Let go of the center of my entire universe.

How does a person even go about doing that?

"I don't know who I am if not Ainsley's father."

Ave laughs. "We do."

"Yeah. We do," Dom adds. "You're the guy who jumped into the quarry to fish out my kid sister after Sam dared her to go in there with only a pair of water wings." He elbows Sam, who looks sheepish.

"You're the guy who paid to rebuild the school in Saubry when the hurricane took it out our second year here. And added a second level and three new outbuildings," Sam says.

"You're the guy who took it upon himself to build a sex dungeon in the Merit house instead of partying with all the hot chicks I brought over. And you've only used it once," Ave offers with a sly grin.

I cock my head. "Twice."

All three sets of eyebrows shoot up in unison, an act so comical that I almost crack a smile. I shake my head and turn my gaze down, finding it difficult all of a sudden to take a full breath in the face of the love and understanding written across my friends' faces.

"We know you, all right? And we know you're a beast when it comes to change of any kind. So, we'll let you take your time with this one. But now that we know old Ben is still in there somewhere, we're not going to put up with your stone-faced bullshit much longer. We get that you're the caretaker. You always have been. But you've been leaving yourself out of that love and that shit ends now." Ave steps forward and grips my shoulder hard enough that I can't shake him off. "Head on back to the city. Do what you gotta do. But just know that we're watching."

I huff out a laugh. "Is that supposed to be a threat?"

"If it needs to be," Dom answers, dead serious. "And I think we need to bump our quarterly meetings up to monthly. Now that we know you're capable of having a good time down here, we're going to need you to fly down more often."

I can't help the smile that breaks through as I finally meet the eyes of my lifelong friends. "I think I can probably work that into my schedule. If the resort demands it, of course."

"Well, we should get back to work," Dom says, glancing back at the crew that's been on a break since the leaders all wandered off.

I nod. "Sorry I'm not sticking around to help out."

"No worries, man. I'll save you some sanding and staining work for when you're back next month," Sam says with a smile before pulling me into a tight embrace.

I take a deep breath before relaxing into it. When I step back, Dom and Ave are waiting with side hugs and back claps.

"Have a safe flight," Sam calls out as I walk back to my cart. I turn and wave, catching one last glimpse of the trio before they start chiding each other back to work.

Rule #26

STOP PLAYING THE PART

BEN

"Come in," I say, not looking up from my desk.

"Morning, sir. I just wanted to drop off the new batch of intern applications. I put a few good ones on the top."

"Thanks, Cynthia, you can leave them here."

In the six weeks since I came back to the city, my life has settled into a nice little routine. Not at all like the routine I used to have though.

On the plane ride home, instead of just working, I took some time to think about my life and myself and what I really want. What do I want the last half of my life to look like?

The guys were right about me neglecting myself and my own needs, and I want that to change.

During my extended vacation, I started thinking my life would include a certain dark-haired beauty, but even without her, I still want more for myself.

I just about gave my assistant a heart attack when I called to tell her to cancel my weekly standing grocery order. I went to the store myself and picked out food for the week. I've been cooking for myself and listening to music in the kitchen. The other night I went out for dinner and drinks with some old friends.

In other words, I'm living.

And it feels good. I may still know more or less what's going to happen each day, but I'm automating less of it. Getting more hands on. Who knows, I may even start cleaning my own house here soon.

Well, let's not get carried away.

I've got a new lease on life. I can see it. Everyone around me can see it as well. My time on Merit with Victoria changed me. And even though I didn't get the fairytale ending I'd started to allow myself to believe was possible, I'll be damned if I'm going to let this opportunity to have more joy in my life go to waste.

Speaking of which, I glance at my watch, it's about time to clock out to be in Brooklyn in time to meet Ainsley for dinner. He's preparing to start his first semester at Columbia, and I couldn't be prouder. We went apartment hunting together last week and found him a nice one bedroom close to campus.

It's all very different from the life I always planned for him—brownstone in Cambridge, Harvard law—but now that I see him here in the city, picking out his books and preparing to start his degree in environmental health engineering…well, it all looks so right.

When I ask him about what he wants, what he's interested in instead of just telling him what to do, he opens up to me.

I've learned more about my son in the last two weeks than I have in the last ten years. He's kind, funny, and cares deeply about underprivileged communities. Where my upbringing and fortune created a wall around me that I always hid behind, Ainsley had the opposite reaction. He wants to reach down to bring others up.

It makes me want to do the same.

I think a lot about the conversation I had with Victoria on the patio of the Merit house, where she told me that if I really cared about the future of young people, I'd be setting up college scholarships for kids who actually needed them, instead of chasing my own kid around the globe. Obviously, she was right. The woman was right about a lot of things.

Even if she was wrong in one very fundamental way.

I'll probably never know if she planned on telling me about her past with Ains, or if she actually felt the things she seemed to be feeling for me. She had to have known it would end just like it did, so what was she thinking? That we could just live in a bubble forever? That I would never find out?

The hard truth of it all is that she spent the whole of our short relationship knowing it had an expiration date in the near future. She knew it would end.

And I didn't.

While I'm holding myself back from making any comparisons to my only other relationship in this life, the similarities are there. Breanna was taken from me so suddenly, without notice, after a decade of thinking she'd be with me forever. I planned on it. I had our whole lives, and Ainsley's, mapped out. We were going to follow the plan together. And then she was gone.

I haven't let myself enter into planning like that with anyone since…until Victoria. Even though we never talked about the future, the reason why being obvious now, I was still building one for us. We would move back to New York. Victoria would go to college to become a physical therapist or even a doctor. We would live on my estate and play our scary, sexy games forever in perfectly contented bliss.

Yeah, yeah. I hear it.

Just another snow globe life I dreamed up. And when reality didn't fit into my carefully constructed mold, I bailed.

But how could I have done anything different? How could I live with myself knowing that I stole my partner from my nineteen-year-old son?

I know that's a bit dramatic. Ainsley has tried to tell me plenty of times that they weren't a couple in any sense of the word, although I tend to shut those conversations down.

He says they were always just friends.

He says that she seemed good for me.

He says that I should call her.

I didn't tell him that she's called dozens of times since I left, and I just watch the phone ring. I'm not sure I'm ready to admit to that level of masochism.

I flip open the folder my secretary set on my desk and glance over the first few résumés. She wasn't kidding when she said she put some good ones on top. I see the name of one of our partner's sons. The guy knows me well enough to send his own kid through the usual channels, without asking for a favor. He'll get an interview for that, probably a summer internship.

The next résumé catches my eye for a different reason. Harvard law, academic honors, Peace Corps, volunteering to read to the blind. I scan from the bottom up, and when my eyes reach the name at the top of the page, I smile to myself and toss the folder back on my desk.

Leaning back in my chair, I laugh.

Rule #27

YOU DON'T HAVE TO BE READY—JUST WILLING

VICTORIA

"I'm going to miss you so much!"

I give hugs all around the fitness center as the students from my very last class file out the door. It's been a great few months here at The White Sands. I learned a lot about running my own classes, handling client injuries, and working with people on their goals. I know I have a handful of fantastic references for my résumé as well.

That's what secured me the teaching position in New York. One of the managers here on Faraday made a few calls and got me a spot at Lotus Studios, a rehabilitation and Pilates center in Brooklyn. I'll be starting as a junior instructor, but the center has its own education program, so I'll be able to take classes and move up. They certify instructors to do the exact kind of work that helped me come back from my injury, and I'm excited to finally get to help others who really need it.

Ainsley helped with the apartment. We made a deal that day on Merit—he would go back to New York if I would go too. I have a sneaking suspicion he was already planning to start classes that semester, but I don't mind. It was the push I needed to take the big leap and finally go after what I want in life.

To help people.

And to get Ben back.

Part of my deal with Ainsley was that I had to try. When Ben left me on Merit that day, I felt completely helpless, like I had no way to get him back. He made the decision to end our relationship and that was that. The fact that I probably deserved exactly what I got didn't help with my feelings of hopelessness.

One of the parts of being with Ben that I loved so much was how empowered I felt. He seemed to be learning from me. He was coming out of his sheltered little life and having fun. I helped the perfect, almighty Ben. But that feeling came to an end when he walked away. I was blindsided by just how powerless it made me feel. The only future I could see had me running off to the next chapter in my life with my tail between my legs.

Hoping I could manage not to screw up the next thing.

Ainsley gave me the kick in the pants I needed to get off that train and start thinking about what I really want. And he gave me the confidence boost I needed to actually go for it.

I guess the guy isn't so bad after all.

I don't have much to pack, so a golf cart is able to take me and a few other guests to the water taxi together. I watch the resort get smaller and smaller as we bump down the dusty road toward town. This has been a grand adventure for me. Wonderful, hard, and really eye opening. I'm leaving this island a different person than I was when I arrived.

And maybe that kind of growth is all one can hope for.

When I say Ainsley helped with the apartment, I mean that he used his connections to secure me a spot and fronted the first and last month's rent and the deposit. For the most part, I'm still on my own. The city is cold, loud, and busy—a far departure from my little island home. But it's where I need to be. And, if I play my cards right, I'll be back on Merit with Ben before long.

My tiny walk-up came furnished with a single bed, small

dresser, and a desk. It's stuffy and smells like it's been empty for a while, but I pull up the lone window, and the fresh air rushes in. There's a tree outside the window and a small coffee pot on the counter. Things are going to be okay.

As I'm putting my clothes away in the dresser drawers, worrying about whether my fitness outfits will be up to par at a big city studio, my phone rings.

"Hello, is this Victoria Easton?"

"Yes."

"Hello, Victoria. This is Cynthia from Covington, Schwab, Bartlett, and Adams. How are you doing today?"

My breath catches in my chest as shock rolls through me. When I sent that résumé into Ben's firm, the most I expected was for him to finally return one of my calls or texts. I hardly expected an interview for a position I'm in no way qualified for.

But then a sinking feeling settles in my gut. This is a secretary or assistant calling me. Was I a total fool to think that a senior partner would even look at law clerk internship résumés? This poor woman probably chooses all the candidates and thinks she found a great one in me.

"I'm doing fine, thank you. How are you?"

"I'm fine, thank you for asking. We are setting up interviews for next week with the partners, and I would love to get you on the schedule. Do you have time Thursday at one?"

I should say no. I should tell her the truth right now.

But this could be my chance to finally see Ben.

"Absolutely. Thursday at one sounds just fine."

"Perfect, Victoria. We'll see you then. When you arrive at the firm, you can check in at reception, and they'll send you up to the right floor."

"Thank you. See you next week."

I hang up and toss my phone on the bed, followed by my whole self.

What am I doing?

It's going to be okay. This is what I wanted…kind of.

When I was considering different ways to get Ben to see me, like placing myself in cafés around the firm, jogging by his house, or showing up on his damn doorstep, none of them seemed right. I needed something that would make a splash. Prove to him that I'm serious about talking this thing through and getting us back on track.

It might be a total pie in the sky idea, but I like it.

Or I did…until it all became too real. Now I need an outfit for an interview at a law firm and a plan for what I'm going to say when and if I finally get to see him.

Rule #28

VIBE CHECK

VICTORIA

"This is insane, you know that, right?"

I shrug, handing Ainsley my iced coffee so I can sift through the racks with both hands. "Is it insane or genius?"

"Like your plan to fool the guy into dating his son's ex?"

I turn to glare at him over my shoulder. "It's different. That was more like temporary insanity. This, however, this is genius."

I've had three whole days to freak out and settle back down, fully convinced that my plan is going to work. When I called Ainsley and explained the whole thing, he offered to take me shopping for an outfit in Manhattan.

I'm happy for the company, but since I insist on paying for my own clothes, we're in Queens, searching for buried treasure in the discount racks.

"I mean, it's sweet. But I still think we should have gone with my plan."

"For you to let me into his house so I could be waiting there for him when he got home?"

"Waiting for him naked, yeah."

I roll my eyes. "You just wanted to think about me naked."

He shakes his head fervently. "No way. I will never think about you like that again. In my mind, you're already my stepmother, so thinking about you naked means I'm thinking about my dad naked. So, no…just no. Besides, I have a girlfriend now."

I wait for the pang of rejection to hit, the one that always strikes me down when I hear about one of the guys I chased after, one of the guys who 'wasn't looking for a relationship,' being in a relationship with someone else.

But it doesn't come.

For once, I know what I want, and I'm going to get it. Come hell or high water. Well, maybe not the high water. I think I've had enough flooding for one lifetime.

"I think I can pull off hot stepmother."

"That sounds like a Halloween costume," he jokes, leaning on the wall beside me sipping coffee.

I pull an outfit off the rack and turn to him, holding it up to my body. "What about this?"

His face twists into an expression that I can't quite read. "Are you going for hot stepmother or law clerk?"

I look down at the tight black skirt and fitted jacket set, imagining the sheer blouse I could tuck underneath. "Hot law clerk?"

Ainsley nods. "Yeah. I think that'll work."

I let him buy me dinner and accept all of his good luck and good wishes.

Honestly, if nothing else comes of this whole experience, I will have gotten a great friend out of the deal.

Rule #29

ENTER AT YOUR OWN RISK

VICTORIA

When Thursday finally arrives, I'm feeling less confident. I pack on deodorant to keep from sweating through the hot, synthetic fabric of my cheap suit, wishing I'd caved and let Ainsley buy me something nice. But it's too late now.

"Victoria Easton. I'm here to see Cynthia."

"Perfect. She'll be expecting you. Head up to twenty-eight, and you'll see her at reception just outside the elevator."

I thank the woman and make my way to the bank of shiny, gold elevators.

When the doors finally open on the twenty-eighth floor, I'm a nervous wreck. I suck it up and smile, though, stepping out of that lift like I own the damn place. The woman behind the reception desk looks up from her computer and smiles. "Victoria?"

I nod.

She rises to her feet and comes around to join me on the plush rug surrounded by expensive, comfortable-looking chairs, hand outstretched. "Cynthia."

I shake her hand politely and wait.

"Mr. Adams wants to meet with you personally, and I can't say I'm all that surprised."

Her words catch me off guard. I'm not exactly sure what I expected to happen when I finally made it up here. I hadn't even really expected to make it this far, truth be told. But to be taken straight to Ben's office as soon as I enter the building? It seems like a stroke of good luck.

Or my worst nightmare about to come true.

Either way, I'm about to find out. The tall, blonde actual professional in her expensive outfit and designer heels leads me down the hallway toward a set of double wooden doors.

She knocks and then opens the doors without waiting for a response, holding one open for me to pass through ahead of her. I walk into the large, airy, bright room with my eyes on my shoes.

"Mr. Adams, this is Victoria Easton," Cynthia announces as if to the king.

"Thank you. You may leave us," Ben dismisses her like an actual king.

The sound of his voice after so many weeks threatens to derail my confidence, but I suck the emotions down into the pit of my belly. And, with a deep breath, I finally look up.

Cynthia must leave, and the door must click closed behind her. Possibly, she even says something. I hear none of it, aware only of Ben. His presence is like a magnetic black hole, commanding all the energy in the room.

I stand dumbstruck by the sight of him for a long moment before he clears his throat and stands. I click back into motion and take a step forward. For better or worse, I'm here now. Whatever's going to happen is going to happen right now.

"Hi," I say, determined to be brave enough to speak first, even if it's just one stupid word.

"Hi." His eyes never leave mine as he walks around his desk and leans on the edge facing me, arms crossed over his chest.

After a long moment, he reaches behind himself and lifts a

sheet of paper from the desk, holding it up between us. "This is an incredible work of fiction, Vic. You missed your calling as a novelist."

"Yes, well. I'm multitalented."

Ben lets the hand holding the paper drop to one of his thighs and looks down at it, shaking his head.

I'm paralyzed with fear and trepidation, dreading every single life choice I made up to this point, but after a moment, I realize he's laughing.

Laughing.

He doesn't look up at me, just continues to shake in near-silent laughter. After a moment, the tension in my chest breaks, and I start to laugh as well.

Only then does he seem to remember I'm there and look up at me, his face spread wide with a smile and still laughing. He tosses the paper back onto his desk and crosses his arms, trying to get ahold of himself.

It only partially works. "What did you hope to gain from sending this in? Certainly not a job here." His voice is still full of laughter.

I shake my head. "Not a job. Just…this. To be here with you. You never answered my calls or texts."

"I blocked your number."

Oh, damn.

The thought of him never having read or listened to my texts and voicemails hits me right in the gut like a sucker punch.

Silly little Victoria, operating under the naïve, romantic idea that he has been lying in bed, listening to my voicemails and pining over his long, lost love.

He never heard any of them. Never read any of my well thought out reasons or explanations or apologies.

He just hit block and moved on with his life.

"Why…" I struggle to get the words out, struggle to recover from that blow. "Why would you do that?"

Ben's not laughing anymore. "It seemed like the best thing for both of us."

I shake my head in disbelief. "The best thing for both of us? I poured my heart out into those texts and voicemails, and you never even got them? I fail to see how that was the best thing for me."

"Fine. It was best for me, then. I'm not sure what I would... I'm not sure how I would have..." He trails off, uncharacteristically at a loss for words.

"You're not sure how you would have what? How you would have handled me apologizing and begging you to call me so we could talk? Not sure how you would have reacted to me telling you I was coming to New York?"

I'm getting emotional, and I can't help it. I have this one shot to get through to him, and right now, he seems so untouchable.

"You thought I knew you were coming?"

I can't read his tone, and I'm getting desperate. "I thought...I don't know what I thought." My eyes fall to the floor, unable to watch him stand there, unmoved, for another second. "I guess this was a mistake. I'll go."

I turn and wait for him to stop me. I reach the door, my hand reaching out for the handle. Still nothing.

I grasp the cool metal and start to turn it.

"Wait."

Relief nearly sends me to my knees. I wait, hand still gripping the handle.

"Let's just...I don't know, Victoria. Don't go, though. Stay a minute."

It's something. I turn and lean against the door, watching him go through whatever he's going through. In true Ben form, he's still very well composed, but I can see the cracks. I can see him leaning toward me just enough, as if he wants to close the distance between us.

The man reads my mind.

"I need you to know that I could never be seen sharing any kind of personal touch with an intern candidate in my office."

"Even if that intern candidate is a liar?"

Ben cracks a small smile at that, and my heart leaps. "There would still be a lot to explain."

"Take me home with you, then." It's bold, but I'm feeling bold these days. I've already lost what I want most in life, there's no reason to hold back.

He closes his eyes briefly and shakes his head, inhaling slowly and exhaling just as slowly. I'm buoyed by the thought that he's just as flustered as I am, even if he hides it better.

"There's a café across the street from the building with a red and white awning. Go over there and wait for me."

My heart is now dancing in my chest. "What should I tell Cynthia?"

"Tell her you made it to the next round."

I suck in a breath and try to stay calm as I nod and exit the office, closing the door softly behind me. He's obviously not talking about the next round of interviews, so he must be talking about…

It's all I can do not to dance down the hallway.

All I wanted was a chance to speak my heart to this man. To plead my case. And it looks like I'm going to get it.

Rule #30

DON'T FORGET TO GOOGLE THE MAN YOU'RE DATING

VICTORIA

A little bell jingles over the door as I enter the café.

"Good morning," a woman's voice rings out.

I look around the cozy space, filled with red and white booths and a long counter with low red stools. A gray-haired woman appears from behind a wall with a tray of white porcelain coffee cups her hand. "You can grab a table anywhere you like. I'll be right over."

I thank her and slide into a booth far away from the windows that face the high rise across the street.

"What can I get you?"

"Oh, I'll just have coffee, please. Cream and sugar. Maybe food in a little bit, I'm meeting someone."

The woman sets down her order pad and leans on the booth across from me, smiling conspiratorially. "Big interview? Business meeting?"

I blush and look down at my law intern disguise. "Kind of. I'm meeting Mr. Adams from—"

"Oh, Bentley. Yes, I know him well. He gets his coffee here

every morning. You don't have anything to worry about, love. His bark is worse than his bite, which isn't something you can say about all the partners over there." She trails off and gives me a look that lets me know she's got all the good gossip.

"Thanks," I say, not sure how much I should tell her.

"I'll send him over when he gets here."

Bentley Adams.

I had just assumed Ben was short for Benjamin, but now I've got a whole new set of questions to ponder.

I'm still mulling it over when the man in question slides into the booth across from me. "Hey," he says.

"Hey."

He smiles up at the woman as she sets down two coffees, one with a side of cream and sugar for me, and just a cup of black for Ben.

When she's gone, I narrow my eyes at him. "You couldn't touch me in your office, but you're comfortable having a personal meeting with an intern candidate in the café across from the firm?"

Ben smiles and looks around. "This place is a time warp. Things that happen here don't count."

I cock my head to the side. "I'm not sure that's true. The waitress seemed to have the tea on all the partners over there."

Ben lifts his brows in surprise. "What did she tell you about me?"

"That your bark is worse than your bite."

He laughs and shakes his head. "I guess I should watch out. I wouldn't want her telling that to just anyone."

We fall into silence after that, neither of us sure how to move forward. I expect Ben to speak first, but he doesn't. Finally, I can't keep my mouth shut any longer.

"Your name is Bentley?"

His head cocks to one side as he processes my words. "Yes," he says, but it sounds like a question.

"I didn't know that."

"Oh."

"I just figured it was Benjamin. What kind of name is Bentley? That's a car."

"It's a family name. I've always gone by Ben."

"You gave me your own name as a safe word?"

It's a sudden way of bringing our past relationship into the conversation, but I'm tired of waiting. Good or bad, I want to have this out with him right now.

"Yes."

It seems like he's going to stop there, and my own eyebrows go up in impatience. Ben's eyes go up and to the right, not quite an eye roll, but at the very least an acknowledgment of my annoyance at his unsatisfactory answer.

"I..." he takes a deep breath and lets it out in a rush. "I was concerned from the beginning about how my position would affect your decision-making abilities. You seemed to want things to be secret, and I was never sure exactly what that was about. I know now, of course, but back then, I worried that you were concerned for your job or your reputation at the resort. But I couldn't stay away from you. You affected me in ways no one ever has before. I worried that I was going to act out of character in some way that would make you uncomfortable in your workplace, and you wouldn't feel like you could tell me. It's a balancing act to be the one holding the most power in a relationship. I had to be sure you had a way to release yourself from situations in public places if you needed to. In BDSM, safe words are used for that very reason. I figured if yours was my full name, a name you didn't normally use, then you could call it in public if you needed me to back off. You calling out Bentley casually in a conversation wouldn't seem odd to most people. It would be more appropriate than you calling me Ben, honestly. Bentley Adams is the name on the firm's website. On my Wikipedia page. When employees who I'm not personally acquainted with call me by my first name, they often say Bentley."

"I forgot to Google you."

Ben smiles again, but it turns sad as he shakes his head. "And thus, my perfect plan for protecting you was foiled. I thought you knew."

I can't think of anything to say, so I take a sip of my coffee and don't meet his eye.

"But I guess in the end, it didn't matter, did it? You weren't concerned about your job. You were worried that if people saw us together, they would tell me about your history with my son."

It takes all my strength, but I look at him. I can't shy away from this if I want to have any chance of moving forward with this man. I have to own my mistakes. "It was totally and completely fucked up of me to lie to you about Ainsley."

Ben's mouth quirks to the side as if I surprised him with that.

I hurry to go on. "I knew it was fucked up when I was doing it, and I knew it was going to end badly, but I never could have prepared myself for how hard I was going to fall for you. And falling so hard and knowing that you would never have me if you knew the truth, well, it drove me to make some bad decisions. I regret hurting you with my behavior. But I do not regret a second of the time I got to spend with you. I'd do it again."

Ben looks at me for a long time, his face unreadable. I nearly buckle under the pressure, but I'm rewarded for my patience.

"I would, too."

The sky parts and the holy rays of sun shine down on me. "Give me another chance."

The pensive look twists into anger at my words. "How am I supposed to do that, Victoria?" He shakes his head and drags a hand down his face. "What would I even tell people?" He shakes his head again, not looking back at me.

"You tell them the truth. Who cares what people think? Or you tell them nothing. No one here knows me."

"Ainsley does."

"Yeah, and who do you think helped me move here? Found me an apartment, picked out this ridiculous suit?"

Ben's hands drop from his face, and he finally looks at me, mouth hanging open. "You...he...?" he shakes his head and drops it into both hands, propped on the table by his elbows. "I'm going to have a nervous breakdown."

I laugh at that, leaning back in the booth and shaking my head. "You are not. You're fine."

"I'm pretty sure this is what a nervous breakdown feels like."

I cross my own arms over my chest and wait. Finally, Ben seems to catch his breath and looks up at me. He's looking frazzled and clearly exhausted, but he's staring at me with those eyes that I remember from Merit. The ones that aren't so concerned with the world around him. The ones that are free.

"Ainsley knew you were here the whole time?"

"It's only been a couple of weeks, but yeah."

"Why? I thought he was pissed about this whole thing. I haven't brought it up a single time."

"He's not pissed. He wants to help. He knows we're good for each other."

Ben groans at my words, but I press on.

"He showed me the texts you sent him over the last year when he was traveling. I saw how they changed once we got together. Being with me changed you. He thinks it was for the better, and I agree. You were happy. Even if it's hard to remember that now with all the bullshit that went on, it's true. You felt it, too."

"He showed you my texts? You two have been talking about me? Jesus, I don't know how to feel about all of this."

"You can feel good about it. We both love you and want what's best for you." There. I said it.

Ben's mouth drops open, and he snaps it closed. "You what?"

"I love you."

He rests his head back into his hands without responding. It's not like I was expecting him to say it back, but I was expecting him to say something.

When he finally does, I kinda wish he hadn't. "How can you just say something like that with all that's gone on?"

He's looking at me though his fingers, so I shrug. "I'm in my truth telling era."

His head sinks back down into his hands. I can see his eyes close as his chest rises and falls slowly with each breath. Finally, he lifts his face to look at me, rubbing both hands down his cheeks and up through his now messy hair.

He sighs and shakes his head. "I've been grocery shopping."

I close my eyes and whisper, "Ben."

When I look at him again, he shakes his head. "I can't even remember the last time I went to the grocery store. Like actually went there myself and picked things out."

I wait in silence, afraid to even take a loud breath and interrupt whatever Ben is about to say. The air feels heavy, ripe with something. Whatever it is, I want it.

"I'm different. I can feel it in all sorts of ways. The grocery store is one of the more obvious ones, but it's everywhere. I've been leaving the office on time every day. Somedays I just go for a walk in the woods on my property before dinner. I put on music in the house while I cook. I've been watching movies."

"Scary ones?" I whisper.

Ben catches my eye, and I see the tiniest smile tip the corners of his mouth. He nods.

Well, shit. The first tear rolls down my cheek before I realize it escaped. I hurry to brush it away, but it's no use. Ben saw it.

His smile grows a bit, but it's sadder this time. "I know it's you. You broke something open in me, Vic. I still have my shell, but there are cracks and little parts of the old me are escaping. The weight of the world on my shoulders is lifting. It's scary to let this stuff out, but I don't think I could hold it in now if I tried. Now that I remember what it feels like to be happy. To laugh and feel free. I feel like such a fool for living this way for all these years. It's no wonder I drove my son away."

His head slips back into his hands, and I reach over, braving a touch for the first time since seeing him again. My fingers curl around his and slowly pull his hands down to the table, away from his face. His head still hangs, but he tips it up just enough to catch my eye.

"You didn't drive anyone away, Ben. Ainsley is right here in New York, going to school."

He nods, looking down at where our hands are still touching on the table in front of him. "I don't know how to do this, Victoria."

A rush of adrenaline hits my system at the words. Do they mean he's willing to try? "I don't either. But we can figure it out together."

His eyes close again, and I take a deep breath. It's time for me to say the words I came here to say.

"You've told me over and over that I changed you, Ben. But what I've never said is that I feel the same. You can't understand what it's like to be a woman my age, faced with life and choices and the enormity of it all on my own. My family isn't rich or well-educated or even particularly interested in what I do. I have to make all my own decisions, and it's fucking terrifying. Around every corner is a new decision, and there's no one to help. If I choose wrong, I fail at life. But then I met you. And sure, you questioned some of my decisions at first, but it never stopped you from treating me like a whole person. After a while, I started to realize that it wasn't my decisions at all that were driving my self-worth. It was something else. Something innately me. You practically said as much when you told me that the women you usually date are doctors and lawyers or whatever. And you chose me anyway. It couldn't be my life path. It had to just be me. Somehow, I was good enough, just for being me. As soon as I realized you seem to think that, I wondered if maybe I could think it too."

My voice is rising, but Ben doesn't look nervously around like I would if an overenthusiastic woman was ranting at me. He watches me with rapt attention.

"And I might have made the worst decision of my life choosing to keep something so important from you. Choosing to lead you on and lie to you. But by the time you found out, I had already learned that my decisions didn't create my self-worth. It was separate. I could still like and love and believe in myself even after I made that mistake. And so that was the choice I made. And it's the choice I'm asking you to make."

His eyes meet mine, and I see nothing but questions there.

I panic.

"I know this is a lot to put on you at once. You don't have to give me an answer right now." I pull my hands back, icy cold with the loss of his touch, and clasp them nervously in front of me. "We can just start slow. I'll go, and you can think about this, and…" I trail off, unsure of what to say.

"You'll go where?"

I lock eyes with him once more, biting my lip. "I'll go home. Back to my apartment."

"Which is where?"

"Brooklyn."

Ben grimaces, and I laugh. "This isn't the eighties, Ben. Brooklyn is very nice."

"I'm just imagining the nice Brooklyn apartment you're paying for with your Pilates salary." He looks up at me, narrowing his eyes. "Unless Ainsley is paying for it."

I roll my eyes. "He's not paying for it. And it's okay. It's fine," I add quickly when he balks. "I can take care of myself. I'm perfectly safe."

"Says the woman who gets off on danger and fear."

My face spreads into a smile at his mention of our intimate past. Maybe this isn't such a lost cause after all. "Why don't you come over and see for yourself how safe it is."

His face twists into an evil grin. "If you mean you want to lock yourself in your apartment and see if I can break in, I think that's a game best played at my house where there's no risk of me getting arrested."

His words suck the air right out of me. I blink a few times in shocked silence before I can get a single word out. "Okay," I say.

Ben leans back in the booth, eyes locked on mine. He still looks exhausted, but at least he's holding his head up now. His eyes carry questions, uncertainty, but he doesn't look like he's about to bolt. I hold his gaze and wait patiently.

Finally, after what feels like an eternity but is probably only a minute or two, he looks away and reaches into his pocket to draw out his phone. "It's probably best for me to check out this apartment. I'll call my car."

I smile. "Not driving yourself around, huh?"

He snorts out a laugh and shakes his head, tapping on the phone screen. "I have to draw the line somewhere."

Rule #31

ALWAYS NAIL THE INTERVIEW

VICTORIA

Ben follows me up all five flights of stairs. I can feel his body heat close to mine. A few times, his hand grazes mine on the handrail. By the time I unlock the door, I'm on fire with need for him.

But I can't rush this. I told him we could take it as slow as he needs. I asked him to trust me. I have to let him come around in his own time. The fact that he's standing here with me right now is a great sign.

He walks right into the center of the small, single room and spins in place with his hands on hips. I hit the lights and toss my bag onto the wooden chair just inside the door. Ben walks over to the window and looks out before examining the lock. He then walks to the door that I just closed and examines those locks as well, locking and unlocking each one and trying the door to make sure it doesn't open.

When he seems to be satisfied, he turns to where I stand, leaning against the wall in my tiny kitchen and nods. "You're right. It's okay."

I hold in a smile at the way he seems to be taking care of me, but as soon as the thought crosses my mind, it turns a bit sad. I suppose he's always been taking care of me. I think back to the food that appeared in his fridge when I started coming over. The cream and sugar. The way he drove me to the helicopter that was always waiting for me when I needed to leave. How he took me in with no question when my house flooded.

This man is a nurturer, a caretaker. He has so much love to give, it breaks my heart that he's spent so many years alone, trying desperately to be the perfect role model for his son.

I watch as he sits down on the small bed in the corner, the only furniture in the room other than the small desk and dresser. He folds his hands, looking up at me.

"I'm not really like that, you know."

I open my mouth to protest but then realize I don't have any idea what he's trying to say. "What do you mean?"

Ben lets out a sigh and looks around the room again before meeting my eye. "That guy on the island, vacation Ben. I've never met him before. I liked him, and I know you liked him, too. But that's not me."

I shake my head and start to speak, but he raises a hand to stop me.

"One of the first things that went through my mind, when I realized that you and Ainsley knew each other, was that he was going to tell you the truth about me."

Tears spring to my eyes, and I hold my breath. He has something he needs to say, and it's time I started listening.

"The shame of being with someone he dated came later. It was followed by the shame of being lied to." He shakes his head once more to stop my protests. "I know. I know what I said. What I always say about going for what you want in whatever way you need to. But I wasn't prepared for how it would feel to have it turned on me like that. To realize that this person who I thought I was forming a deep connection with was someone I didn't know at all. It only shined a light on the fact that I was just as big of a liar. You might have fallen for vacation Ben, but that guy doesn't exist here. So, unless you want to move to the Merit house and see me twice a year when I can get away from this mess, I don't see how we move forward."

My breath is coming in short, shallow gasps as I try to keep myself from losing it completely. The sadness of this situation is threatening to eat me alive, and I'm not sure I have the words to fight my way out of it.

But I've made my decision. I have to try.

I walk over and sit beside him on the single bed. He doesn't reach for me, but doesn't shift away, so I take that as a good sign. I lay a hand on his shoulder and let it run down the smooth fabric of his suit jacket until it's resting on his hand. When I glance up, he's watching me.

"I didn't fall for vacation Ben. I fell for this, right here." I lay my hand on his chest, right over his heart. After a second, he places his hand on mine.

"You showed me how deeply you can care about people, how deeply you love. You showed me a world where people matter so much that you're willing to scour the globe for them. You are so caring and so loyal. You dropped everything to help your employees when they were in need. You opened your heart and your home to me, showed me a kind of love that I've never experienced before. Even if you didn't call it love, I knew it was. I—"

I break off and close my eyes, taking deep breaths to try to get through this without sobbing. "I've never had anyone care for me like you did. I've spent my time dating being dragged through short 'take it or leave it' flings with guys who couldn't care less if I was even there. I thought that's what love was. I thought that's what I had to look forward to my whole life. But then you came along. I knew who you were, and I never intended to fall for you like I did, but when I saw the man you were, the man you are, it showed me a world that I never imagined possible. A world where someone saw me and cared for me."

Ben's eyes are closed when I glance up, but he's still holding my hand tightly over his heart. "Ainsley did tell me about you. He told me that you're the greatest man he's ever known. That you're strong and loyal and kind. That you're fair and level-headed. That he aspires to be like you when he grows up, just in a different work outfit." I break off and let out a small sad laugh, which sounds a lot like a sob.

Ben's eyes open, and he looks right into mine.

"He told me that any woman would be lucky to have you. And at that moment, even though you were gone, and I thought I'd lost you forever, I still felt lucky."

Ben's lips hit mine with a force that would have knocked me onto my back if he didn't also wrap an arm around me. The feeling of him pressed against me feels like a rush of pleasure and a dam breaking. All the tears I'd managed to hold back come rushing out. He kisses me anyway, his cheeks getting as wet as mine. The taste of salt filling both of our mouths.

When he pulls away, I'm panting.

He presses his forehead to mine, and we breathe together for a long moment.

"My life is so boring," he says finally.

I laugh in surprise, reaching up to wipe my tears and pull back to look at him. "What do you mean? You just told me that you went grocery shopping."

Ben's eyes close as his mouth spreads into a real smile. The first I've seen in a while, and I rejoice.

"I put my whole life on hold to take care of my son. I focused all my energy on that. Focusing on other things is new, and I'm not sure how good I'm going to be at it yet."

"We'll figure it out together."

He pulls away from me then and holds my head in both hands, facing him. He's shaking his head, but it seems more resigned than anything. "I'll just hold you back."

I shake my head so quickly it breaks free from his grip. "That's impossible. You can't hold me back if you're the life I want."

"You can't know if this is the life you want."

"We can't know anything about the future. All we can know is what we want and how we feel, and then we go from there."

Ben says nothing so I go on. "We can start over."

I stand abruptly and have to steady myself before I stick out my hand. Ben looks at it for a long second before taking it in his own. "I'm Victoria. Nice to meet you."

Ben stares at our locked hands and takes a deep breath. When he exhales, he meets my eye. "Ben."

I smile. "Ben, is that short for Benjamin?"

When he returns my smile, a tiny bit of my broken heart heals. It's a start.

"No. It's short for Bentley. A family name."

"Well, it's nice to meet you, Ben. I look forward to learning more about you."

He doesn't let go of my hand when I loosen my grip, so I retighten it, taking a step closer.

"You know," he starts, looking down to our hands and then up my body in a way that sends chills through me. "The first time we met, you seduced me."

"Is that what happened?" I ask, narrowing my eyes at him.

"I'm pretty sure that's the only way I would have ended up in that hotel room with you."

"Well, since we get a do-over, maybe it's your turn to seduce me."

"I would, but…" Ben drops my hand and pats his pockets. "I didn't bring any snacks with me."

I laugh then, in surprise but also in pure joy. The weight of the last few weeks has been heavy on my shoulders, and I just felt a bit of it lift. I know this isn't the end of what we need to work through, but the fact that he's willing to start that journey with me is music to my soul.

I feel a bit like singing.

Instead, I unbutton the stiff suit jacket and let it fall to the floor behind me, seductively reaching for the buttons of the silk blouse.

Ben groans. "You can never, ever tell anyone how much I'm about to enjoy this law clerk intern strip tease."

I scoff and try to look scandalized. "I thought this was part of the interview."

Ben groans again and covers his face with his hands. After a moment, though, I see him peeking through his fingers.

"Do I need to take it all off? Or would it be okay with you if I just unbutton my top?"

Ben shakes his head and pulls his phone out, holding down the button to power it off. "Thing's always listening," he mutters.

I want to laugh at his unnecessary precaution, but I stay in character. "I really appreciate this opportunity, sir."

When he looks up at me, I can see the change in him. He's going to play. Adrenaline shoots through me, and I suck in a breath to keep from reacting.

He stands and buttons his suit jacket, just the way I've seen actors do it on television law shows. Again, I want to giggle, but I keep it together.

"On your knees."

I drop to the floor in a rush of desire.

Here we are, right back to where we started, Mr. Adams.

But so much has changed since that night. It seems like a million years ago that we were in that hotel room on Faraday. I never could have imagined being here now, still with Ben. Getting a chance to make this crazy thing between us real.

But here we are, in my shabby studio apartment, with him standing over me in his fancy suit, getting ready to make me earn a clerk job the hard way.

And he says his real life isn't any fun.

I beg to differ.

"You better get that shirt off. I don't have all day."

Gone is the funny, kind, uncertain Ben from moments before. He's replaced with the powerful, take no shit, Mr. Adams the lawyer.

Heat pools between my legs as I struggle to unbutton the blouse as fast as I can. When I toss it to the side, I glance up and find him appraising me, hands on his hips.

"You wore a bra like that to a job interview? You were expecting to end up on your knees, then?"

"I just wanted to be prepared." I try to sound as meek as possible, when inside, passion races through me. I only hope I can behave myself long enough to get what I want.

"Well, I had a chance to look over your résumé, and it all seems very impressive. But I need you to know that as a clerk in this firm, you will have other duties."

"Like filing and getting coffee?" I ask timidly, eyes on his shiny shoes.

Ben laughs darkly. "You will certainly be getting coffee. But there will be times like this, when I call you into my office, and I need to know that you are willing and able to perform the duties asked of you."

"I graduated top of my class, sir. I'm sure I'll be able to perform any duties you need."

"I can tell you're just playing coy. You know exactly what I'm talking about."

"Like I said, sir, I will be happy to perform any duties you need."

I peel my eyes away from Ben's shiny dress shoes and let them drift up his body. His desire is evident in the front of his pants, and I don't want to let my attention hover there for too long, but he catches me.

"Something interesting down there?" His voice is low and rough. Mean, even a little cruel. I can't get enough. It wasn't my intention to provoke him, but I can't help myself.

"No, sir."

No sooner have the words left my mouth than he has my chin in his hand and is tilting my face roughly upward. "No? I thought we had an understanding."

He tosses my face to the side, and I have to catch myself with one hand to keep from falling over.

"I—"

"Get it out."

"Sir—"

"You know, there's an allotted amount of time for these interviews. If you think wasting my time is going to work in your favor, you are sorely mistaken."

Bastard.

I love it. I love him.

I reach up to grasp him by the belt, pulling forward with a jerk and forcing him to take a step toward me. I start to unbuckle it, but he stops me with his hands. "There's no need to take my belt off. Just pull down the zipper. I'm not the one who gets undressed in this office."

Heat rushes through me once more at his command. I fumble trying to get the zipper down quickly but finally manage. I reach inside and grasp him, shifting his pants to the side to wrestle his erection out. He's rock hard for me, just like I've been dreaming about.

Anticipating his next command, I take him straight into my mouth, licking up and around his head and sucking him deep inside.

"Choke yourself."

My jaw drops open around him, and I sit back slightly, his cock coming free of my mouth as I look up in surprise. "What?"

"You heard me, girl. I'm getting really tired of this innocent act. You have two seconds to choke—"

He cuts off as I go for it, driving my head forward onto his waiting cock. I succeed, kind of, hitting the back of my throat hard enough to gag myself.

He laughs darkly at my attempt. "Get it down there."

I try again, slower this time, angling my head back so his cock can slide down, mimicking how he's positioned my head in the past when deep throating me.

I still fail to get his tip to pass the top of my throat. After an embarrassing third and fourth attempt, I sit back on my heels, wiping away my tears and looking up at him from under my lashes. "I can't."

"Can't or won't?" he replies, completely unsympathetic to my plight.

"Can't, sir. I tried."

He takes his cock firmly in his own fist. "Well, consider that part of the interview failed."

My mouth drops open as I gasp. Ben catches the back of my head with his other hand and drives himself into my gaping mouth. "I'll show you how it's done."

Straight fucking down.

I only get a second to marvel at how powerful he is, easily accomplishing the task I failed at. After that first second, my mind becomes otherwise occupied with survival instincts.

He pulls out just enough for me to gasp in a large breath before penetrating my throat once more. Once inside, he stays there, pumping deep into my body as my reflexes try to swallow repeatedly to dislodge the intrusion.

"Fucking hell that feels good."

His words are a balm, and I rise up a bit on my knees to take him deeper.

"That's right, take it."

I can't see through the ocean of tears, but I imagine him up there, eyes rolled back, lip clasped in his teeth, watching me like the sex goddess that I am.

He's pumping faster, giving me less and less opportunity to breathe. I can tell he's close, so I reach up to grasp his balls just like he showed me.

"Damn it, girl. Are you trying to make me come?"

The way he's fucking me right now tells me I'm not the only

one with that end in mind. I brace myself, preparing to take him, when all of a sudden he pulls out.

"Goddamn, that was close." He releases my head and takes a step back, leaving me bowed and heaving on the floor in front of him. "You know as soon as I come, the interview's over. You wouldn't want to end yours on a failure, would you?"

"I..." I swallow a dozen more times, still trying to catch my breath and calm my nervous system back down. When I can finally manage, I peek up at him. "I don't think that was a failure. You seemed to be enjoying it quite a bit."

Ben laughs again in the evil way he's been doing since this game started. "The order was to choke yourself. It doesn't count if I do it for you. Get up and get your hands on the desk over there. Get your skirt up, too."

I struggle to my feet and make my way over to the desk. Using both hands, I pull my skirt up around my waist, exposing my garters and bare ass.

Ben lets out a low, objectifying whistle. "She showed up at her interview wearing garters and no panties. I knew from your résumé you would be one to meet with personally, but I really had no idea, did I?"

"I just wanted to please you, sir."

"What will please me is if I walk over there and find a tight, wet pussy waiting for me. Is that what I'm going to find, Victoria?"

"Yes, sir."

In fact, I think I might be dripping down my thighs as we speak.

I'm facing the window, so I don't see the smack coming before it lands on my ass. I cry out, mostly in surprise, and turn to look at him. "Have I been bad, sir?"

He smacks me again, and I stifle a gasp, burying my face in my arms on the desk. Next thing I know, Ben's lifting my head up by my hair, his face tucked down next to mine. "Good or bad, it doesn't matter. I don't need a reason to punish you. Once you're my employee, I can do anything I want to you anytime. Got it?"

"Y-yes."

"Yes, what?" he growls, still holding my head tightly by my hair.

"Yes, sir."

He gives no warning before driving his cock straight inside me.

I cry out in surprise, and he laughs. "That is a tight little pussy, isn't it?"

My scalp is beginning to burn where he's pulling my hair, and my tears start to flow anew.

"Hurts, does it?" he asks.

I know he's referring to his cock, which doesn't hurt a damn bit—quite the opposite—but I nod.

"Hurts when I stretch that pussy wide open with my cock. It's something you're going to have to get used to working here."

He releases my head, and I catch it just in time before my forehead hits the desk. With both hands holding my hips as I bend over, Ben starts to slide himself in and out of me faster, driving deeper as my body relaxes and opens for him.

"That's right, take it all," he growls out. I can hear the breathiness of effort in his voice.

I touch my forehead down on the cool wood and tilt my hips up just so. He's fucking me just how he knows I like it, and I'm not going to last long.

I wonder if I'll get bonus points on my interview for coming on his cock.

It's time to find out.

I clench down and cry out as the wave of pleasure breaks over me. It's dark where my head is tucked, but I squeeze my eyes closed anyway, holding my breath and biting down on my lip as I careen through the ecstasy.

"That was so fucking hot, girl. I'm about to fill you up."

I can just barely hear his words over the ringing in my ears.

With a few punishing thrusts, Ben comes inside me, pressing himself deeper and deeper as the slickness grows. He stills and holds himself there, bent over my back with his forehead pressed just under my shoulder blades, hands still holding me by both hips.

I wait for him to pull out, but he doesn't. After a moment, I feel myself sliding off the desk. When daylight reaches my hooded eyes, I realize I'm sliding down to the floor with Ben. He's still inside me, and his arms are around my center, holding me tightly on his lap.

When he finally relaxes his grip enough that I can take a full breath, my anxiety decides a joke is the best course of action. "See, Lawyer Ben can be fun."

Ben, to his credit, gives me a small laugh, not releasing his arms from around me.

"Lawyer Ben doesn't take on a case he doesn't think he can win."

It takes a moment for me to process his words, but when I do, I struggle free of his embrace and turn to face him. His now soft cock lays in his lap. I can see that he did take off the belt after all. His pants are around his ankles as he sits on his heels, kneeling before me where I sit.

He looks perfect and sexy and handsome and sad.

"What does that mean?"

He shakes his head. "It means…I just don't know."

"That's right, Ben. You don't know. We can't know. You can't know that you'll win a case before you take it. You can think you'll win, but you can't predict the future. It's the same with us. Whatever reservations you have, you have to give us a chance. I know you want to. And I know you're going to be brave enough to try. I wouldn't have come here to the city and set up my whole life around this if I didn't think it would work."

Ben cocks his head to the side and gives me what could be a little smirk. "I'm the case you thought you'd win?"

"You're the prize I'm here to fight for."

"I'm not sure anyone's ever fought for me before," he says.

"Well, same here. You and I have come down different roads in life, but those roads brought us right here. You can't tell me that you don't feel what I feel."

"I can't tell you that. You're right."

"Okay. That's a start. I'll take it."

Ben climbs to his feet. I think he's going to take my hand and pull me up to him, but he doesn't. "You make one hell of a case, Victoria."

I smile up at him as he pulls up his fancy suit pants and buckles his belt. The wrinkles in his perfect suit make me swell with pride. I love the idea that he's leaving here with the evidence of me all over him.

"Does that mean I get the job?"

He laughs and shakes his head, turning back to the bed where he left his phone. I watch as he switches it back on and tucks it into his pocket. "I can't stay."

"Oh. That's fine. Just, you know. You have my number. You can unblock it if you want."

He pauses by the door and looks back at where I still sit. If he was expecting me to get up and run to him, he doesn't show his disappointment. "Bye."

"Bye." My word is practically a whisper compared to his firm command.

I watch the door close behind him.

And then I collapse.

I'm on the floor with my skirt around my waist, dripping cum, and he just walked out. The tears are automatic, heaving out of my chest in sobs so loud I wouldn't be surprised if Ben could hear them from the street.

This is my lot in life, I guess. The woman who gets tossed aside. Unwanted. Good enough to fuck but never good enough to date. Nothing serious.

How could I have let this happen? I was so sure that my plan would work.

I guess I was wrong.

After a while the tears dry, and I lay quietly on my back, looking out the window at the clouds. The catharsis from the punishing game with Ben and then the actual punishment of being left and crying my soul out leaves me feeling gutted, tired, and somehow calmer. Free.

I gave it my all. I gave him my best. I owned up to my mistakes and apologized. I told the truth about my feelings even when I wasn't sure they'd be returned.

I showed up here as the woman I want to be in life.

I wasn't handed the grand prize, but I'm still that woman. Even sitting here alone, unsure of how to go on, I'm still her.

And I think I like her.

Rule #32

CONTROL'S AN ILLUSION

BEN

"Why didn't you tell me Victoria was in New York?" I bark into my phone as my driver closes the door behind me in the backseat of the town car.

It's not much of a greeting, but I'm not feeling particularly cheerful after this new bout of deception.

Ainsley laughs. "You saw her, huh? How'd you like that suit we picked out?"

I grind my teeth and try not to yell. I will not talk about her with him like we're pals. I cannot. This whole thing is just…too much.

"She told me you helped her get moved and whatnot."

"Yeah."

"Why?"

Another laugh. "Why not?"

My anger seethes at his flippancy. "I can think of a few reasons why not. First of all—"

"Oh, save it, Dad. You and your reasons. You act like you've got all the time in the world, but I'm here to tell you that this silver fox stage you're in right now, it won't last. You're just going to be an old man soon, and don't you want to be an old man who snagged himself a girl?"

My mind can't stop tripping over those words long enough to form a coherent sentence, so I just clench my eyes closed and try to pretend this conversation isn't happening. Ainsley, of course, doesn't take the hint to shut up.

"She's good for you. Anyone can see it. I talked to Cynthia last week, and she agreed."

"Why were you talking to my secretary?"

Another carefree laugh. "We talk, man. I've known her since I was a kid. She's the closest thing you have to a friend in this city, so we chat sometimes and exchange news about you. God knows you don't tell either of us everything."

Another bombshell to process later. "I don't need your assistance with my dating life, Ainsley. I appreciate the gesture, but I have everything under—"

"Don't say control. If we're having this conversation right now, it means that Vicki's not there, which means that your dumbass left her behind somewhere, and that is an indication that you don't have anything *under control.*" He mimics my voice on those last two words.

I grind my teeth harder. "I just need more time."

"And how long do you think a girl like that is going to wait around for you to get over your hang-ups and decide to let her make you happy?"

"She seemed very interested in working together to secure some kind of future for our relationship. I got the impression that I could take some time to think it over."

The kid might die of hilarity at my words.

"Jesus, Dad. You are a lost cause. *Working together to secure some kind of future for our relationship.*" He does a poor imitation of me again and laughs. "The girl is gaga for you, and I know you feel the same way. Cynthia told me that you've been clocking out before six every night. What the hell's that about?

And I've been seeing the movies you're watching. It's like you're running through a list of Vicki's favorites."

"How do you know what movies I watch?"

"I use all your streaming logins. They're right there on the home page."

I should have known that. I should have known a lot of the things the kid's telling me, but I didn't. I didn't know he was in contact with people close to me to exchange information. I didn't know he paid any attention to my life at all.

It makes me wonder what else I don't know.

And if I want to find out.

I grimace at the thought.

"I'm doing some life reevaluation right now. And yes, I am considering whether Victoria could be a part of that."

"What's to consider? You date a girl, it works out, or it doesn't. This idea you have that you need to know the end before you begin is what's holding you back. Just take the leap and see what happens."

"It's my careful deliberation over possible endings that has gotten me to where I am right now. I don't just leap into things without doing my research and making sure I can contain any collateral damage."

"Oh, give it a rest, Dad. That's all bull, and you know it. You can't live your life in a bubble where you only interact with possibilities that have predictable outcomes. I've only just started statistics class, and even I know that. I get that you feel like you have a lot to protect in life, but maybe it's time to let some of that stuff go."

He's right, of course, but I can't help arguing the point until it's dead. I want to stop. I want to let him win. But I still hold the trump card. I beg myself not to play it.

But in the end, I do.

"I promised your mother that I would take good care of you. Every decision I've made has been to provide you with the best possible opportunities and future."

I pause and wait for him to concede the argument to me and apologize, but the kid just sighs.

"Dad, you did it. I survived. I'm an adult. I'm in college, and you're rich as fuck. Everything's fine. It's time to let go of the words that have haunted you for the last thirteen years and start living your life. Mom's gone. She's been gone a long time, and you did everything you promised her and more."

He's so right it nauseates me.

I take the coward's way out.

"I've got another call coming in. I'll talk to you soon."

He's still talking as I end the call.

I don't even set the phone down in my lap before it's buzzing again.

Avery.

He's been calling every day since I left Faraday, but I haven't had the energy to face what could be waiting for me on that line. I let out a sigh and hit accept.

If I blow him off much longer, the guy is going to show up on my doorstep, and I'm not sure that would be better.

"Hey," I say, and prepare for the worst.

"Hey," Avery replies. "I talked to Ainsley."

At least he's not going to drag this out.

"Oh?"

"You should have told us."

I can't imagine saying the words aloud even now that he knows, so I'm not sure how I would have pulled that off. I huff a laugh in response.

"Seriously, man. We would have been there for you. It sounds like that was a rough day. I wish I'd known. I know the guys feel the same."

He told them.

I close my eyes and take a deep breath, waiting for the shame to overtake me. It ebbs, but it's not the rib cage crushing wave I experienced back on the island. Maybe the distance is helping.

"Yeah, well."

"Talk to me, Ben. Or I'm coming up there."

I smile to myself at Avery being so predictable. "There's not all that much to say. I got taken by a pretty woman. I'm still working it all out."

"What's there to work out?" He sounds confused, and I guess I would be as well. The most likely thing for me to do in this situation is move on and never speak about it—or to her—again.

But it's not that simple.

"She's here. She and Ains worked out some kind of plan where he helped her get moved to the city so she could try to get me back."

Avery laughs on the other end of the line. "Really, now? He told me he was just headed back to start at Columbia."

"He did that, too."

"Okay, so the girl—"

"She's a woman, Ave. An adult woman."

"Right, my bad. So, this woman packs up her life here on Faraday and moves to the city to get you back. Is she succeeding?"

Is she? For a moment at that café, I thought for sure I'd let her win. But now, trying to explain this all to my friend? I'm just not sure. "What if she did?"

"That would be great, Ben. We'd all be very happy for you."

I scoff. "Happy for me and my son's ex-girlfriend."

Avery's having none of it. "If you're going to stay on this pity train, you're not going to get anywhere, and you know it. I talked to Ains. It sounds like they were really more like friends. And we all need friends in life, don't we?"

I huff again, considering that the opposite might be true as my own best friend is giving me the third degree.

"If that shit hadn't happened out on Merit, would you have taken her home with you?"

"Yes." There's no point in lying now.

"So, she's the one."

I grind my teeth and lay my head back on the seat. "There is no *the one*."

"How can you say that? Have you met my perfect in every way for me girlfriend?"

I shake my head and sigh. "Fine. You found the one. Congratulations on winning life, Ave."

"You found Breanna."

Only Avery would dare to say something like that to me, even after all these years. "Perfect. I found the one, and she died. Thanks for the pep talk."

"She was the one for you then. Breanna swooped in when you were going through some heavy family shit and pulled you right out of it. Helped you stand up to your parents. Helped you get through law school after you thought you were going to fail. And she gave you Ainsley."

I close my eyes and take a deep breath, letting it out long and slow. "You're right. She was the one."

"And what if you've found the one for the man you are now? You're in a new chapter. Stepping away from some of the firm responsibilities as the younger partners step up. Sending your kid off to college. Committing to being at The Sands more. This is a fresh start for you, and what do you know? The perfect woman for your new start shows up right on time."

I don't have to think hard to know Breanna would agree wholeheartedly with him right now. I can see them in my mind, laughing over this whole thing and telling me not to screw it up.

"I think it's perfect that Ains brought her to you. It's a fucking love story, man. Like a movie."

"Glad I'm keeping you entertained."

"Don't fucking do this. Don't do the thing where you decide one problem is big enough to kill everything good in your life. It's too short."

I don't have a response for that, so I say nothing. I'm sure Ave's just getting started.

He doesn't make me wait. "If this shit with Ainsley hadn't

gone down, and Victoria was living at your house with you right now, would you tell me she was the one?"

"Yes."

"Okay, then. You've got your answer."

Smug fucking bastard wraps the whole thing up with a box and hands it over, expecting me to thank him.

"When are you coming back up to New York?" I ask.

Ave is quiet for a long moment, and I know he's deciding whether to let me change the subject. Finally, he relents. "Ains and I have tickets to see The National next month."

"Let's get dinner."

He laughs. "We're going to get a lot more than dinner, Ben. I'm staying at your house. I'm going to be all up in your bullshit."

I laugh then, shaking my head. "Sounds good, man."

"Tell Vicki I said hi."

Arriving home is usually my favorite part of the day, but today it just feels heavy.

I set my briefcase down on the entryway table with a thud that echoes through the empty halls. As I walk, lights gradually brighten to greet me, something I generally enjoy, but today it just seems pathetic.

I have my house programmed to greet me because I'm always alone.

I mentally curse Ainsley for sending me down this path of morose thoughts. I'm not pathetic. I'm doing just fine. I'm a partner at the largest, most prestigious firm in the city. I have everything I could ever want in life.

So why am I standing in the doorway of the kitchen, holding down a rush of emotions at the thought of cooking dinner for myself and settling down on the couch to watch TV?

I don't bother offering myself multiple choices for my emotional state. I already know the reason.

I shouldn't have left her there like that.

I could have said something to indicate my predicament and mental gymnastics. Let her know how deeply I'm considering her offer. Let her know how much she means to me.

Instead, I just walked out with only a single word.

Bye.

The thought haunts me.

I cross the kitchen and pull a bottle of beer from the fridge before heading to my study. As I sink into my favorite chair, the one that faces a massive window overlooking the forest on the back half of my property, I pull out my phone.

My plan is to call her and explain why I left, explain that this whole thing took me by surprise but I'm working through it.

But first I have to change her contact info back to Victoria, and away from Do Not Answer, which was what I changed it to while waiting for my helicopter on Merit.

It would have been simpler to actually block her number, like I told her I had, but I couldn't give up the test of my control I'd undergo by having her texts and voicemails sitting in my phone and not reading or listening to them.

I'd won the game. I never opened a single one, but I hate thinking about what the prize for that kind of behavior could be.

A lifetime of loneliness?

Congratulations, Ben. You're the most in control man alive. You can now die alone in your giant house.

I curse myself for once again allowing those despondent thoughts to sneak through my mental firewall and take another long sip of beer.

I'm in no state to talk to anyone, not after those two conversations in the car. I've got some real thinking to do.

With a heavy sigh, I hit play on the first voicemail.

Rule #33

DON'T BE LATE FOR CLASS

VICTORIA

"I usually do three-quarters bright at the very front, and half bright for the rest of the room. Especially for these early morning classes."

I smile and watch my trainer, Sandra, adjust the lighting in the cool, quiet studio.

I'm getting set up for my first class at Lotus Studio. It's an intro to Pilates class, and I'll be observed by Sandra the whole time, but I'm still really excited. This is the first step toward becoming certified to teach the kind of rehabilitation Pilates that got me back on my feet. I'm overjoyed and grateful that the nice people at Lotus took a chance on me and put me right on the schedule.

"We've got a handful of students signed up for this class, so why don't you go out to the front desk and help them get signed in and grab their props. I'll take care of getting the air turned on and sweeping the room."

"Okay. Thanks, Sandra." I smile and head out to the lobby

where I can hear the bell on the door announcing the first student's arrival.

I'm just turning the corner to greet them when I stop dead in my tracks.

It's Ben.

We haven't spoken since the day before yesterday when he left my apartment. I'm not sure if I expected him to call, but he didn't. I didn't have the heart to try calling and getting his voicemail for the millionth time.

I committed to being patient. I told him that we could take it slow, and I plan to keep that promise.

Right now, though, with him strolling into the Pilates studio to take my class, looking fine as hell in his gray joggers and hoodie, the last thing I want to do is take it slow. I want to take a running leap into his arms.

"Morning," he says, and I curse myself for not getting my shit together fast enough to greet him first.

"Good morning," I say with a big smile. "Welcome to Lotus. Is this your first time in?"

He pauses next to the check-in counter and narrows his eyes at me for a moment. Then he nods. "First time in. I've taken a few Pilates classes before, though."

"Well, let's get you signed in."

I stand next to the iPad stand on the counter. Ben walks over and stands right next to me. I sneak a glance down at my shoulder and see only a millimeter of space between our bodies. Wild electricity jumps the gap from his skin to mine and sends chills down my spine.

When I look back up, he's watching me. The intensity of that stare takes my breath away, and I shift uncomfortably, needing to dispel the feelings I now have swirling around in my belly. I do have a class to teach, after all.

"I'm glad you came."

He smiles, and I melt a bit more. "I couldn't miss your first class."

He definitely could have, but he didn't. Somehow, he found out about my new job and my first class all on his own and took it upon himself to show up here. The stark evidence of him thinking about me—caring about me—threatens to derail me once more.

I've got to get this under control.

"You have to behave yourself in there, okay? It's really important that this goes well."

His smile turns sly. "I'll be the perfect student."

I don't want to look away from those dark eyes, but the iPad screen catches my eye as it falls asleep. I jump and turn my focus to waking it back up and getting him signed in. I grab a mat, band, and ball for him without meeting his gaze full-on again. I do let my hands graze his gently as I pass the items over and instantly regret it.

I'm going to be hot and bothered all class long.

This class is nothing like the punishing workout routine I put him through on Faraday. I try not to follow his body for the entire class but spread my attention throughout my students.

After class, he files out of the room with the rest of them, and I have to force myself not to chase him down the hallway.

Patience, Victoria.

I'm putting away the mats and sweeping the floor when Sandra comes to find me. "Your boyfriend's waiting for you in the lobby. If you want to head out, I can take care of the sweeping."

My eyes go wide, but I snatch back my composure quickly. If there was ever a time to be professional, it's here at this job. "My boyfriend?"

"Ben? I was just chatting with him about the class. Sounds like he's going to start coming regularly. I recommended that he try out a few of our more challenging classes, considering his fitness level, but I'm not sure I convinced him."

I can feel my blush burning my entire face. "Oh, yeah. He does like coming to my classes."

Sandra smiles at me conspiratorially. "That man is a catch, girl. Let me know if he's got any single friends. I'd jump on a double date anytime."

I grin and nod, happy that this woman seems to trust me enough to offer personal information about her life. I might have just made my first female friend here in this giant city.

"I got all the mats and props put away, and I did this whole side of the room already," I say, gesturing to the area I swept.

Sandra takes the broom from me and mimes sweeping me out of the studio. "Go on then."

Ben's sitting in a chair in the lobby area when I emerge with my bag and sweatshirt. "Hey."

He looks up from his phone, pocketing it when he sees me. "Hey."

I put my hands on my hips and cock my head, tossing him a sly smile. "Sandra, my trainer, thinks you're my boyfriend."

I want the joke to lighten the tension a bit, to take the edge off my big, scary feelings of uncertainty.

But he doesn't laugh. "I told her as much."

My mouth opens and hangs there for too long of a moment before I catch myself and snap it closed. "What do you mean, you told her as much?"

He stands and walks over until he's chest to chest with me, looking down as I look up. "I mean, I told her that I was your boyfriend. Not that I like the term, but it'll do for now."

"What makes you think that you can just walk in here and proclaim yourself my boyfriend? Isn't that something we need to discuss? You never even asked. I didn't know if I would ever see you again."

Ben sighs and nods. "I'm sorry about that."

I bite my lip and wait in silence, not trusting myself to speak. I know for sure if I opened my mouth, a sob might escape. Or possibly a scream.

After a long, heated stare, he surprises me once more by dropping to his knee on the wood floor of the lobby. He takes one of my hands in both of his and holds it up to his lips. Eyes locked, he smiles. "Victoria, will you be my girlfriend or possibly another word we come up with together?"

I can't help but laugh…and cry. "Are you proposing dating to me right now?"

Ben looks sheepish, but only for a heartbeat. His confident expression returns in force. He knows he has me, but he's still willing to defend his decision. I've never felt so special. "I fucked up. I never should have walked away on Merit, and I definitely shouldn't have walked away from you the other day. Can you forgive me?"

Tears blur my vision, but I don't look away. "It's you who's supposed to be forgiving me."

"I forgive you. Do you forgive me?"

I nod.

"And you'll come home with me and live in my house?"

My eyebrows go sky high, but I nod again.

The relief is obvious on Ben's face. "Thank God. I wasn't sure how I was going to flood a fifth story apartment in Brooklyn, but I would have tried."

My surprised laugh is loud, echoing through the quiet lobby.

"If you're all finished here, my car's waiting out front."

Rule #34

WE ARE FAR FROM RATIONAL BEINGS

VICTORIA

Ben's house is almost exactly how I pictured it.

Old world exterior of gray and red brick, immaculate landscaping, and windows with white shutters. There's even a damn turret.

The inside is like walking into a near future sci-fi film. The house unlocks with his fingerprint and greets us with slowly illuminating warm lights. I glance around to see the outside of the home reflected in the antique looking dark wood furniture and parquet floors. The effect is softened with modern touches that speak instantly of Ben—bold modern art prints and athletic shoes on a rack.

I marvel at all the space. The seemingly never-ending hallways leading off in all directions. I thought the Merit house was big, but that was a dollhouse in comparison.

"Why do you live in such a huge house?"

Ben turns after hanging his jacket in the entry way closet and reaches for mine with a shrug. "I've never really thought about it. My grandparents built it, and it was my parents' after that. I inherited it when they passed, and it just seemed right to move here."

Wow. "So, you've lived here your whole life?"

He smiles and comes over to take my hand, leading me down the hallway into the kitchen. "Not exactly. I grew up here, but I moved to Boston for college and had an apartment there. When I got married, I was still in grad school, so we stayed in Massachusetts. It wasn't until about ten years ago that my father passed, and I took over the estate. Ainsley and I lived in an apartment in Manhattan, close to the firm, before we moved here."

He sits me down on a stool at a high eating bar with a marble counter and walks over to the massive stainless-steel refrigerator. "You know," he starts, looking around, "it seemed so natural to move here, I never really gave it much thought. But I guess Ains and I were city boys at that point. And the estate is in the city, but it's not like our apartment in Manhattan. Moving here was a big transition for both of us, and a hard one for Ains with the school change and all that. But it never occurred to me that not coming home was a decision I could have made."

It's just a taste of the man's past, and I want more. "And your wife?" He's never brought her up, but somehow, I get the feeling it's okay to ask.

Ben's back is to me as he stands at the fridge, and he's quiet for a while as he digs out supplies. Turning back to me, eggs and veggies in hand, he smiles. "Hungry?"

I nod. "Always."

I watch him get out the pan and start chopping. After a few moments, he answers my question.

"Breanna died of cancer when Ains was six. We still lived in Boston at that point. She went fast. By the time we knew anything was wrong, it was far too late to intervene."

The veggies sizzle as they hit the pan. Ben stirs them with a spatula.

"Back then, I didn't worry so much about things going wrong. I had no idea how bad it could be. Up to that point, things had been pretty rosy. Perfect upbringing, finest education, happy marriage to a lovely woman, and a healthy son. We had bright futures. All of us."

He stirs the pan and adds the eggs, lifting it and swirling them around to cover the bottom. I don't dare to even breathe, not wanting to risk interrupting whatever little bit of Ben I'm about to learn.

"All of a sudden, she was gone, and I had to start over. It's like you said at the café. All of my decisions had to be made by me, alone. And I now knew how much I had to lose by making the wrong ones. It was even worse because I had this kid to keep safe as well. The world was a minefield of possibilities. I was paralyzed with fear. Avery was living with me and Ains in Boston after Breanna passed, and it seemed like the three of us would hunker down there together and heal, but that's not how it happened. Avery can't really hunker down anywhere, and his healing was something that needed to happen far away from his father. But it was Avery's dad who stepped in and started showing me how to make decisions. I have a lot to thank Frederick for. I'm not sure why he took me under his wing after abandoning Avery for his whole childhood, but that's another conversation. I started at his firm. Ains and I lived at his estate for a bit before settling into our own apartment after I landed at the Manhattan office. And life went on. But I never lost sight of the fact that everything I loved was just one mistake away from being ripped from my life."

"Your wife dying of cancer was hardly a mistake you made."

He nods, using the spatula to slice the omelet in half and slide it onto two plates. "Rationally, of course. But we are far from rational beings."

I close my eyes to hold back tears as the heartbreak of his statement washes over me. The years he spent blaming himself for not catching the cancer earlier. How he must have decided that it was his job to keep anything else terrible from happening.

"This was all a long time ago, Vic."

I nod, finally opening my eyes when I hear a plate being set down in front of me. I smile at the lovely breakfast. He even tossed a little cheese on mine when I wasn't looking. "Thank you."

Ben sets his own plate on the counter in front of him, so he's standing face-to-face with me as I sit at the bar. We eat in silence for a few minutes. The food is truly delicious. I could get used to this.

"I never did this again," he motions between the two of us with his fork, "because I was too scared of it all repeating. Relationships just seemed too volatile. People are too fragile. I already had to be worried about Ainsley every second of the day, I didn't think I could make space in my psyche to worry about someone else as well."

He shakes his head, looking down at his plate for a long moment before meeting my eyes. "But I don't worry about you. And that's not to say I don't care about your wellbeing. I care very much. But it's a different kind of care. It's less like something I need to manage and more like something I'm watching go on. With Ains, I feel like if I take my eyes off the road for one second, he'll careen off an overpass. But with you I feel like I could be the one reclining in my seat, putting on music for the road trip of our lives. And I don't know exactly what that means because I've never felt anything like it before. But for the first time since I lost my wife, I'm thinking about being in a relationship and feeling something other than dread. It's more like excitement."

I don't know what to say so I wait, holding his gaze as best as I can with the tears blurring my vision. When I glance down, I realize that he's reached over and is holding my hands. I squeeze my eyes closed and let the tears fall, unwilling to let go of him for even a second to wipe them away.

"And I made you cry, which wasn't my intention."

I shake my head fervently, preparing to argue, but he shakes his own, quieting me. "That's not what I meant to say. What I meant was that I've been listening to your voicemails, and I read your texts. And the feeling of someone being willing to fight for me like you're doing means a lot to me. I'm a stubborn old man with control issues who has been alone for more than ten years. I can't tell you that I'm going to be a great partner for you at first. But I'll learn if you'll give me time."

"And call you on your bullshit?"

Ben laughs. "And call me on my bullshit. Although, if I start listening to reason now, my son's going to be pissed. He's been trying to talk me out of my castle for years."

"He's a smart guy."

Ben nods. "He is. And you know what, he brought you to me. And maybe that's what was meant to happen all along."

I slide off my chair and come around the counter, pressing myself right into his waiting arms. "What you're saying is that this was meant to be?" I ask, looking up at him from where my chin rests on his chest like I've done so many times before.

I get a little smirk and a narrow-eyed glare in return. "What I'm saying is that we've been living in la-la land for the last few months, and if this thing between us has a chance of transitioning into the real world, I'm going to have to start showing you how things work around here. It can't all be scary movie scenes and role playing."

I smile and cock my head to the side. "What else is there?"

"Well, there's me cooking dinner for you every night."

"Which you pretty much did already on Merit."

"And there's my strict fitness regimen."

"God, you say the sexiest things."

"And there's my bedroom upstairs which is now our bedroom, and my shower which is now our shower."

"Mmm..."

"Where you better be waiting for me naked in exactly five minutes."

I narrow my eyes once more. "I don't even know where the stairs are in this castle. How am I supposed to know where our bedroom is?"

Ben spins me in his arms but continues to hold me tightly to his chest. He leans down and whispers in my ear. "The clock starts now."

Then he gives me a little shove.

I shake my head and toss an eye roll over my shoulder before hurrying back down the hallway we came in. I jog up the main stairs and find my new bedroom without much difficulty. It's the master suite at the end of the wide hallway with the doors flung open.

The inside is so perfectly Ben that I know without even having to think it that I won't be changing a single thing about it. It smells like the woodsy, pine essence of him, with deep green rugs and dark brown leather furniture. Even the headboard is leather. The bed is made perfectly with a magnificent forest green down duvet and a folded throw so fuzzy and cozy looking that I almost toss myself on it and wrap up like a burrito.

But then I remember my task.

The ensuite is the size of my apartment on Faraday, with a walk-in shower complete with four shower heads and steam nozzles. It's open to the rest of the room with drains in the green tile floor. I kick on all the shower heads to hot and strip off my Pilates clothes, tossing them on the leather love seat just outside the bathroom.

When I stand in the very center of the shower, all four waterfall shower heads pouring down on me at once, I close my eyes and moan in pure pleasure.

"That's what I like to hear."

I open my eyes and wipe the water away, watching Ben approach through the steam. He's naked as well, and hard as a rock, erection bouncing with every step.

He steps into the water and pulls me to his chest. We're quiet for a long moment like that, allowing the hot water to soak us.

Finally, I can't stand it any longer. "What game are we playing?"

Ben pulls my face from his chest and wipes the water away from my eyes and cheeks. More rushes into its place. "No game."

"No game?" I whisper, holding his deep, dark gaze.

He shakes his head. "No game. Just you and me."

I'm not sure how to start so I wait, letting my hands drift over his naked body. Ben does the same. The sensation of his smooth, wet skin under my fingers merges with the feeling of him touching me in the same soft, loving way. The tears start to rise once more. I don't think Ben will notice with the sheer volume of water already pouring down my face as I stand tucked into his chest under the shower heads, but he does.

"If these ever become tears of sadness or fear or unhappiness, you tell me, okay?"

I nod.

He wipes his thumbs under my eyes and smiles down at me. "I feel it, too. I want you to know that. The feeling that makes you cry while you smile like this, I feel it."

Which, of course, only makes the tears bubble up faster as I smile up at him.

After a long moment, he breaks our stare to lean over and grab a bright green loofah, holding it under a built-in nozzle on the marble wall. The automatic dispenser offers a squirt of what I can already smell is lavender body wash. Ben lathers it in his hands and starts to wash me, beginning at my shoulders and continuing until he's kneeling before me, rubbing soap in between each of my toes with his fingers.

The continuous stream of water from overhead does a great job of rinsing me as I stand and watch him, so by the time he's done, I'm relatively soap free, and he's kneeling in a pile of bubbles. I can tell the second his soft, loving caress turns to something more. His fingers press harder as he drags them back up my legs, leaning in close to follow behind with his lips, pressing kisses in a line leading up toward my hips.

He touches down between my legs first with the tip of his tongue, a little hello to my nerves that makes me gasp.

"Sit," Ben says, and I glance backward toward the built-in bench on the wall behind me. I slowly back toward it, not taking my eyes off the man before me, crawling on his hands and knees to follow me there.

"You know, I could get used to seeing you on your knees." It's a joke, but Ben isn't laughing.

"You will."

I gasp again as he pushes my knees apart, baring me fully to him. I lean back in the sloped seat and watch as he grazes his lips up and down both of my thighs, nearly reaching my center, but pulling away each time.

"Tease."

"You have no idea."

It's true. As fully and completely in love with this man as I am, he was right before when he said we have a lot to learn about each other in real life.

I plan to make studying him and how we work together a lifelong academic pursuit.

He finally gives me the touch I've been burning for, landing his tongue down once more on my clit, sliding up and around, tasting me.

My body is warm and pliable from the long, hot shower, and my knees fall even further to the sides as I moan in pleasure.

I'm so worked up from having his hands on my body for so long already that I know I won't last long like this. I try to steady my breathing to prolong the pleasure, but Ben increases his ministrations at the same time. His fingers slide into me, deep and slow. It's all I can do to keep my eyes open, but I fight for it. Watching this beautiful, strong, sensitive man feast on me is not something I want to miss.

He says I'll get used to the sight, and I'm sure that's true. But I'm not used to it yet.

His eyes are closed, brow slightly creased as he swirls his tongue up and around, matching the pace of his fingers. I can't control my breathing any longer with the wave building in my stomach, so I let go.

And I crash.

My head falls back as I tip over the edge into orgasm. I can feel Ben holding me tightly in place, working me through it, but I lose connection with reality for a moment as the pleasure overwhelms all my senses. On and on it goes. I'm wrung out and gasping but the sensations continue to fire though my nerves, keeping me trapped in my little bubble of ecstasy.

He stills when I do, and I somehow make my way back upright, make my way forward until my mouth finds his. My own taste is sweet and tangy on his lips and tongue, and I suck him into me, biting his lip and losing myself in the kiss with reckless abandon.

I'm so absorbed in getting every taste of him on my tongue that I don't notice he's lifting me until I'm already in his arms. I wrap my legs around his waist as he turns us and sits down on the bench, settling me on his lap.

I break away from his lips to look down at his hard cock jutting up between us. Kissing is instantly forgotten as a new need overtakes my mind.

I lift up and seat myself on his tip, my hands on his shoulders steadying myself as I slowly, so slowly, sink onto him.

His eyes are closed and mine follow suit, shutting out everything but the sensation of him entering me. The glorious fullness of us together. When my hips reach his lap and I settle my weight, it occurs to me that this is the first time I've really been in charge. Not that he couldn't take over at any moment, but for right now, I'm on top. I'm the only one moving as I explore the angle of my hips, the way I can swirl him around inside me, gripping and loosening and tilting our connected bodies back and forth.

Ben is strong and steady. He grips my hips firmly to keep me safe as I slowly find my rhythm, but other than that, he seems to have melted from the combination of heat and pleasure.

I'm nearly at a melting point myself but the power of the moment is too good to let go.

I lift up further than before, taking his tip to my clit and gasping as I rub myself with it, then I slide it back in. A long, low moan from Ben brings a smile to my lips, and I do it again. And again until I'm fucking us, leaned forward and gripping his shoulders with my fingernails for purchase.

Ben still doesn't take over, allowing me to use his body all on my own, but his eyes are open now. As my breasts bounce in front of his face, he captures my nipples one at a time, licking and giving a little bite when he can.

I can't take my eyes off his mouth, his hooded eyes, the place where our bodies connect between my legs. I rest my forehead on his as we both watch.

I've been working myself in just the right ways since I started, and I'm on the edge once more.

"I'm going to come," I whisper, grinding myself harder, deeper, barely able to get the words out before my breath catches.

"You better," he growls back, tightening his grip on my ass and preparing to take over when I lose control.

It's a slow slide into madness, a far cry from the cliff Ben usually pushes me over. With my body rubbing slow and hard, I slip into orgasm gradually, the pleasure starting as a little seed and growing up my spine like a vine. I hang my head forward and clench down on him as it overtakes me, feeling his strong hands start to move my body back and forth as I hold on with my core.

"Fuck, girl," Ben hisses into my wet hair as he follows me into orgasm.

I can't stop, can't breathe, can't force my eyes open, even though I want nothing more than to watch him break. The heat and the pleasure and the closeness all combine, and we're one person for a moment in time, two bodies locked together.

When my lungs finally release, I lift my head and find Ben still holding his breath.

"Together," I say, meaning our orgasm.

"Always," Ben whispers back, and I can tell he means so much more.

He pulls me tighter to him, both arms wrapped around my ribcage. I'm not sure how long we stay like that, with him buried deep inside me, the hot water from the shower beating down on the tile floor and creating a fog of steam.

I'm going to need to move my legs soon, so I start the process of rousing him by nibbling softly on his jawline. That gets me a smile and a moment later, his deep brown eyes find mine.

"I've never let anyone else fill me like you always do." I remember how he told me he liked to be my first anything, so I'm happy to offer this little bit of myself to him.

"And you never will," he says back.

I smile and lift my head so I'm looking him straight on. "What's that supposed to mean?"

"It means you're mine."

"Oh, really?"

"Yes, really."

"And you're not worried about getting me pregnant?"

"I'm not worried about anything when I'm with you."

"That's not really an answer."

"It wasn't really the right question, was it?"

"I guess not," I admit softly, taken aback by the directness of the last few moments. I know what he's trying to get at. "I'm not sure I'm ready to ask."

Ben stands and lifts me with him. I release my legs and stand, still held tightly in his arms. "Well, when you're ready to ask, the answer is yes."

Time stumbles as yet another unimaginable promise escapes the lips of that man.

How did I get so lucky? How do I deserve this?

"I'm getting overheated," I say, feeling a bit lightheaded now that we're back in the stream of hot water.

"Perfect timing," he answers cryptically.

And then he reaches out and turns the faucet as if he's turning it off but stops when it's ice cold. I shriek and try to escape, but my strong man has too good a hold on my body.

"It's good for your nervous system," Ben replies, holding me tightly as I squeal and squirm.

"I hate you!"

"You'll get used to it."

I'm still shrieking when he finally hits the handle and turns the tortuous shower off.

My anguish turns to laughter as he brushes my hair off my face and kisses my forehead. I might be a teeny bit hysterical.

"C-c-can I have a towel?" I ask, grinning up at him even though my teeth are chattering. I'll never admit it to him, but the blast of cold water made me feel amazing. Maybe not in the moment, but now that it's over, all of my senses are online, and I feel a lot less foggy-headed than I did two minutes ago.

"We'll dry off in here." He pulls me across the wet tile and through the glass door of a dry cedar plank sauna.

"Jeez, Ben. You dry off like a crazy rich person."

It's his turn to laugh as he stretches out on the top bench and motions for me to take the lower. "My grandfather would be rolling over in his grave if he knew."

"They had to have been pretty extravagant to have built a house like this. You think he'd disapprove of your sauna?"

"They were old-fashioned. He may have sprung for the estate, but he was a penny pincher."

"You didn't inherit that gene?"

He's shaking his head and smiling, eyes closed. "I only use about a quarter of this house, but the part I live in, I made just the way I want it." He rolls to his side and looks down at me. "Speaking of which. You have free rein of the place. It could use a bit of freshening up. It's quite the bachelor pad."

"It's beautiful, Ben."

"Yeah, well. Let me know."

"I'm going to suffocate to death in here."

Another laugh and I find myself being lifted and carried from the sweltering hot tomb. When Ben tosses me on the bed a moment later, I'm amazed to see that I'm almost completely dry, other than my hair.

"I was dreaming of wrapping up in that fuzzy blanket earlier, but now I'm too hot."

"Allow me." He pulls open the window over the bed a large crack and cool air rushes in, sending goose bumps over my body.

My nap overtakes me before he even gets the fuzzy throw tucked in around us. I dream of being a queen and wake still feeling like one.

Is this really my life now?

We spend the rest of the afternoon in bed. I admit a few of my deepest darkest secrets, and in return, Ben entertains me with stories about growing up in a palace like this with his three best friends, thick as thieves.

Reality is starting to tap at the window of my mind, and I can't help but wonder if I should be doing something useful right now. Getting my stuff from my apartment, working out, figuring something out. It seems like my whole world has just been flipped on its head, and though it's exactly what I wanted, I'm a bit disoriented.

Ben's solution is a plush robe and a tour of the estate. I follow him through room after room as he points out paintings that he likes or hates, places where he got in trouble or got hurt as a child. I find one room in the south hallway that's decorated almost exactly like a room in a dream I had once. I make a mental note to come back soon and claim it for my own.

Once we're back in the main foyer, I'm starting to get my bearings. Ben leads me straight down a hallway to a dim room filled with leather and books, and into a wide, comfy chair in front of three floor-to-ceiling windows looking out into seemingly never-ending evergreens. I watch as he works the latch on one of the windows and swings it open, creating a doorway that leads out onto an open porch with a few steps leading down to a path into the forest.

I walk outside and stand at the top of the steps, sinking into his body as he embraces me from behind.

With the trees looming tall and ancient before us, I finally feel strong enough to believe that this is all true. I feel free enough to take my first deep breath in what feels like hours.

"This is amazing," I say, the words swallowed up by the magnificence of the forest.

I feel him murmur his agreement into my neck where his face is tucked. "Seven acres of forest and trails. All ours."

I look back toward him without pulling away. "No one else is out there?"

"They better not be."

Something in his tone, and the words themselves, send a shiver down my spine. I must shiver a bit in his embrace because he rubs his hands briskly up and down my arms for a moment.

And then pulls my robe off and tosses it onto the deck, leaving me in just my panties and a thin tank, wide eyed and aghast in the cold twilight.

"What are you—"

I don't get the words out before he has me turned around and marching down the stairs, toward the tree line, arms held tightly behind my back.

The cold, damp earth squishes softly beneath my toes.

Once we reach the edge of the forest, Ben stops and lets me go so suddenly I almost fall forward onto the trail.

"Now we're playing a game," he says darkly.

My breath catches in my chest as I consider the winding path before me that leads into the trees.

I glance back at Ben and find him watching me. Waiting.

I bite my lip and narrow my eyes at the rapidly dimming sky. The forest is almost completely dark.

"W-what kind of game?"

He leans down and whispers the words right into my ear. "One where you run."

Rule #35

THIS IS WHAT IT MEANS TO BEGIN AGAIN

BEN

Eight Months Later

I lean against the doorway of our bedroom, watching Victoria fuss with her earrings, then her hair, then her eyelashes. I would interrupt to tell her she looks beautiful, but even in these short months living together at my house, not even a full year, I've learned to let her process. She gets there in her own time, her confidence waning and waxing like the moon until she's full and bright.

As much as I would like to say that I learned to be patient, to allow life to unfold naturally, from decades of being a parent, I'm not entirely sure that would be the truth.

Did I ever sit back and let Ainsley figure things out for himself like this? Did I ever once patiently wait for him to change his outfit six times until some mysterious approval level was reached, and we were able to leave the house? Never. His clothes were laid out for him by me. If there was ever a problem, he was reminded of how lucky we are to have the things we had and that he should fall in line.

What a joke that was. What a joke to think that having such an excess of money would somehow make up for the fact that our hearts longed for connection and softness.

It would be easy to let myself wallow in the missteps of my past, but even I can see the futility of it.

I made mistakes in my marriage to Breanna. We were so young, and I was chasing down the world. Never a second to spare for frivolities like days off. Thinking of all those wasted moments I could have spent with her used to drive me to madness, but time was merciful, allowing the pain to ease.

I made mistakes in my cold, systematic upbringing of my son. I needed so badly for him to grow into the kind of person anyone could see the value in that I failed to account for the innate value he, and everyone, was born with. But he doesn't hate me for it, which, I suppose, is the biggest miracle of them all. He blessed upon me this woman, offering me a lesson in letting go that I probably would have died without learning had it not been for him.

And for her.

Victoria's dark hair is expertly tamed this evening, shining nearly black in the golden lamplight. Her gown, chosen carefully with the help of her new girlfriends from the Pilates studio over the last few weeks, fits her like liquid mercury, draping over her curves and pooling behind her tall, black heels in a puddle of starlight.

"What time is it?" she asks, drawing me out of my meditative adoration.

I glance down at my watch. "Quarter to seven."

Her face expands in all directions with surprise. "Weren't we supposed to leave at six-thirty? You should have told me I was taking too long."

I push off the doorway and cross the room to take her hand

and twirl her before pulling her into my arms. "It's my party. We'll arrive fashionably late."

I watch her eyes search mine for any hint of condescension. She finds none because there is nothing but love and adoration on my mind.

The party tonight is celebrating my ten years as partner, a milestone generally marked by choosing a mentee from the pool of lawyers working their way through the ranks. I'd be lying if I said I hadn't harbored fantasies over the years of bringing Ains up on that stage and presenting him that honor, but I can see now how ridiculous and self-indulgent that idea was.

Once again, the ocean of regret for having ignored the kid's true nature and potential for his whole life threatens to overtake me, but Victoria's at my hand. I give hers a squeeze, and she returns it, smiling up at me as I lead her down the sweeping staircase into the main foyer.

"I'm a little nervous about tonight." Her eyes avoid mine, and I can see her biting the inside of her red-painted lip.

This is going to be the first official appearance we make together as a couple. We've been spotted lunching and shopping around the city before, and I've made no secret of my new relationship to anyone in my office or extended circle. But this is the first time that I will help her out of a limo and walk into an event with her on my arm. Introduce her to the whole community.

I've never been less nervous about anything in my entire life.

"You look amazing. They're going to adore you."

Her lip-biting persists.

"What are you worried is going to happen?"

"They're going to think I'm too young for you. That I'm a gold-digger."

I crack a smile as the words take shape. "Shall I offer you a romantic quip about your heart of gold and my pan?"

Finally, her smile returns. "You mean your pickaxe?"

"Is that how this went, lover? I spotted a promising looking rock and broke it apart to find my treasure? I don't think so. My metaphor with a pan and a gently babbling river seems more succinct."

She just shakes her head, heading for the front door, where our car is waiting, but I can tell I've set her at ease.

I wonder if I could do one step more.

"Victoria," I call, as she lays her hand on the brass handle. She turns to look at me, and I'm struck with uncharacteristic nerves. "I..." I take a deep breath and collect myself. "I was going to do this at the party, although thinking about it now, I can't imagine why I ever thought that was a good idea."

Her eyes are narrowed as she waits in silence.

I slip my hands out of the pockets of my tuxedo pants as I close the distance between us.

When I drop to one knee, I hear her suck in a breath and smile.

Once again, I was worried for nothing.

"I know this might be a bit sooner than expected. Sooner than we had discussed..." I shake my head to get myself back on track. "Vic, you have changed my life in ways I never thought were possible. You saw something in me that no one has ever seen and fought for me in ways I didn't think I deserved. I don't know if a hundred years would be enough time to repay you for how thoroughly you have saved me, but I want to try. And I want to start now. No more waiting. I love you more than life itself. Marry me."

The ring is in a tiny velvet box, tucked into my jacket pocket. I retrieve it with surprisingly steady hands and present it to her. Its sparkle matches the glimmer in her eyes.

"Ben, goddamn it, I spent an hour on my eye makeup." Her words come with a choked laugh as she shakes her head and dabs carefully at the tears pooling in her eyes.

"You look perfect. You are perfect."

A smile spreads across her face as she looks down at me, makeup forgotten, tears now allowed to escape from her eyes and blaze little trails down her cheeks. "I would have been bawling my eyes out at the party in front of everyone."

"Victoria, if you don't say yes, I might die down here."

"Yes, of course, yes."

She grabs my hands with both of hers and pulls me to my feet. Our lips meet, and a calm washes over me like a cool breeze. This is the rest of my life. I get to have this woman. I somehow deserve this.

She lets me slip the ring on her finger, a delicate gold band holding the largest single cut diamond I could get my hands on, surrounded by a constellation of tiny rubies.

"Ben…" she whispers, turning her hand side to side and watching the gems sparkle. "It's beautiful."

I smile down at her, so much joy running through my veins that I feel buoyant and bulletproof. "It's a beacon, one that will always lead me to you. No matter how well you try to hide."

Her eyes drift back up to meet mine, and I see a flash of playfulness before her gaze softens to reflect my love back to me. A sight I will never tire of as long as I live.

"Thank you," she says finally.

I feel my forehead crease as I draw her now jewel-laden hand up to meet my lips. "You don't have to thank me. This is my way of thanking you."

She shrugs, not pulling her hand away. Not taking her eyes off mine. "I have a lot to be grateful for as well. Grateful that you stepped out of your comfort zone that first night. Grateful that you opened your life to a strange woman after years of being alone."

I watch the emotions rise back into her face, and when she speaks, I can hear them in her soft voice. "Grateful that you saw enough of what I saw when you looked beyond our little games, into the future. Grateful that you took a chance on this."

"The bets with the longest odds have the greatest payoffs, after all."

Her face breaks into a wide grin I can't help but return.

"We were something of a dark horse, I guess."

"I wouldn't want it any other way. Dark horse, white horse, or, as fate has chosen, inside the black limo waiting outside—it's us, together, against the world."

VICTORIA

I began to understand the true meaning of wealth when I came to live in Ben's New York estate eight months ago.

You'd think after all that time frolicking around the Merit Island house like a lady of leisure, enjoying the fruits of someone else's labor, I'd be used to it. But the island life was different. It was easy to slide into the fantasy when everything around me was designed with vacation in mind.

Here in the real world, I feel like a goddamn princess.

Or maybe a queen…

A car delivers me to Lotus Studios most weekdays. I've been working my way through their curriculum and am now certified to teach Level 1 Rehabilitation classes as well as my regular Pilates Mat classes. I love being able to relate to my students on a personal level and share my own journey of healing with those starting at square one. I am a walking success story, and I'm happy to offer people hope.

I've made a small group of girlfriends among the teachers at the studio, and I host lunches and pool parties in my absurdly opulent indoor pool lounge.

My friend Sandra is now two months into a cozy little relationship with one of Ben's work associates. We go on double dates to the theater and to restaurants whose names I used to see in magazines.

I shop with a limitless platinum card.

Growing up in Maryland, we had what seemed like enough to me as a kid, but looking back on it now, I can see the struggle.

My grandparents lived with us for most of my childhood, but I wonder now if we lived with them. It's funny how the world that you're born into seems like the only way people live...until you grow up and learn differently.

The world Ben was born into is one of housekeepers and summer houses. Of leasing cars so you always have a new one and never having to change the toilet paper roll.

It's excessive, and overindulgent, and unnecessary, and I love it with the very marrow of my bones.

I was definitely born to be a queen.

I'm going to do so much good with this fortunate life I seem to have stumbled into. Help so many people and change so many lives. But for now, I'm simply letting myself settle. Letting myself relax and regroup.

Ben, self-proclaimed hard-ass, has actually turned out to be quite the sugar daddy. I love watching him get off on spoiling me almost as much as I like being spoiled. And getting off.

I glance down at the brand-new engagement ring on my finger as I wait for Ben to open the car door for me at the party. It sparkles in the dim overhead lighting, and I feel my heart skip a beat.

How did I ever get so lucky?

It's not just the ring, or the house, or the lifestyle.

It's the man. And it's who I've become in my time together with him. He offered me something I didn't even realize I was missing—a safe place to grow.

"Ready?" Ben asks as he reaches down for my hand.

I nod up at him, feeling calm, solid, and sure. It's a feeling I'm still getting used to, but one I definitely know looks good on me.

And I know it's because of Ben. Love has offered me space to question, to struggle, to worry, and yet to know that this is simply the journey. The human experience. I share my worries and mistakes with Ben and with my friends, and they share theirs with me. I know now that it's okay to not be perfect. I know I'm not alone in feeling this way.

Maybe that's the crux of it. I'm not alone. I never was, not for one moment of my life. I could have leaned on my family. I could have told the truth to my friends. But I never felt safe enough. I never felt secure enough in my own person to allow those faults and weaknesses to show.

What love has offered me is a window into the vulnerability of another person. And what I see there is very familiar.

We breeze through the front doors to the Metropolitan Museum of Art, where the party is being held, security stepping out of the way to let us pass with nods of recognition. I can feel all eyes on me as we make our way down the corridor to the Sackler Wing and the Temple of Dendur, where the party is being held.

The ancient Egyptian temple is stunning and dramatic, taking my breath away as we enter the room. Ben leads us past the reflecting pool and over to where the bar is set up in front of floor-to-ceiling windows overlooking Central Park. I listen to the click, click, click of my heels as I cross the marble floor with a firm grasp on Ben's arm, accepting the eye contact and curious smiles from guests.

With a crystal flute of sparkling wine in hand, I'm ready for the introductions to begin.

Rule #36

HOME IS BUILT BRICK BY BRICK

VICTORIA

Five Years Later

The estate is lovely as ever. Lush, green, and blooming into life everywhere I look.

We set up the small ceremony in the side-yard, with a simple wooden arch under the shade of a cherry tree in full bloom.

It's been quite a week already, the house bustling with guests filling every empty bedroom for the first time since I've lived here. I'm enjoying the fullness. The noise and activity. People have been in and out for long and short stays almost constantly since baby June was born last fall, but this is different. To have everyone we love all under the same roof—my roof—is finally solidifying a feeling I've been chasing since day one of taking up residence here.

Woman of the house.

It's a deep-seated belonging. A deserving I hadn't realized I was missing until I started showing my family to their luxurious bedrooms in the west wing of the estate.

My estate.

The estate where I'm building my own family.

June squawks from the other room and I turn to find my mother already carrying her into the living room overlooking the south-facing gardens where the ladies are all gathered to help me prepare for my walk down the aisle.

"That was a nice, long nap," my mom coos at my baby as she hands her over. "She'll be in a great mood for the ceremony."

"Hello, my love." I smile down at Juney, and she grins back up at me.

My heart swells to bursting with love for my perfect little daughter…

Just as my stomach lurches.

I hold June to my chest in an embrace and close my eyes, taking deep breaths until the feeling passes.

"Let me take her, you sit down for a moment," Reina says.

I open my eyes gratefully and hand the baby over. I'm going to be battling more than just the rush of happy, excited emotions for this wedding.

And no one understands that better than the seemingly ever-pregnant Reina.

"Give your mommy a minute to go barf in the trash can," she coos at June as she dances her away across the floor.

My own mom kneels down beside my chair. "The first four months were the worst for me."

I nod and offer a soft smile, eyes still gently closed. "It wasn't like this with June. I barely noticed her there before she was a bump."

"That must mean this one is a boy!" Sally squeals, getting the whole room of ladies going once more.

I rest in my chair and take it all in. The excited birthdate guesses. The name suggestions. The overflowing river of love and support that I somehow managed to swirl around myself in this lifetime.

Deserving.

"I'm going to take June out to the rest of the kids. See you on the altar," Reina tells me, placing a kiss on my forehead.

I smile up at her gratefully. "Thank you. For everything."

Most of the other women follow her through the white, wooden doors, waving and blowing kisses, until it's just me and my mother left in the now quiet room.

She sits beside me, stroking my back as I continue to breathe deeply.

"I never worried about you, you know that?"

I blink my eyes open and glance over at her in surprise. "Not even when I dropped out of college and ran off to Asia?"

She shakes her head. "You've had this way about you your whole life. You seem to know what's right for you, and you go do it. The rest of us just sat around, doing what we felt we needed to do, but not Victoria." She smiles fondly, faraway look in her eyes. "Victoria was always chasing a dream."

My own eyes start to mist. "I felt lost for a long time," I admit. "I watched everyone around me with their close families and guidance and wondered why no one was helping me."

My mom's smile softens a bit as her own eyes start to well with tears. "You just had it all figured out, Vic. We learned about your plans after you'd made them. You were so sure of yourself. Still are. I spent most of my time helping your sister because she was always struggling. You never asked for help a single time, your whole life. And look at you now."

I huff out a small laugh, wiping my eyes gently with the soft, white hanky embroidered with blue forget-me-nots that Sally, my maid of honor, gave me last night. "Marrying money?"

My mom takes the cloth and uses it to touch up the corners of my eyes. "I'll be the first to admit I'm not sad about having a room in this palace to grow old in."

We laugh softly together, but the feeling is deeper than that. She has expressed this gratitude before, and I feel proud to be able to offer it to her. To my sister. To any of them.

"But you know it's the way that man looks at you that has us all wishing we'd lived our own lives differently. To have someone for whom you're the only star in the sky. Someone who has lived and lost and appreciates you for the treasure you are." She shakes her head and cups my chin in her hand. "That's the kind of love legends are made of, Vic. And you found it."

We manage to settle our emotions—and my stomach—by the time Ainsley comes to get us.

"Well, aren't you two just a vision." He's handsome as ever, grinning in his forest green tux.

My mom places a kiss on his cheek as she takes the arm of Dom, who will be walking her to her place in the front row. "See you on the other side," she calls back to me.

"Ready to do this?" Ainsley asks.

I nod, suddenly exhausted.

He notices, of course, forehead crinkling with concern. "What is it?"

The last thing I want is more tears to clean up before going out there, but it seems inevitable. "I miss my baby," I admit finally, wiping my face gently with the back of my hand.

Ainsley steps up to dab my eyes with his color-coordinated pocket square.

"And my sofa. And Ben. I love you all, but I'm so tired."

He laughs softly. "You've made everyone wait a long time for this, Vicki."

I laugh as well, sniffing back another round of tears. "I know."

Ainsley takes a step back, holding me by the shoulders at arm's length. "It's going to be great. One walk through your yard, a few words, and then you'll get your life back."

Of all the surprises the last nearly six years have brought, this man is top of the list.

He went from being my frustration to my greatest fear to my friend. And now, finally, my family. "Thank you. For everything," I whisper.

Ainsley's smile turns sly. "Well, maybe not everything, huh?"

I shake my head. "Everything. All of it. You gave me this, Ains. And I'll never forget it."

He swallows hard, eyes turning misty as he holds my gaze. "Fate's a crazy, sadistic bitch."

I smile back at him, nodding. "But it's worth it in the end."

I know he agrees.

We pause at the doors to the backyard, waiting for our cue.

Suddenly, Ains drops my hand. "Hang tight," he says, jogging off across the yard.

Fran, who's orchestrating the perfectly timed walk down the aisle, looks like she wants to scream at him, but she can't with the guests sitting just a few feet away.

Luckily, he's only gone a moment.

When he comes back around the corner, I laugh. And yes, cry again.

He hands me baby June and takes my bouquet.

She's smiling and laughing, excited by the sudden change of plans, eyes filled with adoration for her Uncle Ainsley.

"Thank you," I tell him, sinking my nose into the crook of her neck and calming myself with her perfect baby scent.

And that's how we make our way down the aisle. June on my hip, my arm linked with Ainsley, my giant bouquet of roses and hydrangea in his other hand.

It's going to make for some memorable photos.

June reaches for her daddy as soon as I come to stand beside him beneath the arch. He takes her and pulls me close. "My girls," he whispers in my ear.

Sam pronounces us man and wife with June cooing, and cackling, and laughing, the whole crowd laughing softly along with her.

I smile through my tears of joy, accepting my first baby back into my arms as Ben places a kiss on my lips, and then one on hers.

The moment is blindingly happy. A ray of sunshine so bright that takes my breath away.

And as lost as I've felt over the years.
As much as I still don't know what life is going to bring.
I know I'll always remember this moment.
The moment I realized I was home.

A Look At Book Four:

PRESS PLAY

A temporary island escape. Her brother's best friend. A secret video that could ruin everything...

My influencer career crashed and burned, so I fled to my estranged brother's resort, pretending it's just a quiet break. The truth? I'm chasing the memory of one reckless, unforgettable night with his best friend, Sam.

But Sam's not thrilled to see me. He says getting involved again could ruin everything he's worked for. Still, the chemistry between us hasn't cooled, and neither of us is good at staying away. Now we're sneaking around the island, sending flirty texts, stealing kisses, and pretending we're not falling harder every day.

There's just one problem: I recorded our first night together. By accident.

The video no one's supposed to see still exists, and if it ever surfaces, it could destroy Sam's career and any shot I have at rebuilding my own. I should let him go. Keep my distance. Bury the footage and the feelings. But I've never been great at pretending—and this time, the stakes are everything.

AVAILABLE APRIL 2026

Acknowledgments

First, thank you goes out to the authors who came before me, writing sizzling ex-boyfriend's dad romances. Y'all changed my brain. I don't know what it is about a hot dad…or maybe it's the idea of trading in your younger, less worldly BF for someone older. You know how much I love my age gaps!

I love them in real life, too. I've always dated guys older than me, with one exception, a boyfriend I had in my twenties who was just about my age (and it was just as meh as you might imagine. God, I hope he's not reading this!). My hub is ten years my senior, and honestly, I don't even consider that an age gap. We're on the same level.

Speaking of tiny ten-year age gaps, you have one of those to look forward to in the next book, when Sam falls for a lady in her thirties! Can you imagine? I jest, but this is a serious question I get often from readers. Why are my ladies so young?

The simple part of the answer is that I do, very much, think that sexy older guys falling for younger women is super hot. The underlying reason for that might be wrapped up in the less simple part of the answer.

Which is that in my own twenties, I didn't have the space to work out a lot of my mental and emotional issues. This was due to poor choices about my own sexuality that I made when I was much younger, as well as alcohol abuse and unmanaged anxiety. I made it into my thirties without having done a lot of the self-actualization work that people often do at a much younger age. I found myself still faced with a lot of issues that I dragged with me from my childhood and teenage years, and suddenly without alcohol to manage them.

I'm a firm believer that we, as authors, tell the stories we're given, and every time another book starts to take shape in my mind, the woman whose emotional growth I'm about to work through is in her early twenties. This cannot be a coincidence. Rather than fighting it, I simply go with the flow, pouring my own questions about life into the voices of the characters and trying to find some answers for all of us.

A funny thing I discovered when writing *Press Play,* Sam's book, is that it works just the same with a woman in her thirties. We're all doing the same work, no matter what our age. For me, the place where I got stuck in my emotional growth was about nineteen. Maybe it was older for you. I offer this suggestion, if you tend to feel some disconnect with romance starring women in their twenties, make her your own age in your mind. Sure, some of the situations and language will be a bit off, but I think what you'll find is that the life lessons are universal. We're all searching for meaning, for our place in this vast universe. For new and improved ways to make connections with other human beings.

Allowing the characters in romance novels to lead me through their journeys has done wonders for my own personal growth. Maybe you've had a similar experience. Feel free to write and let me know! I'm always happy to talk about books and life with readers. authorloretownsend@gmail.com

And now for our regularly scheduled thank yous!

As always, thanks to Morgan for always being one text message away. Thanks to Karen, for seeing all the places I can expand on the characters' emotional journeys. Thanks to my whole beta team and ARC team, and especially Cathryn, for being the quickest, most thorough, and most brutally honest reader a girl could ask for. I couldn't do this without you.

Thanks to Chipp for always being ready to offer another fabulous title idea. (You all might have Sausage King of Faraday Island to look forward to in the future thanks to him!)

See you in the next book!

Lore

You can learn plenty of normal things about me in my various platform bios, so here's some things you can only learn in the back of this book:

Q: Where do you go when you need a creative reset?
A: For me, reset mostly happens with sleep—long nights with no alarm clock, and afternoon naps—and reading. We don't watch a lot of TV or movies, but recently we started re-watching *Lost*, and I became obsessed with the dramatic, "episodic" storytelling. I think my next series is going to be more like that.
Q: What do you do when you're stuck on a scene or having a hard writing day?
A: Separate answers for these. When I'm stuck on a scene, I will go back (sometimes to the beginning!) and read everything again. It has to be done anyway, for editing purposes, so I let my roadblock become time for different creative work. I have found many times, however, that if I just cannot get a scene to work or can't get started, I'm probably in the wrong POV. Switching point of view unsticks me every time! Hard writing days—I just

do something else. If I want to work on the book, I read from the beginning. Or I read a book or get a coffee and go to the beach.

Q: Where did the idea for Victoria and Ben's story come from?

A: The first scene I knew about this book was that one where Ben and Avery go to the Pilates class. I didn't even know the characters from this series at that point, but I just imagined the tough gym guys walking into the class with the whole *if those ladies can do it, we can* attitude and getting their asses handed to them (like I always do). Bonus fact—Chipp taught Pilates and power yoga for almost 15 years!

Q: Did you always know that Ainsley would get his own book?

A: No. As a matter of fact, when I set out to write an ex's dad book (because I'm obsessed with them) I didn't think much about the ex at all. It wasn't until I was deep into the story that I realized how big a part of Ben's life he was and therefore the book. I was waffling about which character to do next, so I let the readers in my FB group vote, and they chose Ainsley. *A Fool's Game* was born.

Q: What's your favorite scene in *Lying for Keeps* (that you can talk about in public)?

A: I love the scene where Ainsley comes home and finds them. I was nervous about writing it at all because I was worried readers would be mad at me, but it had to come. I am obsessed with the quiet, desperate drama of it. I also tend to freeze in terrible positions like Victoria did. Freeze and then lash out.

Q: Is there a moment from your real life that snuck into the story?

A: Some of the defensiveness Victoria displays about dropping out of college and taking a low paying job hits pretty close to home. I went to a two-year college out of high school and just got a job. Those were my drinking, reckless days, and I stuck with an industry where my behavior would be safe and supported. I wouldn't say I felt judged by everyone in my life, but I do have this vivid memory of years later, sober, back in college, I was at a clothing exchange at the home of a woman I knew from yoga. She was a nurse practitioner, and all of her friends were nurses or doctors or professors. Most of them were younger than me. I left that party angry and sad that I'd spent so many years in what felt like limbo, just trying to survive. Looking back, I'm not sorry I didn't get pushed straight into university by my parents. I'm glad I have the life experience I have and that I get to live the way I do—with as much freedom as I can manage.

The best place to find the most current info about my books and events is here:

linktr.ee/authorloretownsend

www.loretownsend.com

Join Lore Townsend's Romance Club

www.ingramcontent.com/pod-product-compliance
Lightning Source LLC
LaVergne TN
LVHW040215110826
845146LV00005B/1299